PRESUMPTION
OF GUILT

PRESUMPTION OF GUILT

Marti Green

THOMAS & MERCER

Text copyright © 2014 Marti Green
All rights reserved.

Published by Thomas & Mercer, Seattle

www.apub.com

ISBN-13: 9781477825709
ISBN-10: 1477825703

Cover design by Cyanotype Book Architects

Library of Congress Control Number: 2014940449

Printed in the United States of America

To Lenny, the wind beneath my wings

Molly Singer didn't know this would be the last night she'd ever make love to Finn Reynolds. She hurriedly kissed him good night, then exited his car, quietly closing the door behind her. She prayed her parents were asleep. It was well past her curfew and her mother had been on her back about everything lately. She didn't need her scowl greeting her tonight. It would break the magic of the evening.

Molly walked up the bluestone path to her house and, when she reached the front door, turned and waved to Finn. He blew her a kiss, then drove off. Molly put her key in the lock, rotated the latch, and opened the door.

Nothing. No parent standing in the foyer demanding an explanation. Just silence. Molly smiled, slipped off her shoes, and tiptoed up the carpeted stairs.

The upstairs hallway light was on, the signal she knew her mother depended on, when she stirred from her sleep, to tell her if Molly was back in the house. Light on meant she hadn't returned from her date. Light off meant she had. Molly glanced toward her parents' darkened bedroom, the door ajar just enough to let in the telltale hallway light, then switched off the light and slipped into her room.

She closed the door behind her and flopped down on the bed. It was almost one a.m., an hour past her curfew, but she was wide-awake. Her body tingled with the memory of Finn's hands, exploring, caressing.

After a few moments, Molly got off the bed and pulled a tank top and shorts from her dresser drawer. She quickly changed into them, then headed into her bathroom to brush her teeth and wash her face.

When finished, she stared at the medicine cabinet. *Should I?* Inside was a stash of Ambien pills she'd secreted from her mother's supply, a help for those nights she was too wired to fall asleep. She didn't like the way they made her feel the next morning, but still—no school tomorrow meant she could sleep in. Probably the only way she'd get any sleep tonight, she thought as she reached inside the cabinet, shook two five-milligram pills from the bottle into her hand, and stared at them. *One or two?* One usually worked. Mostly, she'd needed it when she was overtired from studying too late into the night. A smile crept across her face as the image of Finn planted itself in her mind. She could still feel his lips on hers. The scent of his aftershave lingered on her. The promises they'd made to each other tonight, to love each other forever, reverberated through her. *Definitely two.* Otherwise, she'd never fall asleep.

Molly popped the little pink pills into her mouth, took a swig of water to wash them down, and got into her bed. Ten minutes later she fell sound asleep.

The sun streaming through her pink-and-green gingham curtains woke Molly. She glanced at the clock on her nightstand and jumped out of bed, startled that her parents had let her sleep past eleven. "There's too much to enjoy in life to sleep it away," her father always said.

Sundays were supposed to be family day, although lately Molly had been pretty successful at finding excuses for avoiding time with her parents. It had been harder when Donna first left for college almost four years earlier. Then, her parents glommed on to her as though she were their intravenous fix. Their attention suffocated her, to the point that she called Donna late one night and begged her to return home. "They're killing me," she'd cried over the phone. "I can't take it anymore. You've got to get them off my back or I'm going to do something drastic, I just know it." Donna had laughed at her. "Give them time," she'd said. "They're just frightened at the thought of the empty nest. They'll let up soon enough."

And they had. They'd let up so much that they'd stopped thinking that Molly walked on water and started complaining about everything she did. And everyone she saw.

She knew they didn't like Finn. *Too bad.* Molly loved him, so much so that her top college choice was no longer Harvard, but Columbia. That way she'd stay close to Finn. And it was still the all-important Ivy League her parents insisted she strive for. It wasn't good enough for her parents, though. They claimed it was because she shouldn't deprive herself of a traditional campus life—the setting of Columbia had its charms but couldn't compare to the campuses of Yale, Harvard, or Princeton—but Molly knew the real reason. They wanted to get her away from Finn.

Molly opened her bedroom door and peeked outside, expecting to hear the drone of the television tuned to the Sunday-morning news shows. Instead, silence greeted her. She looked toward her parents' bedroom and saw a closed door. It was usually left wide open when they were up for the day. Could they have gone back to sleep? Molly wondered. She tiptoed over to their room and pressed her ear against the door. No sound.

Molly bounded down the stairs and checked first the kitchen, then the family room. Empty. I bet they've gone out for brunch, she figured, then headed to the garage to check for a missing car. She opened the door that led to the garage and stood there, confused. All three cars were parked inside. For a moment she had the sickening thought that a carbon monoxide leak had wended its way through the house, rendering her parents unconscious. Then she laughed at her melodrama. It would have knocked her out as well, and she felt fine.

Quietly, she made her way upstairs again, then tiptoed across the floor to her parents' bedroom. Softly, she knocked on the door, then, after no response, knocked again, loudly. Finally, she turned the door-knob, entered the room, and stopped, rooted in place.

At first, her brain only registered the blood. On the quilt, on the walls, on the bed's headboard. Perhaps it was a trick of her mind to protect her from seeing her parents, but soon enough she saw their bodies.

Her father nearest her, frozen in the bed, her mother on the other side, half fallen out.

Her father's head on his pillow, eyes opened in a fixed stare.

Molly screamed, then screamed again, over and over.

TWELVE YEARS LATER

Dani Trumball had just leaned back in her chair and let the sounds of the orchestra wash over her when she felt a tap on her shoulder.

Ignore it, she thought. Jonah's violin concerto had already been performed, brilliantly composed, and expertly played, as attested to by the enthusiastic applause of the other mothers and fathers in the audience. Now she could relax, appreciate the warm evening breeze in her hair, and enjoy the remainder of the concert. The black sky was bursting with stars, and the full moon cast its light over the girls and boys on stage, huddled intently over their instruments.

"Ms. Trumball?" The whisper, barely audible over the sound of the trumpets, came from behind her. "I'm sorry, but are you Dani Trumball?"

How rude. The audience members had driven hours, maybe days, to hear their children perform in Camp Adagio's end-of-summer concert, all of them bursting with pride over their children's musical prowess. Every boy and girl was a Williams syndrome kid, so lacking in other areas of intellectual development, but gifted with this one unique talent. It was hard to imagine a more blissful moment, yet here was this woman, determined to spoil it.

"I'm sorry to bother you, but—can we go somewhere and talk?"

Dani sat up and turned around and saw a woman leaning toward her. "Shh. Please. You're disturbing the others. After the concert." Dani turned back to the front and resumed her reclined position. The full orchestra was playing a symphony composed by one of Jonah's bunk mates. In his letters home, Jonah had gushed about the musical expertise of his friend, and Dani knew he'd question her later about it.

A few minutes passed, and then the annoying whisper returned. "You work for the Help Innocent Prisoners Project, don't you?"

Feeling her husband, Doug, stiffen beside her, Dani turned around again and practically hissed. "Look. Call my office next week and we can talk. I'm not here to discuss cases." She turned back to the front, crossed her arms, and fervently hoped that would be the end of the intrusions. No such luck.

"Please." Her voice, still a whisper, had a note of desperation. Dani wanted to ignore her, knew Doug would be angry if she didn't, yet couldn't stop herself from standing up and moving to the aisle. Dani understood desperation. Quietly, she slipped out of the row of seats, then walked with the woman away from the music. They came to a grove of trees and stopped.

"Thank you. I didn't know who to turn to. I'm so confused."

"What's your name?" The woman towered over Dani by at least five inches. She was stout, without being heavy, and was dressed in crisp linen pants and a flowered blouse. A sapphire pendant hung from her neck, and it was impossible to miss the large, square-cut diamond on her right hand.

"Donna. Donna Garmond."

Dani held out her hand. "Nice to meet you, Donna, but as I said, this isn't the time or place. I'm here for my son, as I'm sure you are for your child."

"Yes, my daughter goes to this camp. Her first year." Donna took in a deep breath. "I know this is an imposition, but I've read about you. I know how you help innocent prisoners and well—it just seemed that both of us here together must mean something. When the concert's over, everyone will scatter, and you'll want to be with your son. If I didn't talk to you now, the moment will be lost. I just couldn't let that happen."

"If you've read about me, you know where my office is. Just call me next week. I'll be happy to speak to you then."

Donna reached out and touched Dani's arm. "I've contacted your office before, asked for their help. They've turned me down."

Now Dani understood the woman's urgency. The Help Innocent Prisoners Project—called HIPP by the staff—had limited resources. They were highly selective about the cases they agreed to handle. More were turned down than accepted.

"Who is it that you believe is wrongly convicted?" Dani asked.

"My sister. Her name is Molly. Molly Singer."

Dani again took in the woman's clothes and jewelry. "I don't mean to be presumptuous, but don't you have the means to hire private counsel?"

Donna shook her head vehemently, loosening wisps of her chestnut hair that had been pulled back and clasped at the nape of her neck. "My husband does well financially and so I haven't had to work. I'm home with Sarah"—Donna gestured to the group of campers listening to the concert—"and we have a son as well, Jacob. I've begged my husband to let me hire an investigator, try to open Molly's case again, but he's adamantly opposed to it. He's convinced Molly is guilty and our money should be used for our children's future."

"What was Molly convicted of?"

"Murder. They said she murdered our parents."

Dani stared at the woman before her. She'd suffered a double loss—the death of her parents and the incarceration of her sister. No wonder she wanted to believe Molly was innocent. A round of applause came from the stage. The concert was over. Dani reached over and touched Donna's arm. Then, her previous annoyance gone, she said, "Call the office next week. I promise I'll hear you out."

As they walked back together to their spouses and children, Dani knew her promise gave Donna more hope than was warranted. The gulf between hearing her out and taking on her sister's case was wide and, most likely, impossible to bridge.

3

Dani breezed into HIPP's office on West Fourteenth Street in New York City's West Village at ten a.m., her usual arrival time. Unless she was arguing a case, or traveling, she always saw Jonah off on the school bus. Doing so served a dual purpose. It lessened her sense—mostly irrational, she understood—that she was abandoning Jonah by going to work, and it helped her avoid the worst of rush-hour traffic driving into Manhattan.

She stopped at her secretary's desk to pick up her messages, then flipped through them as she entered her windowless office. A message from Donna was in the pile. Just her name and phone number on a white slip of paper, with the words "You promised."

Before returning her call, Dani went to the file cabinets to search for any records of Molly Singer. There had to be a file on her if Donna had previously contacted HIPP. She found it quickly, then brought it back to her office.

Inside the folder was a three-page letter from Donna, along with the notation of the HIPP attorney who had reviewed it: "No, with regrets."

Dani skimmed the letter quickly, noting that Molly had been convicted of the double murder twelve years earlier and sentenced to consecutive terms of twenty-five years to life. That in itself was odd. She had just turned eighteen at the time of her sentencing. Most judges would have imposed concurrent terms, leaving open the hope of some semblance of a life after prison.

She stuffed the letter back into the folder, then strolled over to the office of Bruce Kantor, the director of HIPP. HIPP's office space was small, the furnishings spartan, but it hummed with the energy of young people on a mission. At least, mostly young people. Dani could no longer consider herself in that category, but she'd come to HIPP later than most. After nine years at home with Jonah, Doug had practically pushed her out the door, admonishing her that she needed a life of her own and Jonah needed to become less dependent on her. He was right, of course. Both of them had thrived since she began working at HIPP four years ago.

Dani stuck her head inside Bruce's office and saw it was empty. Instead of waiting for him, she made her way over to the office of Melanie Quinn, the attorney who'd initially reviewed the request.

Unlike Dani's own cluttered desk, Melanie's was pristine. Not even a stray paper clip disrupted the picture-perfect orderliness. Not unlike the image projected by Melanie herself.

"Hey, Melanie." Dani placed the folder down in front of her. "Do you remember at all the letter about Molly Singer? Convicted of murdering her parents when she was eighteen? Doing time up at Bedford Hills?"

"Rings a bell. I think we turned her down."

"Right. Well, her sister actually. She's the one who wrote. Do you remember what the thinking was on it?"

Melanie opened the folder and skimmed the letter. When finished, she nodded her head slowly. "I talked this one over with Bruce. I felt sorry for the kid. Concurrent terms!" A look of disgust passed over her face. "What was that judge on? But Bruce remembered the case. It made the city papers even though the trial was upstate. I guess because she was such a pretty girl, you know how the media loves that. Apparently, the parents were well off. The house alone was worth over a million and that's in the country, before real estate prices skyrocketed. Bruce felt they could pay for private attorneys and our resources were better spent elsewhere." Melanie looked at Dani quizzically. "Why are you asking about her?"

"I ran into her sister at Camp Adagio and she strong-armed me into agreeing to meet with her. It'll just be a courtesy interview."

Melanie frowned. "Her child has Williams syndrome?"

Dani nodded.

"I know you, Dani. You're going to identify with her and want to help—but you must realize Bruce won't okay it. Do you want me to see her instead of you, so you'll be off the hook?"

Melanie's offer tempted her. After all, they'd worked as a team ever since they'd taken on George Calhoun's case together a year ago. And Melanie was right—Dani was a softy. She understood how hard it was raising a child with Williams syndrome, a condition that caused varying levels of retardation. Add to that the stress of dealing with a sister locked up for life. But rules were rules. They had to look at cases coldly and objectively, and the ability to pay for private attorneys was a big factor.

Still, she had promised Donna she'd meet with her. She thanked Melanie, then headed back to her office to return Donna's call.

"I didn't always believe Molly was innocent." The woman sitting opposite Dani was dressed just as impeccably as she'd been the first time they'd met. Now, though, her brown eyes were rimmed with red as she dabbed at her tears with a crumpled tissue. "In fact, from the time she was arrested, all through the trial, I'd convinced myself she'd done it. Murdered our parents. After all, she'd confessed.

"But a few months ago, I got this letter. That was when I first contacted your group." She opened up her black Gucci tote, which was adorned with gold-tone studs, and pulled out an envelope. Carefully, as though she were handing over precious jewels, she placed it in front of Dani. Then, with her head hanging low, she whispered, "I should have believed her. She recanted, said she didn't do it. She's my sister, my only sister. I should have believed her." Once again, tears flowed down Donna's cheeks.

Dani pulled the letter from the envelope. It was in a standard font. Nothing about the paper or writing was distinctive. She put on her glasses, then read: *Dear Mrs. Garmond. Your sister didn't kill your parents. I know the people who were responsible.*

That was it. Nothing more. Dani turned over the envelope and saw a postmark from White Plains.

"That's all? Because of this letter you've changed your mind? It doesn't seem like much here. Any one of Molly's friends could have sent this to you."

"Well, that's what I thought at first. Then"—Donna opened up her bag once more and pulled out a second letter—"I got this last week." She pushed the envelope over to Dani.

Once more, Dani pulled a single sheet of computer-printed paper from the envelope and read. Same font, same paper. *Look into the county jail. That's what it was about.* She put the letter down and looked at Donna. "Do you know what he means by this? What would this have to do with your parents?"

"My father's company built the new jail in Hudson County. It was very controversial and pretty much divided over political party lines. After it was finished, the delays and cost overruns were so high the state investigated, but they found nothing amiss."

"So your father was cleared of wrongdoing?"

"My parents had been murdered before the state finished its investigation. But yes, he was cleared."

Dani's fingers found the ends of her long, dark curls and twisted them between her fingers as she thought. She knew what she was supposed to do: commiserate with the woman, make apologies for HIPP, then send her on her way. Yet the letters intrigued her.

The sparkle of the large diamond on Donna's right hand reminded her of her task.

"Donna, I would like to help, really I would. But HIPP only takes on cases of indigent prisoners. And it's clear that you have the money to help. If your husband chooses not to, well—that's not something we can factor in."

"But I'm not the one who'd be your client. Molly is. And she has nothing."

"Your parents were well-to-do," Dani reminded her.

"Molly didn't get any of their money. She couldn't—once she was convicted her share was forfeited."

"So you got it all?"

"Half. And that's gone. My husband used the money to start his business."

"But the other half? What happened to that?"

"It's in a trust. Molly had a baby in prison. A little girl."

Dani knew she was sunk. The thought of a baby, taken from her mother—cruelly and unfairly if Molly had been wrongly convicted—broke down her resolve. "What happened to her daughter?" she asked, knowing she was only digging a deeper hole for herself.

"I tried to get custody, but the father fought me. You know how it is—blood rules. Although if I'm really honest with myself, I didn't push too hard. I had just finished college when she was born, barely able to take care of myself, much less a baby. And I resented Molly for putting me in this spot." Donna reached into her bag once more and pulled out her wallet, opened it, and retrieved a picture. She handed it over to Dani. "This is Sophie. She'll be twelve soon."

An angelic-faced child with straight blonde hair brushing her shoulders and eyes the color of crème de menthe. It looked to be a school photo; Sophie sat erect in front of a generic blue background, her hands clasped in her lap.

"Do you get to see your niece?"

Donna nodded. "Once in a while. If there's something special in our family, Finn will let me take her."

"Finn?"

"He's the father." Donna looked away from Dani and fixed her eyes on the diplomas hanging on the wall. When she finally turned back, she said, "He testified against Molly at her trial. I've never forgiven him for that."

Dani wondered if it was Finn she wouldn't forgive, or herself, for not believing in her sister's innocence for so long. She'd seen so much anger in her job—anger at the lawyers, the judge, the victim, the defendant's own family, her friends. Almost always it was misdirected. The prisoners were really angry at themselves. Even when it wasn't deserved.

"He's married now," Donna continued. "Has a son with his wife. Kim. That's her name. She tries to be a good mother to Sophie, I suppose, but—"

"Yes?"

"But her son is her son. And it's clear she treats Sophie differently."

Dani glanced at her watch. She'd allotted thirty minutes for Donna and they were going on an hour. She wanted to reassure this woman who was so clearly in pain that everything would work out for Molly, even when it was likely it wouldn't. She'd felt this need since childhood—to try to fix things for others, to make them feel better. That's why she entered college expecting to work toward becoming a psychologist, until events steered her onto another track.

"Look, Donna. I can't promise you anything, but I'll talk to our director about Molly's case. I have to warn you, though; it's unlikely he'll change his mind."

Donna grabbed Dani's hands and squeezed them. "Please, try to convince him. The police homed in on Molly almost immediately and never looked for anyone else. There's something going on; I know there is. Why else would I get those letters?"

"Well, it could be from some crackpot. I'll press Bruce on it, I promise. If he okays it, then whatever attorney is assigned will follow up with you."

The color drained from Donna's face. "But wouldn't you handle it? I'd want you to be the attorney."

"I'm sorry. I'm a capital appeals specialist. Prisoners on death row. But all the attorneys in the office are excellent."

"No," Donna said, shaking her head. "Can't you make an exception? I feel comfortable with you. You understand what it means to have a child that needs help, just as I do. And Sophie needs help."

Dani sighed. "Let's take one step at a time. First, let me talk to Bruce about HIPP taking the case."

"Thank you."

"If he gives the go-ahead, we'll need Molly to sign a retainer letter. I assume you've talked to her about this."

Donna stiffened. "Molly doesn't speak to me." Suddenly, the small office filled with silence. Donna stared at her hands, which were folded in her lap, then looked back up at Dani. "At first, when I thought Molly had murdered our parents, I was furious. How could she do this to me?" She shook her head. "I only thought about myself, never about what Molly was going through. Even when I learned she was pregnant, I refused to visit her in prison. In the beginning, she begged me to come. Wrote me letter after letter saying she was innocent. I never answered.

"After I married and had children of my own, I realized how cruel I'd been to her. Even if she was guilty, she was still my sister. I tried to see her then, but she wouldn't put me on her visitor list. We haven't seen each other or spoken since she was sent away."

Dani eyed the woman sitting opposite her. Life seemed full of conflicting emotions, she thought. The excitement of a new job coupled with the fear of not performing well. A young teenager's wish for independence coupled with the need for parental approval. A working mother's enjoyment of a fulfilling career coupled with guilt for leaving her child's care to another. Dani could see how Donna's conflicting feelings for her sister had wreaked havoc on her. The sadness in her eyes attested to her pain.

Dani wasn't certain where to go with this matter. The likelihood of Bruce agreeing to take it on was small, but even that slight chance disappeared if the prisoner didn't want help.

Her intercom buzzed and broke the silence. She picked up the phone and heard her secretary say, "Don Phelps is on line three."

"I'm finishing right now. I'll get back to him." When she hung up the receiver, she told Donna she'd let her know the agency's decision, one way or the other.

"Just one more thing," Donna said as she stood up to leave. "Whatever hard feelings Molly may have for me, only one thing matters. Sophie needs her mother. Her real mother."

Dani returned her phone call, then dictated a letter to a prisoner whose plea for help had been granted. She enjoyed giving good news, and cringed when she had to turn down a prisoner whose case had merit. It often seemed arbitrary to her, the choices that were made, just as the justice system itself at times seemed arbitrary. Was every last defendant guilty because twelve men and women had deemed it so? Judges certainly treated it that way. A defendant who showed no remorse at sentencing was often rewarded with a stiffer term. Yet, at such times, contrition was impossible. A wrongfully convicted defendant raged at the injustice. That very rage, that lack of remorse when a jury determined guilt, led to more years behind bars. Guilt or innocence wasn't an absolute truth. It was what a jury found as its truth.

As the afternoon wore on, Dani tried, unsuccessfully, to push back thoughts of Molly. Her love for Jonah was so overwhelming that the thought of losing him was honestly unimaginable. If Molly hadn't murdered her parents, if she'd been thrown into a prison of hardened criminals, deprived of her youthful promise, that was an injustice. To have her daughter taken away from her, raised by another woman, made it a tragedy. Dani didn't know if she could find out the truth. And in any event, Bruce was certain to deny her the chance to try.

Finally, her desk cleared of the pressing matters, Dani made her way back to Bruce's office. He sat at his desk, his long legs stretched out to the side, his eyes buried in a brief.

Dani stepped inside. "Got a moment?"

Bruce put down the thick set of papers and looked up. "Sure. Take a seat."

She eased herself into the chair opposite his desk.

"Uh-oh. Something's bothering you," Bruce said.

"Why do you say that?"

"Because every time you're worried, you twirl your hair."

Dani smiled. "I think we've been working together too long. You know me too well."

"Well enough. What's going on?"

Dani unwrapped her strands of hair, took a deep breath, and leaned forward. "Remember Molly Singer? Melanie talked to you about her case a few months ago?"

"Not really. What's it about?"

"A young girl, at least she was young back then, when she was convicted. Just eighteen. She confessed, then recanted. Found guilty of murdering both parents and sentenced to consecutive twenty-five-to-life terms."

Bruce was quiet for a moment, then he slowly nodded. "It rings a bell. We turned it down. No DNA in that case, if I remember correctly. Without that it would be hard to disprove. It was the sister who wrote, right?"

"Yes, that's the case. I met with her sister today. Donna Garmond."

Bruce looked startled. "Why? I already said no." He already had his back up.

"I ran into her at Camp Adagio. Her daughter is a Williams syndrome child, too. I guess I felt a connection with her and didn't want to just brush her off."

"Okay. You've done your good deed and met with her. The answer is still no."

"There's been a new development. Donna's received a couple of anonymous letters that suggest a new angle."

"Unless the new angle gives the name of the real murderer and the evidence to back it up, we don't have the resources to take it on. Send her a letter with regrets."

"But—"

"I don't have time to argue over this. And I didn't think you did either. Send her a letter." With that, Bruce picked up the brief and returned to reading. Their meeting was over.

At twenty past nine, during the time Dani and Doug called their "honeymoon hour," when all work was pushed aside to spend time with each other, Dani lay slumped on the couch, her head leaning against Doug's chest.

"I understand where Bruce is coming from," she said. "We have to be practical when it comes to selecting cases. But she was just a child herself when it happened."

"If you really want to take the case, push him back on it."

"That's just it. I don't know if I want the case. I don't even know if Molly wants HIPP to represent her. Or if I think she's guilty. But without Bruce's go-ahead, I can't even do the preliminary work to figure out those questions."

The curtains lifted with the evening breeze. Nights had finally started to cool down, and they'd been able to turn off the air conditioner. It was Dani's favorite time of year, when the seasons passed from the hot, humid days of summer to the crisp days of autumn.

"Unless you're going to try to persuade Bruce to reconsider, you've got to put her out of your mind."

Dani agreed; she needed to move on. Change what you can, Ted Kennedy had said at his brother Robert's funeral, and know what you can't. The office was too busy for Bruce to alter his position. She had to accept that.

"I'm going to turn in now," Doug said. "How about you?"

"Soon. I'll be up in a bit."

Dani headed to the kitchen and filled the teapot with water, then sat reading the *New York Times* as she waited for it to boil. When the familiar whistle sounded, she poured the hot water into a mug hand-painted with the words "World's Best Mom." It had been Jonah's Mother's Day gift to her when he was seven, the result of a school project. One edge was chipped, but she couldn't bring herself to discard it. If it wasn't in the dishwasher waiting to be cleaned, it was the first cup she grabbed when she needed a hot drink.

She dipped a green-tea bag in the water several times, discarded it, and added lemon juice. She sat back down at the kitchen table and pushed the newspaper away.

The hot steam filled her nostrils. She loved the feel of the warmth on her face, even on the hottest summer day. Usually, it soothed her. Not tonight. She couldn't shake the look on Donna's face as she pleaded for Dani to take her sister's case. And she couldn't shake the feeling that the anonymous letters were the key to something. But what?

CHAPTER

5

It was Saturday, family time. Time to spend with Jonah and Doug doing typical family activities, some mundane, like shopping, some fun, like visits to the Bronx Zoo, a favorite of Jonah's. Instead, Dani drove on the Saw Mill Parkway north to the Bedford Hills Correctional Facility. The only maximum-security prison for women in New York State was a half-hour drive from her home. Its closeness was how she justified to herself going to meet Molly Singer when she'd been expressly told to turn down her case.

She had done as instructed. A letter had gone out to Donna advising that HIPP would not represent her sister. It was only when Donna received the letter and called up, crying, begging Dani to reconsider, that she agreed to meet Molly. And didn't tell Bruce. Instead, she sent a letter to Molly saying that she'd been asked to look into her conviction and would like to meet with her. Today she was doing so.

Traffic was light and she made good time. Dani pulled up to the visitors' entrance just before ten a.m. She hoped to get in and out quickly and be home in time to take Jonah to the movies. Most thirteen-year-olds wouldn't be caught dead with their parents at the movies, but Jonah still wasn't capable of independent activities. One day, Dani hoped, but not yet.

She passed through security, then was directed to a waiting room. It was her first time in this facility—she had far more male clients than female—but it smelled like nearly every other prison she'd been in throughout the country. It had the same odor of disinfectant, used to cover something unpleasant. She couldn't place what—maybe sweat? Urine? Rodent droppings? She entered the room, which had one couch, a low rectangular table in front of it, and numerous chairs spread about. The sign on the door read "Attorneys Only." The room was empty, and she made herself comfortable. She pulled her iPad from her briefcase and clicked on the Kindle app, hoping to use a few moments of downtime to catch up on her reading.

"We're ready for you now."

Dani looked up and saw a uniformed woman standing in the doorway. She followed her down a hallway, through another security checkpoint, and then to a small room, empty except for a square table with two chairs on one side, a single chair on the other. All of the furniture was bolted to the floor. Outside, she could hear the usual prison cacophony—guards yelling, TVs blaring, metal clanging. Five minutes passed before she heard footsteps approach the door on the prisoner's side of the room. When it opened, a female guard stepped inside, her hand on the arm of a woman whose hands were shackled. The guard nodded to Dani, then brought the prisoner over to the chair opposite Dani. She unlocked the woman's handcuffs, then stepped outside the door, where she remained posted.

Dani was used to interviewing prisoners. Whether men or women, they usually had a pasty pallor and an institutional slump. Not Molly. Her fair complexion glowed, despite the windowless room, and her green eyes shone with a sparkle that defied her surroundings. Her blonde hair was cut short, which highlighted the perfect features of her face. She looks like an actress playing the role of a prisoner, Dani thought.

"Molly, let me begin by saying I'm here unofficially. HIPP must be very selective about the cases it accepts, and yours didn't fall under its guidelines. I'm sorry."

The smile on Molly's face dimmed, then returned. "I understand. I'm just happy to have a visitor. I don't get many now. But . . ."

"Yes?"

"Don't get me wrong. As I said, I'm glad to see anyone. But why did you come if you can't help me?"

"Your sister was very persistent."

Molly squirmed in her seat, then crossed her arms over her chest. "Very guilty, you mean."

"Guilty? Are you suggesting Donna murdered your parents?"

"Oh, no. Of course not. Donna was away at school when it happened. I meant she feels guilty that she abandoned me for so long. Did she tell you that we don't talk anymore?"

"She did."

"So I guess this is her way of atoning."

"Maybe it is."

Dani wasn't sure herself why she was sitting across the table from this woman. Normally, she'd ask questions, try to elicit the inmate's version of the events that led to incarceration. But to what end with Molly? Dani couldn't take her case. Bruce hadn't even permitted discussion of the matter.

Suddenly, Dani felt indignant. How dare Bruce dismiss her so perfunctorily! He was wrong to foreclose a conversation. All the angrier for being made to feel like a child sneaking behind her parents' backs, Dani decided to forge ahead. Even when they accepted a case, it was always a preliminary decision. Only after they investigated the client's claim of innocence and found grounds to believe it to be true would they make that final determination to challenge the conviction. Well, she was just doing a preliminary investigation. On her own time, to boot. Too bad if Bruce had a problem with that.

Dani looked Molly straight in the eye. So much could be read in a person's face, she thought. Tommy Noorland, the HIPP investigator she preferred working with, believed prisoners could lie through their teeth and still look like the most innocent angel. Not Dani. There was almost always something that gave them away when lying. The smallest twitch, the tapping of their fingers, even their smile. Sure, she could be fooled. But her track record had been pretty good ever since she stopped working only on appeals and began investigating prisoners' claims.

"Molly, defense attorneys don't like to ask their clients if they've committed the crime. If they confess, then their attorney can't put them on the stand and let them lie. It's different with HIPP. We only take cases if we believe our client was wrongfully convicted. So, tell me, did you murder your parents?"

Molly's smile dimmed, her shoulders slumped, and the glow of her rosy cheeks disappeared, as though an internal light had been switched off. "It aches when I think about my parents. I loved them so much. Sure, we had our fights. I mean, I was a teenager when they died, and I behaved like a teenager. But kill them? I could never have done that."

"When the police took you in for questioning, you confessed."

"I kept telling them I didn't do it. Over and over. They told me they found the knife used to stab them and only my fingerprints were on it. They said fragments of my skin were under my mother's fingernails. And I did have a scratch on my arm, but I always scratched myself in my sleep. The police said I didn't remember doing it because I'd taken Ambien. After hours of going around and around, I felt so confused. I began to think I must have. They wrote something out and I signed it. I didn't even read what they wrote.

"After they locked me up, after I'd eaten and slept, I knew no drug could make me forget doing something so horrible. But it was too late." A desperate, tortured look overtook her. "You don't think it could, do you?"

"Could what?"

"Make me forget murdering my parents."

"I don't know."

It made it so much easier for Dani when the prisoners shouted their innocence. She wanted to believe everyone, even though she knew some—most—were lying. Yet, when a truly innocent person looked her in the eyes and said, "I didn't do it," when his or her body language spoke to that truth, then Dani knew she would fight relentlessly for that person's freedom.

Was Molly innocent? The answer wasn't clear to Dani. She had no business sitting across from this woman and giving her false hope. Bruce didn't want HIPP to take her case. Molly couldn't even state with conviction that she hadn't murdered her parents. The smart course was to pick up her briefcase, give Molly her regrets, and leave.

Instead, Dani smiled and said, "Let me read up on your case. I'll get back to you soon."

On the drive home, Dani knew she was in trouble. Given Bruce's adamancy, any work on Molly's case would have to be on her own. At least until she could figure out whether she believed in Molly's innocence. And if she got to that point? Well, she guessed she'd figure out then how to convince Bruce to take her on.

The clouds had crept across the sky during the hour Dani spent inside the walls of the prison, and now drops of rain began to splash against her front window. She turned on the windshield wipers, and the rhythmic swoosh pushed aside her worries about Bruce. September rain smelled different than spring rain, she thought. It carried the odor of dying leaves instead of spring's new buds. It signaled an ending of warm summer days, of sandy beaches, of family vacations. Some people looked forward to winter—to building snowmen and schussing down ski slopes, to huddling with their partner in front of a fireplace crackling with burning logs. Once Dani had enjoyed those activities, too.. But as she'd grown older, she'd begun to dislike the cold, the ice, the treacherous roads. From time to time she entertained the thought of moving to California, away from New York's harsh winters and humid summers. Any law school would grab Doug up. And she could get another job, maybe in a large law firm, defending white-collar criminals. No one was sentenced to death for competing unfairly, or defrauding customers, or attempting to monopolize a market. She wouldn't have to face the prospect of failing to free an innocent client, knowing that he would be executed if she didn't succeed. She wouldn't have to feel her heart break a little more each time she turned down a request for help from someone facing the rest of his life in jail because there wasn't enough money or enough time to help every wrongly convicted prisoner. And she wouldn't have to tell a woman languishing in prison since she was eighteen that she would never get to know her daughter because Dani wasn't permitted to help her.

She arrived home to an empty house and a note attached to the refrigerator door with a magnet. "Gone to the movies. We'll be home before dinner."

"Damn," she muttered. Jonah had been pestering them all week to see *Despicable Me 2*. At first she wondered why he hankered for a children's film, until she realized she wanted to see it herself. Now they'd gone without her.

Without them home, the house seemed eerily quiet. No television blaring in the background, no music blasting from the radio, no sound of feet traipsing across the wood floors. The silence engulfed her and created a sense of disquiet.

Dani fought it off. She plopped down on the living room couch and wondered what she'd do with this gift of time to herself, a rarity since she'd started working again. She knew what she should do—begin researching Molly's conviction. Or get ahead on some of the cases awaiting her in the office. Instead, she rested her head on the sofa's pillow, closed her eyes, and drifted off to sleep.

6

Dani dreaded her inevitable confrontation with Bruce. She'd sped past his office when she arrived an hour earlier, with just a quick wave and a mumbled hello as she made her way to her own space. None of the usual Monday-morning pleasantries were exchanged. She didn't pop her head inside and ask about his weekend. She didn't wait for him to ask about hers. They'd worked together over four years and had long ago progressed past being mere colleagues. Although they rarely socialized outside the office, they were friends. They exchanged stories about their families, laughed at each other's quirks, shared a familiarity that was bred from working closely together over life and death matters.

After two hours spent on an appeal for one of her clients, Dani ambled over to Bruce's office. She stopped along the way to chat with Vicky, her favorite paralegal, sitting at one of the many desks crowded together on the open floor. Unable to stall any longer, she stood outside his doorway. As usual, Bruce's door was open, and he sat with his chair turned toward the only window, dictating into a machine. Dani stepped inside and plopped down on a chair.

"Hi."

Bruce swiveled around to face her, replacing the handset of the Dictaphone in its cradle.

"What's up?"

"Molly Singer."

Dani saw a frown cross Bruce's face before he caught himself. With his mouth set, he said, "I thought we already settled that. We're not taking her case."

"I met with her over the weekend." Dani waited for the expected explosion. They were rare with Bruce, but when pushed over the line, whether by an obstructionist warden, a reluctant court clerk, or one of his staff, he could erupt. Afterward, he inevitably described his outburst as a tactic, designed to keep the recipient in check, but Dani suspected otherwise. Bruce was simply human, and as such he occasionally lost control. Despite Dani's fear that this would be one of those times, she was met with silence.

"I think she was railroaded, Bruce. And whatever you think of her sister's resources, they're not available to Molly."

Bruce continued his silence. He picked up a pencil from his desk and fiddled with it between his fingers, all the while glaring at Molly.

"Say something."

After what seemed like an interminable stretch of quiet, Bruce said, "There's nothing to say. I've given you my decision."

Now it was Dani's turn to glare silently. Finally, Bruce picked up the Dictaphone. "I have work to do. I assume you do as well." He swung his chair around to once again face his window.

Dani stood up to leave, then stopped. She was a fighter. She fought with judges and prosecutors for her clients' freedom; she fought with school administrators to get Jonah the best teachers. She'd never fought with Bruce before—they were allies. But she wasn't ready to walk away from Molly Singer. She sat down again.

"You're wrong."

Bruce swung his chair around. "Excuse me?"

"You made a decision when you didn't have all the facts. From the beginning, the one point you've drilled into me has been, 'Dig for the facts.' We're supposed to make decisions based on the facts of the case, not some preconceived notion of a client. You based your decision on what you remembered reading about Molly's case when it was first tried."

"You're off base."

"I don't think so. Melanie told me you turned it down because her parents were wealthy. But you didn't know then that her inheritance was forfeited when she was convicted. And you didn't know that her sister wouldn't pay for her appeals."

"I also remembered that she confessed to the murders. What makes you think she's innocent?"

"I'm not sure. None of us are ever sure until we start digging into the case. All I'm asking is to start digging."

A smile slowly crept across Bruce's face. "Okay. Go ahead."

"And also—wait. Did you just say we could take the case?"

Bruce nodded, his smile broadening. "I just wanted to see how hard you would fight for it."

"You skunk. Why did you put me through that?"

Bruce's smile disappeared. "This isn't a DNA case, Dani. You'll have a tough challenge proving she's innocent—if indeed she is. I needed to see if you were fully committed."

Dani walked back to her office, unsure if she had won a battle that she would come to regret.

Settled in her chair, Dani began where she always did—with an Internet search of Molly's conviction. She started with newspaper accounts.

Hudson Valley Dispatch, September 24, 2000
Molly Singer Guilty on Two Counts of Second-Degree Murder
Byline: Shannon Evans

After three weeks of testimony, the jury took only four hours to return a guilty verdict for second-degree murder against

18-year-old Molly Singer, arrested five months ago for the murder of her parents, Joseph Singer, 48, and Sarah Singer, 46. Both were found dead in their Andersonville home on May 2 of this year.

The only solid evidence presented by the prosecution was her confession, recanted almost as soon as it was given. With a paucity of forensic evidence to back up the confession, the district attorney's office relied on testimony from Ms. Singer's classmates at Munsee High School to show her long-standing resentment toward her parents and the restrictions they'd placed on her. Classmates described her as a spoiled rich girl, used to getting her way and prone to angry outbursts when she didn't.

Although Robert McDonald, Ms. Singer's attorney, elicited testimony from Molly's closest friends that painted a different picture, it wasn't enough to overcome the most damning witness: Molly Singer's boyfriend of two years, Finn Reynolds. Mr. Reynolds told the jury that he was with Ms. Singer the night before her parents were found dead in their beds. He stated that Mr. and Mrs. Singer were trying to separate the couple, but Molly told him that night that she would do whatever she had to in order for them to be together.

Sentencing is scheduled for September 28.

Dani pushed away from the computer. Donna had mentioned that Finn had testified against Molly. The prosecutor couldn't have known of their conversation without Finn bringing it up, yet the couple were supposedly in love. Dani jotted down a note to ask Molly about Finn.

The rest of the day was spent reading the appellate decisions in Molly's case. Although it gave her some sense of the defense strategy, her real understanding of the case wouldn't come until she got a copy of the trial transcript. Dani had heard of Robert McDonald. He had a reputation as a top-notch litigator. A claim of ineffective counsel wouldn't be available to her as an avenue of appeal.

By the time Dani finished her review, it was past four o'clock, an hour later than the time she usually left the office. It meant she wouldn't be home to greet Jonah when he returned from school. Instead, Katie, his sitter—an absolute godsend—would watch over him.

On her way out, Dani stopped by Bruce's office. "I'm going over to Bedford Correctional tomorrow morning, before I come into the office," she said. "I've decided to sign up Molly."

"So you think she's innocent?"

"I don't know—but those letters, they might mean something. Or lead to something. And I want to find out where."

The buzzer on the intercom didn't stop, despite the county executive's strict instruction to his secretary to hold his calls. Reluctantly, he grabbed the telephone.

"Jeannette, I told you—"

"I know, I know, Mr. Reynolds, but it's Sheriff Engles and he was insistent."

After a moment's hesitation, he said, "Okay, put him through."

When the phone rang again, Frank Reynolds picked it up quickly. "John, what can I do for you?"

"Is the line safe?" Engles asked, his voice barely above a whisper.

"What the hell are you talking about?"

"Is it safe? Could anybody else be listening in?"

Reynolds wanted to laugh at him. Engles liked drama, always finding conspiracies where none existed. Still, even the paranoid were sometimes correct. So he withheld his snicker. "Of course it's safe. Who do you think could hear us?"

"Well, your secretary for one. The woman's the biggest gossip around. I wouldn't put it past her to be listening in on your calls. Especially one from me."

Reynolds sighed. Jeannette was pushing fifty, had worked in government offices for over twenty years, and was the most efficient secretary he'd ever had. It was ludicrous to think she'd monitor his phone calls. Still—he'd been wrong about others before. "If you're so concerned, call me back on my cell. You've got the number."

A few minutes later, Reynolds's cell phone vibrated and he answered it immediately. "This better be important, John."

"Maybe, maybe not. But I thought you needed to know. Molly Singer has a new attorney. From the Help Innocent Prisoners Project. Came to see her on Saturday."

Molly Singer. At first, he'd felt pity for the girl. After all, he'd known her since she was a baby. But twelve men and women put her behind bars and, after many years, he'd decided that it was meant to be. Now he rarely gave her any serious consideration, not even when he saw Molly's daughter. Not even when she smiled the same way Molly used to, her green eyes crinkling at the edges.

"How do you know?"

"I have my sources."

A wave of anger washed over Reynolds. With his voice barely controlled, he said, "What the hell does that mean? Did you blab to someone?"

"Calm down. It's nothing like that. The guards down in Bedford keep me apprised on all the inmates we send there."

Reynolds felt his chest unclench. "Okay. That's good. Anyway, it needn't mean anything, her seeing a new lawyer. Don't most prisoners keep trying to overturn their convictions?"

"Sure. But it's Molly."

"So? She's had other attorneys."

"Not in years. I thought it was over."

Despite his reassurances to the sheriff, Reynolds felt an acidic burning in his gut. He reached into his desk drawer and pulled out a bottle of Tums, popped the lid, and shook two pills into his hand. He listened as Engles jabbered on a bit longer, then cut him off when he couldn't take any more. "Look, just monitor the visits, okay? Let's not get all worked up when it could be nothing."

"Don't you think Alan should know?"

"Not yet." Reynolds needed to think this through before they involved Alan. He had been crystal clear about that—keep him at arm's length unless there was no choice. "Look, I'm up to my ears here. Let me know if you hear anything else, but for now, let's just let it simmer."

After hanging up, Reynolds stared at the budget on his desk. He'd been working overtime getting it ready for the legislature, looking for places to cut. When the county changed to a county executive form of government, the Democrats took the first spot. Everyone knew it was because of that damn jail. But he'd won four years later and had held on every election since, mostly because of his promise to keep taxes down. With real property values in the toilet, property-tax revenue went down the drain with it. Now balancing the budget was like walking a tightrope with no net. The locals demanded services—they just didn't want to pay for them.

He pushed the papers to the side of his desk and opened its bottom drawer. He rarely drank anymore, especially at the office. But he kept a bottle of eighteen-year-old single-malt scotch tucked away for important visitors—those deep-pocketed constituents whose favor he needed to curry year round, election year or not. After buzzing Jeannette and reminding her not to interrupt him again, he pulled out the bottle, slid his chair to the credenza behind his desk, and retrieved a crystal highball glass, then poured himself two fingers' worth. The rich, peaty scotch went down like liquid heat, and he leaned back in his chair as he savored it.

It wasn't like he'd never thought about Molly Singer over the years. It would have been impossible not to. Still, he'd pushed those thoughts to the back of his mind, only brought them forward occasionally, less and less often as the years went by. He'd known she was trouble the first time Finn brought her home. Too smart for her own good, too willful for her parents to control. And too pretty to ignore.

That was the question now: should he ignore this new development? Chalk it up to just another grab by a prisoner for freedom? Or did it mean trouble for him? Trouble for all of them. Reynolds took one more sip of the scotch, then picked up his phone and dialed Alan.

8

The sound of the door slamming shut reverberated throughout the house. At least it was quiet now, Finn thought, the screaming of the last twenty minutes replaced by silence. He knew it wouldn't last. Any moment now Kim would storm into his study, her mouth twisted into the scowl she wore whenever she'd had a run-in with Sophie. It wouldn't matter that he'd told her he shouldn't be disturbed. Kim paid him no more mind than Sophie did. He braced for the inevitable tirade. It wasn't long in coming.

"I can't take her anymore," Kim spat as she burst into the room. "She has no respect for me. None whatsoever."

Finn swung his chair around and looked up at his wife, firmly planted in the doorway, her arms folded across her chest. She hadn't changed from her yoga class at the gym, and the black spandex shorts hugged her body. *She's so beautiful, even when she's angry.* How did she manage it? Even after a baby she'd stayed slim, her skin still smooth and youthful. With her hair pulled back in a ponytail, she looked more like a college coed than a mother of two. He felt like an old man who'd robbed the cradle, but she was only two years younger than he.

Finn looked down at his expanding belly. The buttons of his tucked-in shirt looked ready to pop.

"Well, aren't you going to say anything?"

"What can I say? It's Sophie."

"What does that mean?" The coldness of her tone sliced through the air.

"I mean she's always overly dramatic. You shouldn't let it get to you."

Kim stormed across the room and thrust her index finger at him. "Heaven forbid you should ever take my side. She's a drama queen because you've allowed it. You never see Graham behave that way." Finished with her scolding, she once again wrapped her arms around her chest.

It always led to that. Their son, as rambunctious as most six-year-old boys, had no flaws according to Kim. The perfect, loving child, well-behaved and attentive. Too attentive, Finn sometimes thought. Too attached to his mother. And Sophie? It seemed Kim only saw her flaws, never the terrific things about her.

Graham was a carbon copy of his father, with sandy-brown hair that curled when it got too long, deep-brown eyes with lashes women envied, and a nose that some already described as patrician. When strangers saw the family together, though, it was the resemblance between Sophie and Kim that drew their remarks. When the two females in his life weren't engaged in warfare, Finn appreciated the irony. Sophie shared Kim's silky blonde hair that almost touched her shoulders, her large eyes, and full lips. "How much your daughter looks like you," they'd often comment, and Kim would always reply, "Oh, she's my stepdaughter. Looks like her real mother."

Her real mother. The phrase cut through Finn like a surgeon's scalpel. He'd married Kim when Sophie was only four years old. Before then, Sophie had no mother. He couldn't understand why Kim pushed her away, even before Graham was born. Deny it as she might, Kim was Sophie's real mother—she had no other.

"Look, I've got to catch up on this paperwork. Let's talk about it later."

Kim's mouth clenched tighter. She unfolded her arms and placed her hands on her waist and stamped her foot twice. "No! Not later, now. I'm sick of you coddling her. She wouldn't be this way if you ever disciplined her."

Finn held back a chuckle. Almost thirty, and sometimes Kim behaved like a child having her own temper tantrum. With a sigh, he said, "I'll talk to her. I promise. But I really have to do this work now."

"Just do it. Today," Kim said, then turned and stormed out of the room.

Finn turned back to his desk, papers spread across the top, and ran his fingers through his thinning hair. Life hadn't turned out as he'd expected. Throughout high school, he'd planned on becoming an architect. Then, everything changed with the killing of Molly's parents and her unthinkable arrest and conviction for the crimes. And with Sophie.

His parents thought he was crazy to fight for custody. "You're only nineteen, your whole life is ahead of you," they'd said. "Donna wants the baby; she's finished with school. Besides, she's a woman. She can handle it better." It didn't matter what they said. Sophie belonged with him. Instead of college, he did what he'd done every summer since he'd started high school—worked on a landscaping crew. He enrolled in botany classes at the local community college and by the time Sophie was three, he'd started his own landscaping company. Now he owned the most sought-after landscape design company in Hudson County.

Finn glanced out the window at his expansive lawn. He was a fortunate man, with a family he loved. If only Kim and Sophie could get along, he would be truly happy.

Kim was right, though. He didn't discipline Sophie. He couldn't. When she looked at him with her tear-streaked face, he only saw Molly. And a rush of guilt would flow through him, because he knew it had been his testimony that sent Sophie's mother to prison.

Once again, Dani sat opposite Molly Singer in the austere inter-view room, with a table and their chairs the only furniture. Again, a guard dressed in a starched gray uniform stood outside, able to view the occupants through the square window at the top of the door but unable to hear the soft voices of the two women talking. Dani heard the usual distant sounds, all blended together inside the room. She had learned to push those sounds away, to turn them into background noise, like waves crashing over rocks.

Molly's prison garb was orange, a starkly bright color that made most faces disappear. Not Molly's. Even without any makeup, her freshly scrubbed cheeks glowed. An attorney retention letter had already been signed and put away in Dani's briefcase. Dani chatted with Molly at first to put her at ease. Now it was time to get down to business.

"Tell me everything you remember about that night."

Molly sat erect in her seat, her hands folded in front of her. She spoke softly. "That's just it; there's so much I don't remember."

"Start earlier, when you were out with Finn."

"We were supposed to meet up with friends and go to a movie. But when Finn picked me up, he said his parents decided at the last minute to go away for the weekend. He wanted us to go back to his house instead."

"So that's what you did?"

She nodded. "We'd begun having sex a few months before. Whenever one of us had an empty house, we took advantage of it."

"What time did you get home?"

"It was past my curfew. I half expected my mother to be waiting by the steps, ready to lay it on for being late, but they were both asleep."

"And what time was that?"

"Almost one. I mean, I was supposed to be home by midnight, and it was well past that."

Dani took notes as Molly spoke, only looking up occasionally. "How did you know your parents were asleep? Did you see them in their bedroom?"

Molly paused before speaking again. "No. I mean, I didn't see them. I just assumed they were asleep because their room was dark and the door was ajar, just like they always left it when I was out and they'd gone to bed."

Dani stopped writing. "So they could have already been murdered by then."

Molly flinched at the word "murdered," then looked confused. "I thought they said at trial that the time of death was between two and four a.m.?"

"Medical examiners can be wrong. The science isn't always so exact. If they were off by two hours, even an hour, it's possible your parents were killed before you returned home."

"No, that doesn't make sense. Their door was ajar when I got home and closed when I woke up the next morning."

Dani struck a line through her last note. She'd hoped attacking the time of death might be an avenue for appeal. "Okay, so you got home, your parents seemed to be asleep. Then what?"

"I was really hopped-up from being with Finn, you know, that way, so I decided to take Ambien to fall asleep. I had some in my medicine cabinet and took two of them, then got into bed."

"How strong were they?"

"I thought they were five milligrams. That's what my mother always used to take, and I'd gotten a few from her stash. After, when my lawyer looked into it, it turned out that she'd switched to ten-milligram pills. I guess I hadn't paid attention to the difference in the way they looked."

Occasionally, Dani had to rely on Ambien herself. She'd always been a solid sleeper, until Jonah was born. Then, after months of making sure she awoke at his first cry, the slightest noise disturbed her sleep. When that happened, after Jonah was regularly sleeping through the night, it sometimes took a pill to return her to sleep. She'd only needed the five-milligram pill, though.

"What do you remember next?"

"I—"

A tapping on the door caused both women to look up. The guard stationed outside the interview room was pressing her face up to the window and held up five fingers. Dani nodded. Molly would be returned to her cell in five minutes.

"Let's change gears, Molly. We'll get back to that night and the next day on my next visit. I want to find out more about your father's business, especially the job building the new jail."

Molly looked confused. "What does that have to do with anything?"

"Your sister received two anonymous letters. They're the reason I'm here, looking into your case. They suggest that your parents' murder had something to do with the Hudson County jail. I know your father's company built the jail, and I wonder if you can think of any reason why the two could be connected."

Before Molly could answer, the door opened and the guard stepped inside. "It's time," she said.

"But it's not five minutes yet," Dani said, pointing to the clock on the wall.

"Yeah, well, I still have to get her back."

Dani took a breath. This kind of arbitrary treatment was hardly unusual in prison—if anything, it was pretty much the norm—and it wouldn't pay to antagonize the guards. She turned to Molly. "Just think about what I asked you, okay? We'll talk about it when I return."

"When are you coming back?"

"Soon."

It was almost noon by the time Dani arrived at HIPP. As she made her way to her office, she popped into Melanie's and Tommy's cubicles and asked them to join her in fifteen minutes. She stopped to pour herself a cup of coffee, then finally sat down at her desk. A handful of messages sat on top of her chair, and she used the time before her colleagues arrived to return calls. As she spoke on the phone, she glanced around her office, so different than the spartan interview room she'd just returned from. Like the prison room, her space was small and without a window offering a glimpse of the outside world. Yet it breathed life. A large potted plant stood in the corner. Her law school diplomas graced one wall and on another were framed images of landscapes taken during her flirtation with photography. Pictures of Doug and Jonah adorned her desk.

As she stared at Jonah's picture, it struck Dani again how unfathomable it would be to be separated from her son. He was ten in the picture. His dark-brown hair, its curls covering his ears, glowed from the bright sun, and his smile spread from cheek to cheek. They were at the beach in Montauk when the picture was taken, a favorite destination of Jonah's. During her brief visits with Molly, there had been no discussion of her daughter. Dani had wanted it that way; she wanted to take her measure of Molly, the prisoner, before being softened by thoughts of Molly, the mother, deprived of her daughter. Yet, despite her wish to keep that picture at a distance, it kept pushing its way into her thoughts.

A tap on her door erased the image. Dani glanced up and saw Melanie in the doorway, with Tommy a step behind. Although over the years casual Friday had turned into sloppy every day for the office, unless a court visit was on tap, Melanie always showed up for work looking like she'd stepped out of a Saks Fifth Avenue catalog. Today was no exception. Dani waved them both in.

"Did you learn anything helpful?" Melanie asked as she sat down.

"Not really. The guard took her away before we could get into it."

"But you think she's innocent?"

If Dani was a bleeding heart, and she had to admit she was, the only bigger softy in the office was Melanie.

"I still don't know. I don't think Molly knows either, although she insists she didn't have it in her."

Tommy stretched out his long legs and crossed his ankles. "You two would believe Jack the Ripper was innocent if he had a baby tucked under one arm."

Dani smiled. The three made a perfect team, each challenging the other. Whenever she had a choice, she picked Melanie and Tommy to work with. Dani filled them in on what she knew, then turned to Tommy. "I'd like you to check out the jail angle."

Tommy shrugged. "I'll do it, but the state checked into that business and found nothing wrong."

"It probably has nothing to do with the murders, but we shouldn't ignore the letters Donna received."

After her colleagues left, Dani picked up the phone to call Molly's trial lawyer. As with every appeal she handled, the real investigation began with the search through the first attorney's records. But with a client whose memory of the night was erased by drugs, she didn't hold out hope that she'd get much help there. Bruce was right. Without DNA evidence, proving Molly's innocence would be an uphill battle—and a steep uphill at that. Dani had a sinking feeling that the only way she'd convince a court of Molly's innocence would be to find the real murderer.

10

Frank Reynolds pushed his way through the crowd lined up at the barbeque pit and stepped behind Alan Bryson, whose plate was extended to receive the bloodred burger he'd requested. Bryson, still trim from years of daily jogs despite his love of red meat, turned around when Frank tapped his shoulder, then smiled.

"Frank, you're here. I've been wondering what happened to you."

"We need to talk," Frank said, his voice barely above a whisper.

A cloud passed over Bryson's face, then as quickly passed. "Later. This is a time for fun, Frank. Our friends are here, the music is blaring—I don't know how these young people stand it so loud—and everyone's enjoying themselves." He nodded across the lawn. "Look over there. We got a clown this year for the little ones. They're eating it up." Now the judge lowered his voice. "Whatever's on your mind, stow it. Put on a smile and start pumping some flesh."

Frank nodded, then walked away, irritated that he'd been brushed off so casually. He looked around and silently calculated the number of guests at the annual Harvest Festival, sponsored by the county Republican Party and timed to remind their constituents who to vote for in the upcoming elections. It was a good turnout this year. At least three hundred people, maybe more. A bounce house was set up at one end of the field, part of a county park that bordered the Hudson River, and children were lined up to get inside. At another corner, a volunteer ran relay races for the older children. On an adjoining field, a softball game was in progress.

"Hi, Dad."

Frank turned around and saw Finn. He gave him a hug, then asked, "Where's Kim and the kids?"

Finn shrugged. "Off somewhere. Graham's probably doing the races and Sophie went looking for her friends."

"And Kim?"

"Stayed home."

Frank raised his eyebrows but knew enough not to press his son.

"It's been a little strained lately between us."

"I'm sorry to hear that."

"Nothing to worry about; it'll pass."

Frank held his tongue. He'd never liked Kim. Sure, she was pretty, and had a body to go with it. But that was it. It was bad enough she had no brains, but she had no heart either. Cold as ice. The only good thing she'd done in Frank's view was produce Graham. And it'd be a miracle if she didn't mess him up good with her coddling.

"Mom here?"

"She's helping at the food table."

"I'm gonna go say hello. See you later."

Frank headed over to a group seated at one of the picnic tables—a few lawyers, an accountant, and a couple of local merchants. All big donors to his campaign in the past. He wasn't up for election this year but it didn't matter. Running for office never stopped. As soon as one election was over, he was out hustling money for the next. Only now, his head wasn't into glad-handing some big wheels. The call last night still had him rattled. He needed to tell the judge about it.

"Frank, how are you doing?" Jim Thornton boomed, turning heads all across the lawn.

Frank slid into an empty seat at the picnic table and forced a big smile. "Just fine, thanks. And how are you all doing?"

The men around the table nodded and offered murmured "goods" and "fines."

"You're one lucky bunch," one of the men said to him. "I don't remember one time when it's rained on your barbeque. And I've come to every one for at least a decade."

"The luck of the righteous," Frank said. "And you know, we do right by you folks."

"Oh, we know," said another. "And we remember come election time."

"I appreciate hearing that. I appreciate even more when I hear from your checkbooks," Frank said, his smile widening.

"Oh, you don't let us forget that." The men at the table laughed.

The conversation soon turned to talk of the upcoming World Series. Frank couldn't care less who won. Why was it that every time a group of men got together they talked of sports? He'd never shared that interest. Maybe it was growing up in the country, far enough away from New York City or any other place big enough to have a team. Maybe because, from as far back as he could remember, he'd always preferred academic pursuits to physical games.

Now half the folks in Hudson County had come up from the city. First, they bought vacation homes and just came north on weekends. Then, taken with the beauty of the countryside, the abundance of outdoor activities, the peaceful, laid-back lifestyle, they began moving up to live year round. Housing prices skyrocketed, and before the locals knew what had happened, their children couldn't afford to live there after they moved out of their parents' homes. And even people who'd lived in their homes for generations had trouble paying the property taxes that escalated right along with the increased value of their houses. Still, the newcomers brought wealth with them, and money paid for campaigns.

As the men heatedly argued over their favorite players, Frank could only think about the phone call he'd received. Beads of perspiration formed on his forehead, and he hoped the men at the table attributed it to the warmth of the day. He didn't want to appear nervous in front of them. The chief executive of the county should be confident and in control at all times.

Only he wasn't. Not today. He waited a bit, then stood up to leave.

"Heading off to fleece more pockets?" Jim Thornton thundered, and the men laughed again, but good-naturedly.

"Exactly. I don't want my constituents to think you fellas have a monopoly on that privilege."

With the band having finally taken a break, their noise was replaced by the sounds of children laughing and the cheers of three-legged race spectators.

Frank wandered over to the food tables. He was starting to get hungry. The smell of greasy hamburgers always got his juices flowing. He grabbed a bun, plopped a burger on top, then filled the rest of his plate with a corn on the cob and homemade salads made by loyal volunteers. He sauntered over to a large barrel and pulled out a cold beer, then looked for a familiar face to sit down with. As he scanned the picnic tables, he saw Bryson again, sitting with a group of men and women, all listening raptly to him. He began to walk toward him, then stopped. The last thing he needed was to antagonize Bryson.

How did I get involved in this mess? I didn't start it. It shouldn't be on my shoulders. Frank felt a tide of anger, tried to push it away, but couldn't. With tray in hand, he strode over to Bryson's table and stood over him.

"We need to talk now."

Bryson looked up and smiled blandly at him. "I told you, no shop talk today, Frank. Come by and see me on Monday."

"Sorry, it has to be today."

The judge's smile dimmed. With a sigh, he slowly arose, like a king leaving his throne, and signaled for Frank to follow him. Once they were alone, he turned to face him. That smile was a distant memory now. "Don't you ever contradict me in public again. You hear me? Never!"

"I'm sorry, but—"

"No buts. I don't care what this is about. Come by and see me on Monday and we'll talk. Need I remind you? You're in office because I put you there. And I can just as easily get you removed."

As Bryson turned his back to leave, Frank whispered, "An investigator is coming to my office on Monday morning to talk about the jail."

Bryson swung around to face him. "Who? And why?"

"His name is Tom Noorland. And he's asking because of Molly Singer."

"Damn." Bryson was silent for a moment. "The state already cleared us. He's just on a fishing expedition. It's your job to make sure he doesn't catch anything."

"And if I can't?"

"Then we're going to have more problems than the jail."

With that, Bryson returned to the picnic tables, leaving Frank just as worried as before.

"He'll be with you soon, Mr. Noorland."

It was twenty minutes past the time set for Tommy's appointment with Frank Reynolds, and all he'd seen were the gray walls of the waiting room. He'd arrived on time for their ten o'clock meeting. The secretary sitting at the desk just outside Reynolds's door, like a soldier guarding the castle, said he was running late. Running late, my ass, Tommy thought. He could see the buttons on the phone sitting on the secretary's desk. Not one was lit up. A million to one against anyone walking out of Reynolds's office when the door finally opened. He knew the strategy. Keep an enemy waiting long enough to get fidgety and it throws them off their game. Only it didn't work with him. Ten years with the FBI had familiarized him with every type of deception, every kind of game playing.

It made him question, though, why Reynolds treated him like an enemy.

Tommy reread the report of the state's investigation into the cost overruns on the county jail. He'd gotten a copy easily enough. As a public document, it was subject to the freedom of information laws.

Which didn't mean government agencies didn't usually drag their heels complying with those requests. It often took two weeks or more to find such documents, but Tommy had former law-enforcement buddies throughout the country. One phone call, and the next day the report sat on his desk. As far as Tommy could judge, the report raised no red flags.

Another ten minutes later, the door to Reynolds's office opened. Sure enough, the man standing in the doorway had been alone in there. He looked about Tommy's height, six feet even, but weighed at least thirty pounds more. He was dressed in a rumpled suit, and through his open jacket Tommy could see his stomach hanging over his belt. "Sorry to keep you waiting, Mr. Noorland. Why don't you come in now?"

Tommy held out his hand to shake Reynolds's. "Thanks for seeing me on short notice. I'll try not to take up too much of your time."

He entered the office and sat down on a wood chair opposite a plain walnut-veneer desk. Government offices all looked the same. No frills, even for the guy at the top.

"So," Reynolds said as he took his own seat, "you said you had some questions about the building of the jail. I'm afraid I won't be of much help to you. I wasn't county executive when that came about."

Tommy pretended to look through some papers on his lap, then pulled out one and placed it on top. "I see. That was before Hudson County had a county executive, right?"

"Yes, the county was governed by its legislators. And although I was a county legislator then, I wasn't the chairman. I was just one of forty-eight."

"Well then, this shouldn't take long. Just a few questions if you don't mind. Maybe you could fill me in on the decision to build a new jail to begin with."

"I'll be happy to. But first, I'm wondering what this has to do with Molly Singer. Didn't you say your office represented her?"

Tommy saw Reynolds's fingers tapping on the desk. *He's hiding something. Something about Molly.* "Probably nothing. I'm just following the orders of my boss to check out the jail."

"But why?"

"Molly's sister got some anonymous letters. Whoever wrote them said her parents' murders had to do with the jail somehow."

Reynolds's face blanched, the tapping of his fingers stopped, and he sat up straighter. "That's preposterous. How could that be?"

"That's what I'm trying to find out."

Tommy could hear the soft clicking of the clock on Reynolds's desk. Finally, Reynolds stood up. "I'm sorry. I don't have any information that would be helpful to you. I've a busy schedule."

Tommy remained seated. "You were chair of the appropriations committee in the legislature back then, right? Didn't that committee approve the budget for the jail?" He smiled up at Reynolds. "Well, actually, I know the answer to that." He looked through his papers and pulled one out. "Your group approved payments that were over fifty percent higher than the original seventy-million-dollar budget, didn't they?"

"Look, Mr. Noorland. This was all settled years ago. The state investigated the payments for the jail. They approved all of them. If you have a problem with it, talk to them."

"Oh, I will, Mr. Reynolds. You can count on that. Thanks for your time." With that, Tommy stood up and walked to the door, a smile on his face.

"Wait."

Tommy stopped and turned around.

"I don't know anything about the Singers' murders, that's the God's honest truth." For the first time since he'd showed up in the man's waiting room, Tommy didn't feel like he was being played. "For twelve years, I've believed Molly killed them. But Molly is my granddaughter's mother. If she's innocent, I hope you find who's responsible."

Tommy nodded. "I hope so, too."

An hour later, Frank Reynolds sat in Bryson's office. Unlike his own office, with its cut-rate furniture, this one was replete with rich wooden appointments: a large mahogany desk in the center, floor-to-ceiling wooden bookcases against two walls. On the desk, a Tiffany lamp emitted a soft glow. Bryson sat on a plush leather chair that looked like it would work fine for a quick catnap.

"Did Molly Singer kill her parents?" Frank knew he should have approached the question with more finesse, but his nerves didn't allow it. All he could think about on his walk over from the county office building was the possibility of Molly being innocent. And of his complicity in her conviction.

"A jury said she did," Bryson answered. "Why are you asking now? Did that investigator spook you?"

"You haven't answered me. Forget the jury. Do you think she was guilty?"

"Of course I do."

Frank breathed a sigh of relief. The tightness in his chest he'd carried since his meeting with Tom Noorland whooshed out in a burst, like a balloon stuck with a pin. He sat back in the chair, spent. That whole business of the jail had been a disaster from day one. He hadn't wanted any part of it. But he knew he couldn't buck Bryson. Not if he wanted a political future.

"Anything else on your mind?" Bryson asked.

Don't say anything. You got your answer, leave it alone. Frank dropped his head down and stared at his shoes. He knew he should thank him, stand up, and leave. Molly was rightly convicted, that's what Bryson had said. It saddened him, though. At first he'd tried to keep her away from his son, but only because they were too young. Now he had a granddaughter. Sophie deserved her real mother, not the witch she got stuck with.

His tension, so briefly absent, had seeped back in. He lifted up his head and met Bryson's icy stare. "I know we were relieved when Molly was arrested. It meant they wouldn't go looking into Joe's stake in the jail. But this guy, he's going to dig up the business with the jail now anyway. Molly taking the fall won't stop it. So, I just need to know—"

Frank stopped. He couldn't will himself to say the words.

"Know what?" Bryson's voice dripped with disdain.

Frank's gaze drifted back to his shoes. With his voice barely above a whisper, he asked, "Was he killed to stop him from talking about the jail?"

Frank could feel the heat of Bryson's eyes on him, like lasers burning holes in his chest.

"None of us murdered him. That's all you need to know."

CHAPTER

12

D ani had driven up to Andersonville—with fifty thousand resi-
dents, the largest town in Hudson County—that morning. The New
York State Thruway was flanked with trees displaying the full regalia
of orange, red, and gold that tourists flocked to see each year during
the peak fall-foliage season. She'd smiled, thinking what Jonah would
have said about the show. He might have described the colors as "de-
luxe" or "commanding." Typical of children with Williams syndrome,
he often used complex words that were close to what he meant, but
slightly missed their mark. It was as though someone had dropped a
thesaurus into his head and he repeatedly picked the wrong synonym
from it. This was one of the countless things Dani loved about her
son: his capacity to surprise her, even in the simplest conversation.

Reminded of it again now as she glimpsed the trees outside the
window across from her, she fought back a small smile and turned
her attention to the man seated before that window, and across the
large walnut desk from her. His appearance suggested he was in his
fifties, as did the graduation date listed on the diploma from Albany
Law School, which hung on the wall, nestled among reprints from the

Museum of Modern Art. A well-tailored suit covered his small frame.
Dani thought his eyes looked kindly behind his thick-lensed glasses.

"Thank you for meeting with me, Mr. McDonald."

"Call me Bob. And I'm happy to meet with anyone who wants to
help Molly."

"I've read the file, but maybe you can tell me in your own words
about the case."

McDonald opened up the thick folder on his desk but didn't glance
down at it before speaking. "Well, you know Molly doesn't remember
that night."

"I do."

"Even so, I didn't believe she was guilty then, and I don't now."

Dani felt relieved to hear that. After meeting with Molly and re-
viewing her file, she believed in her innocence yet wondered if her
own maternal instincts had infiltrated her judgment. "Can you tell me
why?"

"For starters, there wasn't any forensic evidence tying her to the
murders."

"But the police testified that she had showered before they arrived
and washed away any blood."

"They tested the shower drain. No blood in it."

That surprised Dani. She hadn't read it in the trial transcript.

"The judge wouldn't let that in. He claimed it wasn't dispositive of
anything."

"You said, 'for starters.' Were there other things that convinced you
she wasn't guilty?"

He nodded. "The weapons. The Singers were bludgeoned with
some heavy object, then repeatedly knifed. The police found neither
weapon."

"But their house bordered the Hudson. The police claimed she
dropped the weapons in the river before she made the call to 911."

"Yes, that's a possibility. But let's look at the police reconstruction
of the case. The medical examiner said a heavy object knocked them
out first, and that's why there was no sign of a struggle when they were
knifed. Don't you think, though, that hitting one of them hard enough

to knock them out would have awakened the other? The perpetrator would need to have moved to the other side of the bed to knock out the second victim. That should have given the other parent enough time to get out of bed, maybe struggle with the perpetrator. Both Singers were found in their bed, on their respective sides. Mrs. Singer had made it just partway out of her side, but still, I think there had to be two people committing the murders."

That made sense to Dani. She knew McDonald presented that theory in his closing arguments. Clearly, the jury hadn't bought it. "Were there any other reasons you believed in Molly's innocence?"

McDonald picked up the coffee mug sitting on his desk and took a sip. "Are you sure you don't want any?"

"Thanks, no." She'd already drunk three cups on the drive to Andersonville.

When he put his mug down, McDonald said, "I've practiced criminal law over thirty years. Even though I don't ask them, I can tell most of my clients are guilty. By and large, the police do their jobs. When defendants come in to meet with me, or when I see them in jail, I can usually tell there's something off about them. Sometimes big, sometimes hardly noticeable. But it's there. I didn't see anything in Molly. Sure, she was spoiled. And I'm sure she complained about her folks to her friends. What teenager doesn't? But she got all As in school, ran on the track team, sang in the chorus. This was a kid who did everything right. It didn't make sense to me that she would suddenly murder her parents."

"But it happens, doesn't it? Some kid who neighbors never suspected of being a monster commits an unspeakable crime and everyone shakes their head in disbelief."

"I suppose so. But if people looked closely, there were usually signs."

"Still, a sociopath can be very clever."

McDonald looked through the opened folder and slipped out a slim file, then handed it to Dani. "I had the same concern. So I had her evaluated by a psychiatrist. That's his report. He concluded she was a normal teenager. No hidden demons."

Dani leafed through the document, scanning the pages until she reached the conclusion.

Molly presents as a young woman of above-average intelligence. She displays no abnormal ideation or inappropriate responses to visual or auditory stimuli. Her affect is within normal range. Testing revealed no underlying psychosis or neurosis.

Dani handed the report back to McDonald. "Were there any other suspects the police considered?"

Once again, McDonald rifled through the papers in the folder, pulled out a sheet, and handed it to Dani. "Here's the police report. They latched on to Molly right away and that was the end of their police work. As far as they were concerned, there wasn't any need to look further."

"Why were they so certain it was Molly?"

"They checked all over the house and found no evidence of a break-in. Molly opened the front door for them but she insisted she'd locked it when she came home the night before. And all the other doors and windows were secure. Nothing was missing from the house either. Since Molly was the only other person in the house, she quickly became their primary suspect."

All of that was so, but it still didn't add up for Dani. A young woman with no apparent psychiatric issues doesn't suddenly kill her parents. "Did you do any investigation on your own?"

Bob nodded. "Fortunately, the family had sufficient resources to hire a private detective. He couldn't find anyone who recalled Molly saying she hated her parents, much less wished they were dead. Just normal teenage resentment, the kind my own kids probably feel toward me every time I tell them no."

"But what about other suspects? Did the police look into whether anyone had a vendetta toward the Singers?"

Bob pulled another letter from the folder. "Here's the investigator's report."

Dani noted the letterhead—Henry Aster Investigations. It was five pages long. "Can you summarize it for me?"

"Bottom line—some questions about Singer's partner, Quince Michaels, but nothing that panned out."

"What were the questions?"

"Quince and Joe had been in business together for a long time. Quince was the public face of the company, the one who schmoozed everyone to get business. And he managed the business as well. Joe was the hands-on guy. He supervised the work, made sure any building that had their name on it was constructed right.

"Molly told me her dad and Quince had a volatile relationship sometimes. So, naturally, I had the investigator poke around the business, see if there had been any hanky-panky with the books, that kind of thing. But he came up empty."

"Do you know what project they were working on when Molly heard them fighting?"

"Sure, everyone knew. It was in the papers practically every day because of the cost overruns and delays. They were building the new county jail."

There it was again. The county jail. The anonymous letter that prompted the investigation into Molly's conviction pointed to the county jail project as the motivation for the murders. But why? Dani couldn't figure it out. She'd read the report from the state concerning the cost overruns. Routine adjustments, it concluded. Shortage of lumber led to higher prices. Weather delays led to unexpected labor expenses. Blah, blah, blah. One hundred pages of numbers and excuses that led to nothing.

She finished up with McDonald, thanked him for his time, then started on the drive back to HIPP's office. She took her time. She wanted to luxuriate in the Indian summer weather before entering the mostly treeless streets of Manhattan. Instead of heading south on the New York Thruway with its mass of cars and trucks, she exited onto Route 9W, a meandering and little-used road lined with tall oaks and maples exploding with autumn colors. As she drove, she thought about Molly's case.

The meeting with McDonald had reinforced her feeling that Molly was innocent, but proving it would be a challenge. McDonald had already appealed those trial-court rulings that had been questionable, including the exclusion of testimony showing the lack of blood in the shower drain. His representation of Molly had been professional and thorough, so a claim of inadequate counsel was out of the question. The letters about the jail were interesting, but not probative. She needed to learn more about the jail, but Tommy's efforts on that front were going nowhere. Did the county executive cut short his meeting with Tommy because he had nothing to offer, or because he was involved somehow? They needed to investigate the jail angle further, push a little harder. Maybe speak with Joe Singer's partner, if he was still around.

Dani turned on the radio and tuned to the classic-rock station on Sirius/XM. There were no other cars on the road, and she let herself get lost in the music, oblivious to the large black SUV with tinted windows moving closer and closer behind her. It came as a shock when it tapped her rear bumper, just hard enough to rattle her.

The SUV fell back then, and she slowed to move onto the road's shoulder to exchange insurance information. Just as she began to pull over, she glanced in the rearview mirror. Instead of seeing the SUV moving off the road with her, she found it barreling toward her just an instant before it rammed into her car, sending it careering off the roadway and straight toward the massive tree in her path.

CHAPTER 13

Finn gripped the newspaper tightly in his hands as he read the story on page twelve.

> Dani Trumball, an attorney with New York City's Help Innocent Prisoners Project, is in critical condition following a crash on Route 9W in Marlboro yesterday morning. Witnesses to the crash described a black, late-model SUV that seemed to deliberately strike Ms. Trumball's car from behind, pushing it into a nearby tree, before it sped off. Ms. Trumball represents Molly Singer, who was convicted twelve years ago of the murder of her parents, Joseph and Sarah Singer. Singer is serving consecutive twenty-five-years-to-life terms at Bedford Hills Correctional Facility.

He slammed the paper down on the desk. Just like that, he felt a headache bloom behind his temples. He rubbed at them with slow, concentric circles. *Damn.* He'd bumped into Donna at the supermarket last week. She'd told him how she'd pushed this same Dani Trumball to take Molly's case, how the head of the agency hadn't wanted to. What would happen now? Would someone else take over or would it be dropped? For such a brief time he'd held out hope for Molly. Hope that she would get a new trial. Hope that she'd be proven innocent. Hope that she would reunite with Sophie. Hope that the melancholy Sophie wore like a shroud would be lifted if Molly were part of her life.

He picked up the newspaper and read the story again. If the witnesses were right, someone had wanted to hurt the lawyer. Even kill her.

Who would want to do that?

Someone who stood to lose from something the investigator was working on.

But surely there would be other investigators at the woman's agency who would carry on her work.

Unless they knew she was the only one there who wanted to go forward with that work to begin with.

In addition to his headache, Finn was now having trouble breathing. He knew who had to be behind the attempt on Dani Trumball's life—and he knew that he himself had helped set it in motion. Finn had told only one person about Donna's intervention on Molly's behalf, and about how the agency hadn't wanted to take her case—until Dani Trumball had pushed them to do so.

In a kind of daze, he picked up the phone and dialed the county executive's office. When Frank Reynolds answered, though, the daze was gone. Finn was screaming at him. "Are you insane? Are you— what *are* you? You'd help *kill* a woman, all so you could sabotage Molly? Sophie's your granddaughter. You're supposed to care about *her*, at least."

"What the hell are you talking about?"

"You told him!"

"Calm down, Finn. I don't know what this is about."

"You told him Ms. Trumball was the only one who wanted to take Molly's case. He must have figured if she were removed from the picture, no more questions would be asked."

Frank didn't speak for a moment, then quietly said, "You saw the newspaper today. That's what this is about?"

"Yeah, I saw it. What did you think? That I'd never find out?"

"Son, that's crazy. I swear to you, Finn. I never told anyone."

Finn didn't believe his father for one moment. He slammed down the phone.

The headache was worse. If he didn't lie down now, it'd blossom into a full-fledged migraine, and he'd be utterly disabled all day and night, curled around the pain in a pitch-dark room, helpless as a baby. He left the office and headed up to his bedroom. The kids were in school and Kim was, thankfully, at the gym. He stepped into the master bathroom, swallowed three Advil, and then ran hot water over a washcloth. After shutting the bedroom curtains, he lay down and placed the warm cloth on his forehead.

Before long, the pain began to subside. A minor miracle.

After less than an hour, Finn got up from bed, straightened the flowered bedspread Kim had insisted upon, and which made him cringe every time he looked at it, and returned to his office. The business's account books were open on his desk, ready for him to send out the monthly invoices. He tried to concentrate but couldn't push away thoughts of Molly. At first, he'd let his father convince him Molly was guilty, and he'd given in to his father's insistence that he testify at her trial. The guilt gnawed at him like a parasite, eating away inside him.

He heard the front door slam, then heard Sophie's footsteps stomping up the stairs to her bedroom. When she was younger, she'd rush into his office upon her return from school, eager to tell him about her day. Now she barely spoke to him. He hoped it was normal. Raging adolescent hormones turned the most rational of children into foreign creatures, mortified by their parents' very existence. When he drove her and her friends anyplace, he'd see her try to shrink into the car's seat, as though she could will herself to be invisible. It was almost comical to watch, but he knew better than to laugh.

He remembered his own adolescent embarrassment when his friends were around his parents and wanted to believe that was all Sophie was going through. Yet there seemed to be more to it than that. He left his office and walked upstairs to her room, knocked on the closed bedroom door, and opened it before she responded.

"Hey, no hellos?" he asked.

Sophie lay on her bed, her arms thrown over her forehead. She remained silent.

"Something wrong, sweetie?" Finn looked around her room, still a child's room, with pale-pink walls and pink-and-green gingham curtains. An oversize stuffed giraffe sat in one corner, and a shelf over her desk held dolls she'd collected over the years. The walls were adorned with posters of Justin Bieber and the boy band One Direction.

Slowly, Sophie moved her arms down, then looked up at Finn. "I hate her."

Finn knew she meant Kim. At times, he couldn't blame her. "What did she do now?"

"Now? What could she do now? She's locked up, where she belongs."

Finn didn't understand. Had Kim been arrested? He went over to Sophie's bed and sat down on the edge. "What are you talking about?"

"My mother, the murderer," Sophie said, her voice filled with disgust. She rolled onto her stomach and buried her face in the pillow. Finn could hear soft cries. Undoubtedly her friends, or their parents, had seen the paper, reminding everyone of the murder that had taken place in their quiet town twelve years earlier. She'd been taunted at school, he figured. It wasn't the first time, but it hadn't occurred in a long while. He lay down next to Sophie and put his arms around her slim body. Soon, he wouldn't be able to do this. She was poised on the edge of childhood, ready to take the leap into becoming a young woman.

"I don't believe Molly murdered her parents," he said softly to his daughter.

Sophie turned onto her back and wiped away the tears with the back of her hand. "But you were against her at the trial."

"How did you know that?"

"I know a lot. Kids talk."

Finn wrapped his large hand around Sophie's. "I spoke about things Molly had told me. I thought then it was the right thing to do, but I was wrong."

"Dad?"

"Yes, sweetie?"

"Do you think there's a murder gene?" Sophie's voice seemed strained.

"Of course not."

Sophie turned to him, leaned into him, and buried her face in his chest. "Sometimes I'm afraid of my thoughts about Mom."

Finn knew she was now talking about Kim. The only mother she'd ever known, she'd called her "Mom" from the beginning. "All kids hate their parents at one time or another. It's natural."

"But I don't hate you."

Finn laughed. "You will. Trust me. When you get a little older and you don't like all the restrictions I'll put on you."

Sophie picked up her head and looked at Finn. "Like what?"

"Well, like you can't date any boys till you're at least twenty-one."

She punched him in the arm. "Oh, Daddy, you're so silly."

They laughed together and relief washed over Finn. It had been a long time since he'd heard Sophie laugh. He gave her a kiss on the top of her head, then headed back down to his office.

Opened on his desk was the newspaper with its story about Dani Trumball. The relief he'd felt moments before dissipated, replaced by a tightening in his stomach. He had to do something for Molly, something he should have done many years ago.

Tommy's face blanched when he saw Dani in the hospital bed, tubes going everywhere into her body, her face and arms covered with bruises. An orange glow from the setting sun streamed through the one window in the single-bedded room and cast its light over her. On every surface in the room stood bouquets of flowers, their sweet fragrance replacing the antiseptic odor of the corridors. He trudged over to Doug, sitting at her bedside, and held out his hand.

"I'm so sorry. Tell me what I can do for you." He knew those were empty words, the murmured condolences of everyone when in fact they were helpless to do anything.

Doug shook his head. His eyes were puffy and rimmed in red.

"She'll be all right, won't she?" Tommy asked.

Doug looked up at Tommy. "The doctors put her in a coma." His voice cracked at the word. "Said they had to, because of swelling in her brain."

Tommy sat down in the chair next to Doug's. "I had a cousin they did that to. He came out of it fine. Good as new, at least after a while."

"They won't know whether there will be any impairment until they take her out of it." Doug picked up Dani's hand and dropped his head to his chest.

"She's a tough broad, Doug."

A thin smile stretched Doug's lips, and he nodded. "She's got a few broken ribs, too, but that's all. I saw pictures of the car. It's a miracle it wasn't worse."

Tommy took in Doug's rumpled clothes and stubble. "You been home yet?"

"I don't want to leave her."

"You got to take care of yourself, if not for you, then for Jonah."

"Katie's taking care of Jonah."

"How's Jonah doing with this?"

"I haven't let him see Dani yet. It would be too frightening for him. I told him she was traveling for a case."

Tommy nodded, and then for a long moment the two of them just looked at Dani, battered and tiny amid her tangle of tubes and wires. "I'm gonna find whoever did this," Tommy said. "You can count on it."

Doug turned to him. "Do you think it's because of the case she's working on?"

"Has to be."

"But why? She's just one of dozens of lawyers at HIPP. If she doesn't handle it, someone else will. What did whoever did this think he'd accomplish?"

"You know, Bruce didn't want to take this case at first. Dani talked him into it."

Doug nodded. "She believes in this girl. No, woman. I guess she's no longer a girl. So what's Bruce going to do now?"

"We met this morning. Everyone wants to keep going. Melanie will take over the lead until Dani's back on her feet." Tommy looked back at his friend, lying still in her bed. He got up from his chair and leaned over the railing, his face inches from Dani's. "We're gonna get her out. I promise you," he whispered to her. He straightened up to leave and said good-bye. As he got to the door, Doug called out to him.

"Just be careful, Tommy. Tell everyone to be careful."

Always be careful. That had been drummed into the agents at the FBI, and it was no different at HIPP. Be careful. But how do you protect yourself from the unknown? Someone wanted Dani off this case and had sent a strong message; that much was clear. It was the "who" that had him stumped.

Before Dani had gotten into her car to make the trip back to the city, she'd called him. "We've got to look harder at the jail," she'd said. "See if you can find Joe Singer's business partner." There hadn't been time for much discussion. She'd said she'd fill him in when she got to the office. But she never arrived. If Dani was true to form, she'd jotted down notes of her visit with Molly's trial lawyer. She always liked to do it while it was still fresh in her mind. Those notes would be in her car, now in the police impound, evidence in a potential attempted murder. He'd have to wait until the car had been gone over completely before he could get Dani's briefcase.

Tommy wended his way through the hospital corridors and out to his car. It was already starting to get dark, a reminder that the shortened days were bringing them closer to winter. Some of his FBI buddies had retired to Florida, spending their time on the golf course instead of shoveling driveways while freezing their butts. Their biggest worry was getting to the restaurant in time for two-for-one drinks, not whether their friend would survive an attempted murder.

He found his car in the parking lot and started his drive home, where his wife waited for him. If it were Patty lying motionless in a hospital bed, he'd be inconsolable. She'd been by his side for more than twenty years, and without her he'd be lost. It was hard enough dealing with Tommy Jr. off at college, the first of his five children to leave the nest. Time seemed to be flying by now, as if the passing of days sped up as he aged. Before long, all of the kids would be gone, his once noisy home silenced with their absence. How could parents bear that? He'd left the FBI to spend more time with his kids, and it was the best decision he'd ever made. Seemed unfair that they would turn around and leave him and Patty, going off to college or getting married. Married? It seemed surreal to Tommy. His dark hair was peppered with gray but he still felt like a kid himself. He prided himself on his fitness, often challenging his sons to basketball games and holding his own against them.

He pulled into his driveway, and as he walked in the door, the smell of garlic wafted in from the kitchen. With the television blaring in the living room, Patty didn't hear him as he snuck up behind her, placed his arms around her waist, and nuzzled her neck with a kiss.

"Great, you're home," she said, leaning into him. "Dinner's just about ready." She turned around to look at her husband. Her voice grew quieter as she studied his face. "It's bad, isn't it?"

"She should be okay, I think. But the docs put her in a coma. You remember, like Cousin Eddie." Tommy went to the refrigerator and pulled out a cold beer, then sank into his chair at the head of the kitchen table. He'd played the optimist with Doug and now continued it with Patty. But he knew Dani's injuries were serious. Sometimes the unexpected happened. Doctors never gave guarantees. He'd always accepted the risks that came with his jobs, but lawyers weren't supposed to be in jeopardy. If Dani's car had missed the tree, it would have gone over an embankment. Instead of seeing her battered and ghostlike, but still alive, he'd have been at her funeral.

Someone had wanted her dead. If she pulled through this, he would make damn sure that person didn't get another chance.

CHAPTER 15

A week after the crash, the police finally released Dani's car, and Tommy had the contents of her briefcase spread out on his desk. He opened the folder she'd marked "trial attorney" and took out the legal pad sitting on top. There were only three words on the page: "Hire forensic accountant." Those didn't come cheap, and HIPP, as a non-profit relying on donations and grants, operated on a shoestring. He'd have to get approval from Bruce. He strode over to his office, knocked on the open door, then stepped inside.

"Dani wants us to hire a forensic accountant on the Singer case."

Bruce perked up. "She's already out of the coma?"

"No, that's still later today. It's in her notes. I got her briefcase back today."

Bruce picked up a pencil and twirled it in his fingers. "Is that about the jail finances?"

"I assume so. She didn't elaborate in her notes."

"I know those letters said the murders had to do with the jail, but the state looked into it. Isn't it a dead end now?"

"Maybe not," came a voice from the doorway. Both men looked around and saw Melanie as she walked into the office. "I was going through Dani's mail and found another letter, still unsigned, but more detailed this time." She handed the letter to Bruce and he read it aloud.

Dear Ms. Trumball: I know that you are now representing Molly Singer. I read about you in the newspaper, about your accident, and hope that you are better now. As I said in my earlier letters, the ones I sent to Donna Garmond, Molly is innocent. Her parents were murdered because of the jail. There are some powerful people in Hudson County who had too much to lose if the truth about the jail came out. I was hoping you'd figure it out on your own but maybe this can help. The cost overruns weren't routine like the state said. It was because people involved were lining their pockets with a lot of money, including Molly's father and his partner. But they weren't the only ones. And the others needed to make sure Joe Singer didn't talk. I hope I've given you enough because I can't tell you any more. I shouldn't even have told you this. But Molly Singer doesn't deserve to be in jail.

Bruce looked up from the letter. "Well, this certainly backs up Dani's call for a forensic accountant. If the state couldn't find wrongdoing, the payoffs must have been buried pretty deeply."

"I know a good one from my days with the FBI," Tommy said. "He's semiretired now. Maybe I can sweet-talk him into giving us a break on his fee."

Bruce placed the letter on his desk. "We're not spending much money on travel to other states with this case, so there's room in the budget. Go ahead. Give your friend a call."

Tommy thanked Bruce, then headed back to his own office. The letter writer talked about powerful people in Hudson County benefitting financially from the jail. *But who?* Even if he hadn't seemed squirrelly when Tommy had met with him, Reynolds the county executive would have been a strong candidate. As head of the legislative committee overseeing the building of the jail, he'd have been in a position to cover up a lot of questionable expenditures. Tommy would check into Reynolds further. It had been a hell of a lot easier when he worked for the government. Then, he could get a court order giving him access to bank records without the target even knowing about it. It was trickier to get that information now, but he'd figure out a way.

Who else, though? Every county in every state had people who ran things, usually behind the scene. If he wanted the scoop on who carried the weight in Hudson County, the person most likely in the know would be the head of the party out of power. He turned to his computer and after a quick Google search came up with a name. Paul Scoby headed the Democratic Party in Hudson County. He reached for the phone and dialed his number.

Black enshrouded her, and wrapped around the darkness was confusion. Dani didn't know where she was, why the slightest move sent waves of pain throughout her body. Then she was aware of the murmur of whispered voices and realized her eyes were closed. Why couldn't she open them? It felt as though weights pressed down on her lids. She pushed, gently at first, then harder, and slowly the light emerged. She was in a bed, in a room painted white, aluminum blinds on the windows. Doug sat in a chair next to the bed, his face turned up to a man dressed in a neatly pressed suit, a folder in his hands. She tried to speak but couldn't form the words. Her hands felt heavy but she managed to lift up her thumb and hold it erect. Suddenly, the man in the suit nudged Doug and said, "Look."

Doug grabbed Dani's hand. "Sweetheart, you're awake." He opened his mouth to say more but stopped as tears rolled down his cheek.

Dani tried to speak again, and this time forced her words out in a croak. "What happened? Where am I?"

"You were in an accident. Your car went into a tree," Doug said. "Do you remember anything?"

Slowly, it came back to her—the black SUV that loomed suddenly in her rearview mirror, the jolt that sent her off the road and into the tree. "It wasn't an accident," she said.

Doug squeezed her hand. "I know. There were witnesses."

"What happened to me?"

Doug looked up at the doctor standing at the bedside. "Dr. Reuben, do you want to explain?"

The man in the suit tucked the folder under his arm and stepped closer to Dani. "Mrs. Trumball, you were very fortunate. Your airbag inflated and saved you from more serious injuries. Several ribs are broken and you sustained some trauma to the head from the impact, which caused swelling in your brain. You were put in a coma to allow the swelling to subside. This morning, I stopped the medication which kept you in a coma. I don't believe there will be any permanent injuries, but I'd like to examine you now if you're up to it."

"How long?"

The doctor looked puzzled.

"How long have I been here?"

"Seven days."

Dani turned to Doug. "I have to get back to work. Without me, Bruce will probably drop Molly's case. I need to be there." She attempted to sit up, groaned from the pain, then carefully lay back down.

Doug laughed. "I don't think you need to examine her, Dr. Reuben. She's back to her old self."

"Well, let's just make sure," the doctor said with a smile. He began by asking Dani simple questions—her name, address and phone number, her date of birth, the name of the current president, the sum of five plus seven. She rolled off the answers easily. He moved then to a physical examination and when he finished, said, "I don't find any neurological deficits, Mrs. Trumball. When your bones and bruises heal, you'll be good as new. But work is out of the question for a bit. You still need complete rest."

"I'll make sure she gets it," Doug said. "Even if I have to strap her down."

Dani turned to Doug. "Have you heard from Bruce? Is he dropping her case?"

He pointed to a vase of flowers on the windowsill. "Those are from Bruce. He was here. So were Melanie and Tommy. Tommy I had to practically throw out, he came so often. I told him you'd rather he were working on Molly's case."

"And Bruce didn't stop him?"

"Nope. He said go ahead."

Dani breathed a sigh of relief. She knew the doctor was right—just sitting upright pained her. She needed to talk to Tommy, though, fill him in on her conversation with Molly's trial lawyer. Before, there hadn't been pressure to move quickly. No clock was ticking toward a date with an executioner, as was so often the case with Dani's death row clients. But the SUV that pushed her off the road changed things. Someone was watching her and didn't like what he saw. She and her team needed to find out who, quickly, before he acted again.

16

Paul Scoby's office was a tiny room at the back of his hardware store, the one desk taking up most of the floor space. It was difficult to believe that the slightly built man, measuring no more than five feet seven on a good day, with a mop of brown hair falling over his eyebrows, was the leader of the Democratic Party in Hudson County.

"Thanks for meeting with me," Tommy said.

"No problem. But I don't know how I can help you. I didn't know Joe Singer and wasn't involved with the building of the jail."

"That's exactly why I'm hoping you can shed some light. I have reason to believe that the people who were involved somehow benefitted financially, in ways they shouldn't have."

"Skimming?"

"That's right."

"If that were true, why do you think I'd know anything about it?"

"Because I think the people doing it were the higher-ups in the Republican Party. And I think as head of the Democratic Party you would keep tabs on them."

Scoby smiled. "Don't you think if I had something on them, I would have used it during election campaigns? I'd love to have that kind of dirt. The state looked into the cost overruns with the jail, though, and they came up empty. So, I'm afraid you've wasted your time with me."

Tommy wasn't ready to give up. Sometimes people didn't realize what they knew. "How well do you know the county executive?"

"Frank? Very well. We went to Hudson High School together back in the day."

Tommy made a note on his pad. "He was head of the appropriations committee when the jail was being built. Any overage approvals had to go through him, didn't they?"

"Sure. But there were Democrats on the committee as well. Frank didn't have the authority to approve bills on his own. The ranking Democrat on the committee had to okay them as well."

"And who was that?"

"Back then? Let me think." Scoby was quiet for a moment, then opened his drawer and took out a book, thumbed through it, then said, "That would be Mary Jane Olivetti. Came into politics after she stepped down from being a nun. You couldn't find anyone more honest than Mary Jane."

"Do you have a phone number for her?" Tommy held his pen in his hand, ready to write.

Scoby's voice softened. "I'm afraid not. She died a while back, a car accident. A terrible loss for us. She would have gone far in politics."

Tommy didn't know where else to go with his questioning. The one person who might have information about wrongdoing was dead. He stood up to leave, then sat back down. "Just one more question. Do you remember how long ago she died?"

"I think it was about ten years ago, give or take."

"That's okay," Tommy said. "I'll look it up. I'm sure the local newspaper had a story about a legislator dying."

"Wait a minute. Now that I think about it, maybe it was twelve years ago. I remember now. Molly Singer was on trial when it happened."

"Mommy, you look damaged," Jonah said when Molly walked into the house leaning on Doug's arm for support. "And your face has purple eruptions. Did you have an accident?"

Dani wanted desperately to hug him, but she knew her knitting ribs couldn't withstand the squeezing he'd give her. Instead, she made do with leaning over and kissing the top of his head, then ruffling his hair with her hands. *Had he grown again?* At thirteen, he was almost as tall as she. "Yes, Jonah, I was in an accident, but I'm okay. Only I need to rest a few days at home before I'm all better."

Jonah's face lit up at the prospect of having his mother at home, and once again Dani felt that twinge of guilt that she wasn't home for him every day. Whoever said women could have it all couldn't have been a working mother. Sure, the once-closed doors to previously male-dominated careers were now opened. But once inside the door, women still had to work twice as hard to make it to the top echelons. And that took away from time spent with her children at home. No one talked about the emotional loss in not watching your child's first steps, or hearing her first words, or being there to soothe him when he scraped a knee. Dani knew her decision to return to work required her to engage in a balancing act, and she wasn't always certain the scales tipped in the right direction.

"I'm going to lie down for a bit," Dani said, after catching up with Jonah on what he'd been doing while she was gone.

"Do you need my help getting upstairs?" Doug held out his arm for her.

Dani shook her head, then walked up the stairs to her bedroom. As she passed the large mirror hanging over her dresser, she glanced at her image and frowned. Splotches of purple bruises dotted her forehead. Her normally olive skin was washed out, drained of all color. Her dark curls hung limply down to her shoulders. She looked all of her forty-three years and then some. *What a sight I am*, she thought as she made her way over to her bed. Well, at least there was one bright spot. The five pounds she'd been trying to lose for more than a year were gone. But the lying-in-bed-in-a-coma diet wasn't one she'd recommend.

After she got settled, several pillows propped up behind her back, she reached for Molly Singer's file, then called Tommy. She'd had several conversations with him since she'd been awakened from the coma.

"So, how does it feel to be back home?" Tommy asked.

"You can't imagine. Just the few days in the hospital after they woke me up were agony. And not seeing Jonah was the worst. Doug thought it'd be better to wait until I was home."

"How long before you're able to come into the office?"

"I'll see how it goes over the weekend, but I should be ready by Monday."

"Good. And how early can you travel?"

"Why? What have you found?

"Joe Singer's partner. He's living in Miami Beach. I'm gonna fly down to speak to him, and I didn't know if you wanted to come as well."

Dani thought about it. If there had been skimming of the jail funds, the anonymous letter writer said Quince Michaels was involved. She'd love to watch as Tommy questioned him; so much could be learned from Michaels's body language. Still, having an attorney in the room could be intimidating. Tommy might be more effective at getting Michaels to let down his guard if he questioned him alone. "No, you go without me or Melanie. And this way you don't have to wait until I'm cleared to travel."

"Okay, then if he's available, I'll leave tomorrow."

"How about with Mary Jane Olivetti? Did you find out any more about her death?"

"Like Scoby said, she died in a car accident."

"Do you think there's a connection?"

"I don't like coincidences."

"See if she has any relatives. Maybe they can shed some light."

"Will do, boss."

As soon as Dani hung up something nagged at her. She needed to tell Tommy something, but what? She struggled to remember, but her memory remained clouded from the days of medication. Soon, she drifted off to sleep, the thought lost in her slumber.

A voice whispered in her ear, "Dinner's ready. Wake up, Dani."

She opened her eyes and saw Doug standing over her, a worried look on his face. "You've been asleep for three hours. Are you feeling okay?"

Dani stretched her arms over her head, then eased them to her sides when the shooting pain reminded her of her injuries. "Just tired, I guess." With her hands, she pushed herself up to a sitting position, then swung her legs over the side of the bed. The odor of garlic wafted up from the kitchen. "Is that Katie's lasagna I smell?"

Doug nodded.

"Boy, I didn't realize how much I missed her cooking until just this moment." Slowly, she stood up and, with Doug's arm around her waist, she walked down the stairs to the kitchen. Katie stood by the stove, an apron around her ample waist.

"I made your favorite," she said when Dani entered the room. Jonah was already seated at the kitchen table. In the center stood a vase of flowers, one of the many she'd taken home from the hospital.

"It smells delicious." Suddenly, Dani felt famished, as though she hadn't eaten in weeks.

"And Katie made a delectable desert, Mommy," piped in Jonah. "Apple pie, and it's still warm."

Dani looked around the kitchen. With its white cabinets and rustic wood floor, vintage stove and gingham curtains, it felt like a country farmhouse rather than a suburban home just thirty minutes north of Manhattan. It was the look she'd wanted, a substitute for the second home in the country she'd once hoped to own. That was when she and Doug both worked for the United States Attorney's Office, when their futures seemed limitless and money plentiful. That was before Jonah was born, before they learned of his condition, before she decided to drop out of the practice of law and become a full-time mother, before Doug left to become a professor at Columbia Law School. At times, when the pressure of work seemed relentless and her conflict over not being home when Jonah returned from school greatest, she looked back on those years as idyllic. There were no hard choices to be made then. Should she stay home with her child or return to work? Whatever choice she made left her with a tinge of regret. Everything for a working mother was a compromise, but one she willingly made. She couldn't imagine life without Jonah, and she relished the satisfaction she felt in her job, especially when she succeeded in freeing an innocent person.

"Katie, why don't you sit down and join us?" Dani said.

"Well, now, don't mind if I do. Buddy is off at a ball game tonight. One of his friends managed to score tickets to the Yankees."

Katie took another plate from the cabinet and silverware from a drawer, and then they all sat down around the kitchen table. Dani relished being back home with her family—Katie was like family, too— yet, as the conversation flowed, her mind kept drifting to Molly's case. She kept thinking there was something she'd needed to tell Tommy.

"And Billy was screaming at Joey and Mrs. Radler made them both sit in the corner," Jonah told everyone, clearly confused by the injustice to Joey.

It hit her then. After making excuses, Dani got up from the table and went into her office. She dialed Tommy's home and when he answered, said, "Molly remembered her father and his partner arguing shortly before the murders. See what you can find out about that."

17

As soon as he stepped out of the terminal, a wave of heat and humidity engulfed Tommy. He'd been to Miami before, but during the winter months, never in October. It felt like the outdoors had turned into the steam bath at his gym. With the rental car's air-conditioning blasting, he headed east on Route 395, across the McArthur Causeway, where azure-blue water sparkled in the midday sun. Once across the causeway, he followed the turns he'd mapped out beforehand, and twenty minutes later pulled up to Quince Michaels's home. He whistled at the enormity of the place, then fell into dazed admiration of the profusion of tropical flowers that adorned the front of the property. He'd studied flowers for years and, over time, learned to identify most. Orange milkweeds, purple coneflowers, pink powder puffs. The display was astounding.

When he finally finished admiring the landscaping, Tommy walked up to the front door and rang the bell. The man who greeted him looked like he'd stepped out of a *GQ* fashion shoot. Dressed in tennis whites, he appeared to be in his mid-fifties, with wavy, silver-gray hair, a toned body, and a tan that rivaled George Hamilton's.

"You must be Tommy Noorland."

"I am, and thanks for agreeing to meet with me, Mr. Michaels."

"It's Quince. No formalities here. Come on in. Can I get you something to drink?"

"A glass of water would be appreciated. I'm not used to this humidity."

As Michaels walked off into the kitchen, Tommy looked around the house. More like a mansion, he thought. The entry foyer led to the massive living room, with ceilings that looked at least twenty feet high and an all-glass back wall looking out over an infinity pool and even more elaborate landscaping than he'd encountered in the front of the house. There was a hot tub in one corner and a waterfall in another. Behind the pool, a dock jutted out into the very water he'd driven over a few minutes earlier. Tied up at the dock was a fifty-foot cabin cruiser.

When Michaels walked back in with a glass of water in one hand, and an iced tea in the other, Tommy said, "Nice digs."

"I got lucky. I bought it after the housing crisis hit. Miami Beach was struck particularly hard by it. The owner had a number of properties he needed to unload, so I paid a fraction of its value. It didn't look anything like this when I bought it. The structure was solidly built, but too small for me. I've doubled the size and probably doubled my investment already."

"Nice deal."

Michaels pointed out the back. "That's the best thing about the house—the view. Let's sit outside and talk. It's too nice a day to be indoors."

Tommy wasn't sure that was the case—the air-conditioning felt pretty good to him—but as soon as he stepped out back, the breeze from the water made it feel ten degrees cooler.

"Have a seat." Michaels pointed to a set of deeply cushioned chairs. Tommy sat down and Michaels did the same.

"Thanks for meeting with me on such short notice," Tommy said.

"Well, I'd do anything for Molly. She was like a daughter to me. Her sister, too. I've known them all their lives." Michaels dropped his head down and rubbed the back of his neck. After a few moments, he looked up at Tommy. "I never believed she'd killed Joe and Sarah. So, if there's anything I can help with, I'm there."

Tommy opened up his briefcase and pulled out a notepad and pen. "How long were you and Joe in business together?"

"Twenty-two years. We started the company a few years after we got out of the army. We'd been friends since college. Joe had the building skills, I had the sales skills. Together we made a good team. Over time, I got pretty knowledgeable about construction, but Joe was the hands-on guy. He oversaw the work of the employees and subcontractors."

"Did Joe put the bids together for a project?"

"We did that together, but Joe's view carried more weight than mine, naturally. He had a better sense of what things should cost."

Tommy wrote on his pad as Michaels spoke. It took all his concentration to keep from sitting back in the chair and just letting the cool breeze wash over him. The water had an almost hypnotic effect. For a moment, he envied his retired friends, having this lifestyle year round. He checked himself. Retired law enforcement didn't have multimillion-dollar homes on the water. The boat alone had to have set Michaels back at least a quarter of a million.

"How did you come up with the bid for the Hudson County jail?" Tommy asked.

Michaels, who'd been rambling easily, stopped short at the question. He picked up his iced tea and took a long swallow before answering. "Like we came up with all other bids. Got estimates from our subs, priced out cost of materials, and took a guess on what our competition would bid. Then we looked at what we needed to cover our expenses and give us a reasonable profit and still come in low enough to win the bid."

"How did you know what the other bids would be?"

"We didn't. As I said, we made a guess. An educated guess, because we always charted what the competition bid on previous jobs."

It sounded reasonable to Tommy. "So, what went wrong?"

"What do you mean?"

Tommy pulled out a folder from his briefcase and flipped through some pages. "You bid $72 million on the jail and the final cost was $107 million. That's almost $23 million more than the highest bid on the jail."

Through the deep tan, Tommy saw Michaels's cheeks turn red. "Listen, I'm sorry, but I'm sick of this bull," he said. "Every other day the newspapers slammed us on the cost. We explained it all to the state auditors and were cleared of any wrongdoing. I'm not talking about it anymore."

Tommy leaned forward and placed his hands on his knees. Softly, he said, "You told me you wanted to help Molly. The only way you can is to tell me about the jail."

"But why? That's over and done with a long time ago."

"It wasn't over when the Singers were murdered."

"But still—"

"Look, I'll be frank with you. We've gotten several anonymous letters saying the murders were tied to the construction of the jail."

Michaels stood up and strode over to the dock. He looked out over the water for a long moment, then turned around and walked back to Tommy. Still standing, he said, "I worked hard my whole life for all of this. I'm enjoying my retirement. Now here you come and start poking into matters that are buried. Leave it alone. The jail had nothing to do with the murders. If I thought it did, I'd be the first person to help you hunt down the murderer. But you're off base here. Now, I think it's best if you leave."

Tommy remained planted in his chair. "Just one more question. Molly heard you arguing with her father shortly before the murders. What was that about?"

"We argued all the time; I can't say what any particular one was about. Usually over minor things. We're both stubborn." Michaels caught himself. "We *were* both stubborn." A look of sadness passed over his face. "Now, really, I'm late for a tennis game. There's nothing I can help you with."

Tommy stood up and Michaels walked him to the front door. As they neared it, the door opened and a striking young woman in jogging shorts and sports bra walked in. Her silky brown hair was pulled back in a ponytail, accentuating large eyes the color of the deep-blue inlet behind the house. Beads of sweat glistened on her forehead. Tommy wondered if she was Michaels's daughter.

The woman glanced at Tommy, then said to Michaels, "Oh, good, you haven't left yet."

"Honey, this is Tommy Noorland. He works with a lawyer trying to help Molly."

The woman held out her hand, as slim as the rest of her body. "Glad to meet you. I'm Lisa, Quince's wife."

She walked off into the kitchen, and Tommy watched her rear sashay as she left. Husband standing right there or not, it was as though he had no choice in the matter. She was that spectacular. When he looked back to Michaels, Tommy was glad to see he'd been taking in the show, too. It wouldn't likely get old, he figured.

As he shook Michaels's hand, he said, "I know you don't want to talk about the jail, but I thought I should let you know that HIPP has hired a forensic accountant. He's gotten all the documents from the state and will be going through them." With that, Tommy released the man, turned back to the door, and left.

"Lucky bastard," Tommy muttered under his breath as he walked to his car. The gal couldn't have been more than thirty-five, if she was even that. He wondered if Michaels had been married before and, if so, what had happened to Mrs. Michaels Number One.

He got into the rental car, started the ignition, and put the air-conditioning on full blast. Once, he would have needed to head to the county clerk's office for his fact-checking. Now he pulled an iPad from his briefcase and typed in a real estate website. Michaels claimed he'd gotten a steal on the house. This website would tell him what he'd purchased it for. Within a few clicks, he had the number—$4.45 million. Didn't seem like much of a steal to him, but he guessed waterfront property in Miami Beach didn't come cheap. The original house was 2,830 square feet and didn't have a pool. A few more clicks told him the current house was 5,850 square feet and had no mortgage. That had to have set him back a few more million at least. Add in the pool, the landscaping, the boat, and the furnishings, and it probably totaled more than $8 million. And he guessed he was being conservative. Not bad for a builder. Maybe Donald Trump made that kind of money, but he didn't know too many other builders who did. So, where did the money come from?

He took out his cell phone and dialed Dani. "How you feeling, doll?" Although she'd gotten used to it and even laughed about it at times, Tommy knew Dani hated terms like "sweetheart," "doll," and "gorgeous." He couldn't help it. It just came out. He was a poster child for political incorrectness.

She took it in stride today. "I can actually breathe today without wanting to claw someone's eyes out," she said. "You finished your interview of Michaels?"

"Yep. I'm still in front of his house."

"Anything interesting?"

"To start with, his house is more like a mansion. Big bucks there."

"Couldn't he have earned it?"

"I suppose."

"Anything else?"

"Yeah. As soon as I started to talk about the jail, he clammed up."

"Seems like everyone clams up about that topic," Dani said. "What did he say about the argument with Joe Singer?"

"Said it was routine."

"What's your assessment of him?"

"Oh, he's hiding something. And I'm gonna find out what."

Bryson picked up the phone in his home office on the first ring. "Why are you calling me here?" he said.

"I just had a visitor."

"How nice for you."

"An investigator, working on Molly's case. She has new lawyers. You know about them?"

"Of course I do."

"It's not going to stay buried. What are we going to do about that?"

"Stop worrying. I'll handle it. Just like I always do."

"I'm going in to work tomorrow." It was "honeymoon hour," and Dani lay entwined in Doug's arms on the living room couch.

"Are you sure? You're still pretty sore."

"It's time."

Doug stroked Dani's hair. The windows were open, and a soft breeze carried into the room the sweet smell of the chrysanthemums and sunflowers blooming in their front garden. "Maybe it's time to think about changing jobs."

Dani sat upright and looked at Doug. "Why would I do that?"

"Because this job is too dangerous. You could go back to the US Attorney's Office. They would take you in a heartbeat."

"It's just as dangerous there, probably more so. With every case, I'd be trying to convict criminals."

"But at least they have the resources to protect you. Or maybe you could work at a Wall Street firm. They pay a fortune there. The only criminals you'd be defending would be accused of white-collar crimes. Not so likely to run you off a road."

Dani lay back down again. "No, I like it at HIPP."

"Then what about going back to writing appeals?"

For many years, Dani had only worked on appeals at HIPP. Last year she had conducted her first investigation into a client's claim of innocence and had continued leading investigations ever since.

"I could be walking down the street tomorrow and have a crane fall down on me," she said. Just that had once happened on a Manhattan street. "I could be driving home from work and skid off the road on my own in the ice. I could fly to another state to argue an appeal and the plane could crash." Dani took Doug's hand in hers and squeezed it tight. "There are no guarantees of safety no matter what I do. But what I'm doing is important. The US Attorney's Office has no shortage of highly qualified attorneys eager to work there. And that's true at the Wall Street firms, too. It's different at innocence projects. There aren't enough attorneys throughout the country to represent all the people incarcerated who insist they're innocent."

"Most of the requests you get are from people who were rightly convicted."

"Sure, but for someone who's truly innocent, we're their last hope." Dani knew nothing she said would ease Doug's worries. If he'd been the target of an attack, she'd be making the same arguments. She couldn't live her life running from potential danger, though. It just wasn't in her DNA. She'd be more alert from here on out, but she wouldn't stop.

Once again, Dani waited in an attorney interview room for Molly. She hadn't seen her since their interview had been cut short almost two weeks earlier. After ten minutes, the door opened and Molly stepped inside. A guard, heavyset and with a sour expression, unlocked the shackles binding her wrists and ankles, then stepped outside the room.

"I was afraid you'd forgotten about me," Molly said, a shy smile on her face.

"I was in a car accident and laid up for a bit. But I'm back at work now."

"And you're okay?"

"I'm fine now." Dani took out her notepad and pen. "When I was here last, we started to talk about the Hudson County jail your dad built."

"I remember. But I was just a teenager then. I didn't pay too much attention to what my father did. As long as he stayed out of my business, I was happy."

"There were a lot of articles in the newspaper about the cost of the jail. Do you recall that?"

Molly shrugged. "I only read the paper when one of my teachers assigned it."

There was nowhere to go with this line of questioning. If Joe Singer had been skimming money from the jail contract, Molly didn't know anything about it. She'd change gears.

"Molly, I hope you don't mind if I ask you some personal questions. It'll help me get to understand you better, especially since your memory of that night is blank."

"Sure, ask me anything."

"Tell me about your daughter."

Molly's body seemed to deflate in her chair. She swallowed and looked down at the floor. "She was such a beautiful baby," she said at last, in little more than a whisper. "She was with me her first year. I shouldn't have been allowed in the nursery program here. Usually only mothers convicted of nonviolent crimes are accepted. But I think the warden felt sorry for me because I was so young."

Dani knew that the nursery program at this prison was the oldest in the nation and the model for other prisons throughout the country. Mothers with their babies were housed in a separate section of the prison.

"When they took her away from me, I wanted to die," Molly continued. "I couldn't bear being parted from her."

"Do you still see her?"

"For a few years, Finn brought her every Saturday. There's a special visiting room here stocked with books and games. Sophie would sit on my lap and I'd read to her. At the end of our visit, when she had to leave, she'd cry so hard." She took a deep breath and went on. "After Finn married Kim, they convinced me it would be better for Sophie if she stopped visiting me, that it was traumatic for her to be wrenched from me each week. I never saw her after that." Tears began to roll down Molly's cheeks. "I still get blue every Saturday. I'll never stop missing her."

"I'm sorry. I can't imagine how difficult it must have been for you to give her up."

Molly wiped her tears away with the back of her hand. "If it's been better for Sophie, then that's all that matters."

"Has Finn written you about Sophie's progress? Sent you pictures, maybe?"

"No. He thought it would be better to cut off all contact."

This was such a bleak statement that it took Dani a moment to figure out how to proceed.

"I was surprised that Finn testified against you at your trial," she said at last.

"He didn't say anything that wasn't true."

"Still," Dani said, "he was your boyfriend. No one but him would know what you told him. If he said nothing, no one would be the wiser."

"He felt tremendous guilt about testifying. He told me his father pressured him and he relented. I forgave him a long time ago."

Dani made a mental note to schedule her interview with Finn soon. Something didn't seem right.

"Do you mind if we talk about your sister?"

Molly stiffened. "There's nothing to talk about. I haven't seen or spoken to her since I came here."

"She'd like very much to visit you."

Molly stared stonily at Dani. Her body language made it clear that her sister was unwelcome.

"If we're able to uncover new evidence that would justify a retrial, it's helpful to have family members in the courtroom," Dani said. "It humanizes the defendant."

"I don't want her help now. It's too late."

Dani knew how hard it could be to forgive. She'd seen over and over petty annoyances tear families apart. Once a barrier was built, the task of dismantling it seemed insurmountable. She also knew the importance of family, especially when, like Molly, defendants had little else.

"Your sister was barely out of her teens herself when your parents were murdered. She didn't have the judgment that comes with age and experience. She loved your parents very much, just as you did. And the hurt she felt from their loss left her vulnerable to the police's certainty that you were guilty."

Molly folded her arms across her chest and continued to say nothing.

"You have a niece and nephew now."

"I know. My aunt told me. And she has a nice, cushy life with a rich husband."

"She loves you."

"Hah!"

"Just think about letting her into your life again, okay?"

Molly shrugged and said nothing more.

"Let's go back to your father's business. You told your trial lawyer you'd heard him arguing with his partner, Quince Michaels. Do you remember what they tended to fight about?"

Molly was silent for a minute, rubbing her wrists where the shackles had been. "I'm sorry. It was so long ago."

"Did they ever fight about the jail?"

"The jail?" Molly shrugged. "I don't know. Maybe. I just don't remember. They'd get loud, though. Sometimes it would scare me." She shook her head. "In those last days, there just seemed to be so much yelling. Me and my mom, about Finn, and my dad and Mr. Michaels, about whatever they were fighting about. They'd be in my dad's office, going at each other. Sometimes it felt like the world was ending."

And then it did, Dani thought.

19

It took twenty minutes for Dani to make her way through the crowd of colleagues wishing her well on her return to work. Once she reached her office, she found a stack of messages on her chair and a dozen folders in her in-box, each containing requests from inmates seeking HIPP's help. She would get to those later. First, she needed to meet with Tommy and Melanie. They both entered Dani's office a few minutes after she'd gotten settled.

"Where are we on Molly Singer's case?" Dani asked.

"We've hired a forensic accountant," Tommy said. "I gave him the report from the state and he's talked to them about getting all the underlying documents. Singer's company was paid on a cost-plus-fifteen-percent basis."

"What kind of documents?"

"As part of the audit, the state got copies of every invoice from subcontractors, as well as records of all payments for materials and labor they provided themselves. The accountant will look for any ir-regularities in all of that."

"Does he think the state will balk at turning them over?"

Tommy shook his head. "If there was fraud, they'll want to know about it."

Dani shifted in her seat. Although she'd felt well enough to return to work, the healing ribs still were uncomfortable. "Anything further with Michaels?"

"Yeah. I found his first wife. Her name is Ellen Michaels. They were divorced eleven years ago and she hasn't remarried. She's still living in Andersonville. I'm driving up there tomorrow to meet with her."

"Great." Dani turned to Melanie. "And on the legal front?"

"I've gone through the trial transcript and appeals. There were a number of questionable rulings by the trial judge, all against Molly, but her attorney raised them all at the Appellate Division and lost."

Dani leaned back in her chair. She had the best team in the office, and they worked well together. But maybe Bruce was right. Maybe they'd taken on an impossible task. It was too early to know. Maybe the forensic accountant would find something the state had missed. Maybe Ellen Michaels knew what her husband was up to. Maybe a miracle would happen.

"Molly told me something this morning that might help," she said. "She remembers her father quarreling with Michaels. Evidently they went at it pretty regularly, but it really heated up shortly before his death." Dani leaned toward Tommy. "We need you to work your magic. This case will turn on what you can uncover."

"I'll see what I can do, although right now my bag of magic tricks seems pretty empty."

The meeting over, Dani turned to the work on her desk. The inmate requests for help didn't take long to go through. Each presented a clear reason not to proceed. After she returned the phone calls that had come in during her absence, she strolled over to Bruce's office

Bruce looked her over when she entered, and the downturn of his mouth told Dani he was still worried about her. "How are you feeling?" he asked. "You shouldn't do too much your first day back. Make it a short day today."

"I probably will. I'm still tiring easily."

Bruce cleared his throat. "You know, everyone will understand if you want to step down from the Singer case."

"You must have been talking to Doug."

Bruce shook his head. "We've never had any attempts on our staff before. It's disturbing to think one of us could be at risk. Your safety, and everyone else's, is more important to me than clearing an innocent inmate."

"Would you back down if it'd happened to you?"

"I'm a single male with no children. If something happened to me, I wouldn't be leaving anyone behind. Jonah is dependent on you."

Dani leaned back in the chair and began to twirl the ends of her hair. She didn't consider herself to be a brave woman. So many things frightened her—flying on an airplane, hiking narrow trails high on a mountain, getting lost with no means to contact anyone, dying before Jonah's future was settled. "I do worry about Jonah. But I can't run away because I'm afraid. It would just invite this kind of attack to happen again. No, I'm committed to Molly's case. And all our cases."

They chatted some more before Dani made her way back to her office and took up her file for Molly Singer again. The last thing she picked out of it was the report of the jail audit by the State of New York. The most recent letter Donna had received said a group of people had skimmed money from the project, and named Joe Singer and Quince Michaels as two of them. Who were the others?

Frank Reynolds certainly was in a position to do so. He oversaw the bills that were submitted for it. But Paul Scoby, the Hudson County Democratic committee chairman, said the ranking Democrat on the committee had to sign off on them as well. And she was dead.

A car accident.

Dani knew that, given recent events—she could still see that murderous black SUV in her rearview mirror, feel it slamming into the back of her, feel the awful loss of control as it drove her off that road—it would be some time before any car accident didn't sound sinister to her. But still: what if Mary Jane Olivetti, too, had been in on the scam?

Were she and the Singers all murdered for the same reason—to keep them quiet? Or was her accident just an accident—an unfortunate occurrence that had nothing to do with the Singers' murders?

CHAPTER

20

"Did any of you kill Joe and Sarah?" The elder man fixed his stare on the face of each of the three men assembled with him in the Manhattan hotel room, a mid-priced property he'd chosen for its anonymity. The men, each in turn, shook their heads.

"Understand me clearly. I'm not just asking if you personally killed them. I'm asking if you are responsible for their murders; if you hired someone to do the job."

Again, the three men shook their heads and murmured, "No."

The elder man sat back in his chair and folded his arms across his chest. He was many things, but not a murderer. Still, if one of the men in the room had overstepped the boundaries, whether out of fear or greed, he knew he would do whatever was in his power to protect him. Were they lying to him? He thought it possible. Which one, though? None of them seemed like he had the backbone for it. A young woman had been convicted of the crime, and they had all breathed a sigh of relief. Whether or not she was guilty had no relevance to them. It only mattered that, with her conviction, their secret remained safe. Now they were once again in jeopardy of exposure. He got up from his chair, went to the dresser, and poured himself a drink from the bottle of scotch room service had delivered earlier.

"Would any of you gentlemen care for another?" he asked.

They shook their heads glumly.

The elder man took his seat again. He took a sip of the scotch, then said, "It doesn't matter to me if one of you handled the matter in the most extreme way. It's not what I would have done, but we can't look back. I need to know the truth in order to ensure our safety going forward. The way in which I handle it will depend on whether the girl is guilty or innocent. Do you all understand?"

The men nodded, then one said, "It's going to come out anyway."

Unable to keep his anger in check, he barked at them, "Do you doubt my ability to control things? If so, you're a liability and no one in this room should trust you."

The men all spoke their reassurances, and the elder man's body relaxed.

"Fine. Then this is what we're going to do. You're all to leave this room, except you," he said, pointing to one of the men. "I will speak to you each one by one. If you've been embarrassed to tell me the truth in front of the others, you can tell me when we're alone. I won't judge you. As I said, I need the truth to know how to fix things."

The men nodded, then two left the room while one stayed seated. After a few minutes, that man exited the room and another went in, and then, finally, the last. When the elder man had spoken to each of them, he understood what he needed to do.

21

Ellen Michaels's home, although stately, didn't come close to matching the extravagance of her ex-husband's Miami Beach palace. Tommy drove up the long, tree-lined drive to a colonial-style two-story home with manicured lawns and a wraparound front porch. Two red rocking chairs on the porch matched the red front door. He rang the bell, and after a few moments the door was opened by a smartly dressed woman. Her chin-length chestnut-brown hair was silky straight, and large gold earrings hung from her ears. Tommy estimated that she was in her mid-fifties, still attractive, and her well-toned arms and slim body suggested she spent time in a gym.

"Thanks for meeting with me, Mrs. Michaels."

"Please, call me Ellen."

Her voice was gentle, her smile was warm, and Tommy felt immediately at ease with her. He followed her into the living room, which was furnished with a deeply cushioned beige-leather sofa and two club chairs upholstered in a brocade fabric. A richly colored oriental rug covered the wide-planked wood floor, and a large stone fireplace took up most of one wall.

"So, how can I help you with Molly's case?" she asked when they were settled.

"Do you mind if I ask you some personal questions first?"

"It depends on the questions."

"When did you and Mr. Michaels divorce?"

Ellen was quiet for a moment. She brushed back her hair, then fluffed a sofa pillow. When she spoke, her voice was shaky. "How can that possibly help you with Molly's appeal?"

"I'm not sure. I'm following a gut feeling. But if I'm right, it may."

Ellen sighed. "Our divorce was finalized eleven years ago."

"Would you mind telling me the reasons for the divorce?"

"I'm afraid I do mind."

Tommy put down his pencil and looked directly at Ellen. "I know this seems off base to you, but it really may help Molly."

"But how? Whatever our differences, Quince adored Molly. And Joe was like a brother to him."

Tommy hesitated. He knew his next question was a leap, but he decided to take a chance. "Did the divorce have anything to do with the construction of the Hudson County jail?"

Ellen blanched. "I—I can't talk about that."

She knows. She's afraid. "We know that your husband and Joe Singer skimmed money from the jail. We know others were involved as well." Tommy paused, then continued softly. "It's possible that the Singers were murdered because of it."

Tears began to roll down Ellen's cheeks. She got up from her seat and went into the kitchen, where she retrieved a box of tissues. When she returned to the living room, her body seemed deflated.

"How did you find out?"

That was it. The confirmation Tommy had hoped for. Until now, all they had were the anonymous letters—worth squat as evidence. "We have a source. I can't tell you who. Charges are going to be brought against your husband. Yourself, too, probably, unless you cooperate."

Now the tears flowed freely. Tommy waited for them to subside before he said, "Tell me what you know about it."

Ellen stuffed the wet tissue in her pocket and patted down the skirt of her dress before placing her hands in her lap and lacing her fingers together. When she looked up at Tommy, her face seemed filled with sadness. "I knew something was going on, but he didn't talk to me about it. The *Hudson Valley Dispatch* ran daily stories about the cost overruns. It wasn't like Quince and Joe. They were good at pricing jobs. Whenever I questioned Quince about it he said it couldn't be helped."

"So when did you learn they were skimming?"

"Quince was off playing golf one Sunday and I couldn't stand it anymore. My parents were coming to visit, and his office was a disaster area. I knew he wouldn't want me to, but I straightened it up anyway. Papers were strewn over his desk, and when I started to put them into one pile, I saw an envelope from a bank in Belize. It had his name over the name of a company I didn't recognize. I opened it up and saw a statement for an account with fourteen million dollars in it. I was shocked. As soon as he came home, I questioned him about it."

"What did he tell you?"

Ellen began fidgeting with her hands. She started to speak, then stopped herself. Instead, she got up from her chair and walked over to the window overlooking the tree-lined backyard. Tommy remained silent, waiting until she was ready. Finally, she turned around to him and said, "This is my favorite time of year. I couldn't bear to miss it." She walked back to her seat and sat down. "Am I going to go to jail? Do I need a lawyer?"

"I'm not an attorney," Tommy said softly. "But it sounds to me like your ex-husband broke the law, not you."

"Even if I kept quiet about it?"

"Even then. There's a marital privilege. You couldn't have been compelled to testify against your husband, much less turn him in."

Ellen exhaled deeply. "He was very angry that I'd been going through his papers, but I wouldn't let it go. I kept insisting he tell me where the money came from. When he said, 'the jail,' I wanted to die. I grew up in Hudson County. My family has been here for generations. Everyone knows me and I know everyone. I begged him to give it back. He laughed at me. It was the beginning of the end of our marriage. When we divorced, I refused to take any money from that account."

Fourteen million dollars. The final tab on the jail was almost thirty-five million over the bid price. Who got the rest? Was it Joe Singer? Was anyone else in on the scam? All these questions needed answers, but one question was paramount: Was Joe Singer killed to silence him? Tommy looked over at Ellen. "Did your husband ever tell you who else took money from the jail project?"

"No."

"Did Joe?"

"I don't know. He was such a straight arrow. I can't imagine him cheating the county, but then I never thought Quince would either."

"Now, here's the most important question. Did you ever hear anyone threaten Quince or Joe about the money?"

Ellen shook her head. "But when I tried to push Quince for more answers, he told me it was better I didn't know, that my ignorance would keep me safe."

Back in the office, Tommy recounted his conversation with Ellen Michaels for Dani and Melanie. "Hey, I thought you'd be more excited about this," he said to Dani.

Dani herself was a little surprised by her subdued reaction. Part of it was certainly fatigue—her ribs were getting better, but it was still hard to get a good night's sleep. "No, it's good," she said, smiling at him. "It means the anonymous letter writer was right about money being skimmed from the jail. It's just—it's a giant leap from theft and fraud to murder. Even if Michaels, and probably others, engaged in massive theft, it doesn't mean Joe and Sarah Singer were killed to keep them quiet about it. We need something to tie the two together."

"Doesn't it create an alternative motive for the murders?" Melanie asked.

"Sure," Dani answered. "And if Molly were being tried now for the first time, it would be great information to have. The jury might believe it more likely that they were killed for that reason than because their seventeen-year-old daughter was spoiled. But it's not a first trial. It isn't even an appeal. 'Might' isn't good enough. We have to convince the judge that this is new information which would probably change the verdict."

"We can't even be sure that Joe Singer knew about the skimming," Tommy pointed out. "Ellen had no idea who else was involved."

Dani stood up and started to pace. "We have a bigger problem. Ellen was still married to Quince when he admitted to the skimming. She can't testify to it because of the marital privilege."

"Yup," Tommy muttered.

"Let's not get discouraged. We still have a lot of work to do, but it's progress. Let's lock it down if we can. Can you get Ellen Michaels to sign an affidavit? Even if we can't use her statement at a hearing, it may be useful in other ways."

"Maybe. She seemed genuinely concerned about Molly."

"Okay. You go ahead with that. And let's all of us try to figure out who else might have been involved."

The meeting over, Dani looked through the file once more. It was her practice to reread documents many times, and nearly always she'd find new tidbits on subsequent readings. When she got to Finn's testimony, she paused. It had never felt right to her that he'd testified against Molly, especially considering that by the time her trial had come up, he'd known she was pregnant with his child.

Finn's father was at the top of Dani's list of potential participants in the theft scheme. Could he have had something to do with Finn's testifying against Molly? She picked up the phone on her desk. It was time to set up a meeting with Finn Reynolds.

Chapter 22

The elder man waited in the hotel room. When the knock on the door came, he opened it to his visitor. "Do you want a drink?" he asked his guest. The visitor shook his head.

Both men sat down in the two club chairs by the window. The heavy curtains were closed.

"Why am I here?" the visitor asked.

The elder man took his time. He was embarking on a course he'd once thought impossible for him. Yes, he'd relished power. And had used that power to obtain personal wealth. But he wasn't a monster. At least, he hadn't thought he was. Still, he'd always known what needed to be done and had taken steps to ensure it happened. This time could be no different. "The investigator knows about Quince's take on the jail."

"How?"

"Ellen Michaels."

"How did you find out?"

"She called Quince and told him."

The visitor spread his fingers and ran them through his thinning hair. He waited for the elder man to continue.

"Quince says we shouldn't worry. He'll say Ellen is bitter over the divorce and made it up."

"Do you think that will end it?"

With a note of sadness in his voice, the elder man said, "No."

"You want me to take care of it?"

"Yes."

"And I have your blessing on this?"

Reluctantly he answered, "Yes."

The visitor nodded. He knew what he had to do.

CHAPTER 23

Finn paced nervously by the front door. That lawyer—Dani Trumball—was due any moment. Almost as soon as he'd agreed to the interview he'd regretted the decision. He felt caught in a tug-of-war, both sides pulling so hard he felt he might tear in two. It was time for him to do the right thing, but what was right? His father had given him life, had nurtured and loved him. Once, he thought it was his duty to protect his father. Was that still true? Or was his duty to his daughter higher? Didn't she have the right to be with her mother?

His pacing stopped when the doorbell rang. He put his hand on the doorknob to open it, yet hesitated. He didn't know what to say. At the second ring, he opened the door and pasted on a smile. "You must be Dani Trumball." The woman before him was smartly dressed in a navy pinstriped pantsuit and a pale-violet silk blouse. Her dark-brown hair cascaded in waves down to her shoulders. Although she only came up to his chin, she had an air of authority.

"And you must be Finn Reynolds."

"I am." He waved her inside and brought her into his living room. He was grateful that Kim was, once again, at the gym. He felt jittery enough without his wife scrutinizing everything he said about Molly.

Immediately after taking a seat, Dani said, "As I told you over the phone, my office is representing Molly Singer. You were her boyfriend when her parents were murdered, right?"

Finn nodded.

"It surprised me that you testified against her at her trial."

She didn't waste any time. Right for the jugular. Finn didn't know what he'd expected, but not this. Maybe some small talk, something to warm him up, put him at ease. Instead, the first comment she made was the one he'd feared. Did he tell this woman the truth, that he'd testified against the girl he loved to protect the father he loved?

He needed to slow things down, to think some more, despite having agonized over the meeting all morning. He blinked rapidly and cleared his throat before answering. "I only told the truth. The district attorney asked me questions, and I answered them." Finn looked down at his hands. They felt clammy; he looked for something to wipe them with, then brushed them against his pants.

Dani smiled. "I'm sure it was a very confusing time for you. You were only nineteen yourself then, right?"

"That's right." He felt unnerved by the way the lawyer looked at him, as though she knew what he was thinking.

"Did you think Molly murdered her parents?"

"Of course not. She loved them. Even when she got angry at them I knew she was just blowing off steam."

Dani's eyes seemed kindly, her smile warm. Finn wanted to tell her everything. He wanted to admit that he'd picked up the phone one evening, anxious to speak to Molly even though he'd just left her fifteen minutes earlier. He wanted to tell this woman who sought to free Molly that he hadn't hung up when he heard his father on the extension. He wished he had. He wished he hadn't heard Alan Bryson tell his father that if Joe Singer talked, it would ruin things for everyone. "Convince him to shut up or someone will shut him up," Bryson said to his father. "You're in as deep as all of us."

Those words were ingrained in his memory, as though deeply etched with a burning stylus. When he heard that the Singers were killed, he knew his father was involved in some way. And he knew he had to protect him.

"It just seems surprising to me," Dani said, "especially since you knew Molly was pregnant by the time of the trial, that you offered up information about your private conversations to the DA."

Finn shrugged. "He asked me, and I answered truthfully."

"No one but you and Molly would know what you discussed. So if you said nothing to him, he wouldn't know about those conversations."

"I suppose."

"I wonder if your testifying had something to do with your father."

Finn blanched. What did she know? Could she have found out his father was involved in something terrible? Even he didn't know what it was—only that it was something that needed to be kept quiet, at any cost. It was time to make a decision. Tell this woman who was trying to help Molly about the conversation he overheard, or continue the silence he'd kept for twelve years.

"What do you mean?" Finn asked, cringing inside, aware that he once again was betraying the mother of his child.

Dani shuffled through some papers in a folder, then pulled out one and placed it on her lap. "When your father was a legislator, he approved payments of more than thirty-five million dollars over budget for the construction of the Hudson County jail. That money went into the pockets of several people. We know Quince Michaels was one of that group. We believe your father was another."

Was that the big secret? Finn wondered. Was his father a thief? He was ambitious, that much Finn understood. But steal money from the county? It didn't seem like his father. Still, he'd been involved in something bad, something so wrong that it couldn't come to light. And this would be something to hide.

"What makes you think he took money? Do you have any evidence?"

"I'm afraid I can't tell you that. But isn't that why you testified against Molly? To protect your father?" Her voice was soft, a siren luring him into her confidence, inviting him to reveal what he knew.

Finn understood this was his chance to right a wrong, to take the first step in bringing Sophie's mother back to her. Still, he hesitated. Life had seemed uncomplicated when he was a teenager. Sure, raging hormones often heightened the importance of every act, big or small, and sometimes left him confused. Even so, his parents had instilled in him the importance of a moral compass, the need to differentiate right from wrong. And, without their saying so, he understood that loyalty to the family trumped everything. When Molly was on trial, his family was his mother and father. He had his own family now, Kim and Sophie and Graham. What would happen to them if he told this lawyer the truth? Would they escape the fallout from his father's culpability or be tainted by it, as Sophie had always been tainted by Molly's conviction? He didn't know the answer. He couldn't take a chance.

"I'm afraid you've wasted your time, coming here," he said. "I testified at the trial because the DA subpoenaed me. He asked me questions and I answered truthfully. I wish Molly wasn't in jail, and I don't believe she killed her parents. But I had nothing to protect my father from. As far as I know, he's never done anything wrong."

The door to Frank Reynolds's office swung open without a knock. When Frank looked up from his desk and saw Finn standing in the doorway, he smiled and motioned his son to come in. Finn entered the room and closed the door behind him.

"This is a nice surprise," Frank said. "To what do I owe the honor?"

Finn's face was set in a rigid mask. He sat down in the chair opposite the desk and began to wring his hands. He'd debated coming to his father's office. The secrets in the family had lasted more than twelve years, and the unspoken words had allowed them to live harmoniously. Now he'd come to ask questions he should have asked a long time ago. And he knew the answers would likely change his relationship with his father forever.

"Molly's lawyer came to visit me today." Finn let his words sink in as he examined his father's face. He saw no reaction.

"Well, I suppose that's to be expected. You were Molly's boyfriend back then."

"She told me Quince Michaels and others pocketed millions from the jail project." Now Finn saw the reaction he'd expected. It was just the tiniest perceptible narrowing of his eyes, tightening of his lips, but Finn saw it. His father remained silent. "You approved the money for the jail, didn't you?" Finn continued.

"Not just me. Mary Jane Olivetti did as well. All the paperwork we got justified the extra payments."

"Her lawyer thinks you took money as well."

"I hope you told her that's ridiculous."

"I did, Dad. That's exactly what I told her. I'm just not sure I told her the truth."

Frank got up from his chair, walked around the desk and sat on its edge, next to his son. "Why would you say that? You know me."

"I do know you. I've known about you for twelve years and let my girlfriend be railroaded because I've known you."

Frank stood up and walked over to the window. He paused there with his back to his son, looking outside without saying a word. Finn let the silence fill the room. The soft tapping of a keyboard could be heard from outside the office. Finally, Frank turned around. "What do you know?"

"I heard you—on the phone with Alan Bryson. Before the Singers were murdered."

"What? What did you hear?"

"I heard him tell you that Joe Singer had to be kept quiet. That if he talked if would be bad for everyone, including you." Finn's voice grew louder. "You took money, didn't you? You lied about the cost of the jail construction and pocketed the extra money. For all I know, the bunch of you killed the Singers to keep them quiet."

Frank came back to the desk and sat down in the chair next to Finn's. He reached over and took Finn's hand in his own. His face looked drawn, his eyes weary. When he spoke, his voice was hoarse. "I did a terrible thing back then, but I had nothing to do with the Singers' murders. I swear to you, I know nothing about that."

Finn wanted to believe his father, this man he still loved and had revered, so much that he'd pushed away his memory of that phone call. "I need to know everything. I need you to tell me the truth."

Frank hesitated. "Okay. I owe you that," he said, then proceeded to tell his son everything he knew.

Tommy drove up to Hudson County with an affidavit in his briefcase for Ellen Michaels to sign. He hadn't called in advance to set up an appointment. He didn't want to give her time to think it over. Present it to her, get her signature, then leave. He thought he might drive over to the county jail next, take a look at it. After all, the jail was supposedly the catalyst for the murders.

Unlike his own town, where remnants of color remained on the trees, the leaves were already dying as he got closer to Andersonville. He pulled into Ellen's driveway, hoping he'd catch her in. He was prepared to wait as long as necessary if she wasn't. Waiting was often the essence of good investigative work. Boring as hell, but necessary.

A car was in the driveway. A good sign, he thought. He parked, got out of his car, then rang the bell when he reached the door. After a few moments, a gray-haired woman appeared. She looked him up and down, then said, "Can I help you?"

"Is Ms. Michaels in?"

"And you are?"

"Tom Noorland."

"Is she expecting you?"

"No, but she knows who I am."

"I'm sorry, she's not seeing anyone now."

This was an unexpected wrinkle. He'd been prepared to wait, but not to be turned away. "Is she ill?" Tommy asked.

"She's fine. Now, really, I have to ask you to leave."

Persistence was another essential for investigators. Tommy rarely gave up easily. "Would you at least let her know I'm here? It's urgent that I speak to her."

The woman hesitated, then said, "Wait here." She closed the door on Tommy and left him outside for almost ten minutes. When the door opened again, Ellen Michaels stood inside. Her eyes were red and puffy. It looked like she'd quickly applied makeup in an unsuccessful attempt to conceal the signs of recent crying.

"I wasn't expecting you."

"Are you okay, Ellen?" Tommy asked, with genuine concern.

At his question, Ellen began crying again. She motioned for Tommy to come in, and he followed her into the living room.

"What's upset you?" he asked softly.

"Oh, it's too awful. I shouldn't be so torn up. I mean, we've been divorced for so long. But we were married twenty-two years."

"Is it Quince? Did something happen to him?"

"He's dead. An accident." Ellen began crying harder, and Tommy put his arm around her shoulder. He stayed beside her, silently, for several minutes, until she composed herself. Finally, she said, "I shouldn't burden you with this."

"It's okay. My shoulders are big enough to cry on. How did it happen?"

"His boat. He was on his boat and it exploded," Ellen said, then began crying again. In between sobs, she added, "The coast guard said it was a gas leak in the fuel line. Oh, it's so awful."

Tommy stayed awhile, consoling Ellen. It would be fruitless to ask her to sign an affidavit now; she was too distraught. He wasn't even sure whether it could still be used, now that Michaels was dead. Dani would have to answer that question. As he got ready to leave, he turned to her and asked, "Did you tell anyone about our conversation last week?"

"Just Quince. I thought he ought to know."

As he walked to his car, Tommy wondered if it really had been an accident that killed Quince Michaels.

His next stop was the Hudson County jail. Inside the entrance, he showed his identification, mentioned his cred as a former FBI agent, and asked if Sheriff John Engles was available. Five minutes later, Tommy was led to his office.

"Thanks for seeing me," Tommy said as he took a seat across the desk from Engles.

"No problem. I like to extend courtesies to other law-enforcement people and hope they do the same for me. What can I help you with?"

Tommy wasn't really sure. He just wanted to get a feel for the place. "Were you sheriff when the jail was being built?"

"Nah. I was chief deputy sheriff then."

"So, what did you think about the whole thing? You know, deciding to build a new jail, all the expense that went into it."

"I didn't think anything about it. That was up to the politicians."

"The newspapers had a field day with it."

Engles picked up a paper clip from his desk and began twisting it. "When newspapers have nothing to write, they make up stuff. I'll show you what we have here. All top rate. Other counties send their prisoners to us and we make money from it. It was worth every penny."

Maybe he was just being a good front man, putting a positive spin on it for an unknown visitor, or maybe he meant what he said. Or maybe he had a hand in the pot. The last anonymous letter had made Tommy suspicious of everyone in high places.

They chatted some more, then Engles led Tommy on a tour of the jail. They walked past the cell blocks, all of them occupied, then entered the dining room, which was immaculate. A library was filled will law books on one side, fiction and nonfiction titles on another. The place wasn't a country club, but there was an auditorium for weekly movies and a gym to work out in. The sheriff was right—it was all top-end. Tommy might have appreciated it more if he hadn't known that two people were likely killed over it.

Let's go over what we have," Dani said to Tommy and Melanie as they pulled their chairs close to the conference-room table.

"We have confirmation that Quince Michaels padded the bills for the jail project," Tommy said. "That's from his wife. We don't have an affidavit from her, but she gave me the name of the bank in Belize where he'd stashed it twelve years ago. It's Allegiance Bank."

Dani frowned. Belize was a country that adhered to secrecy laws. It would be difficult, if not impossible, to confirm Michaels's account there or the amount of funds in it. "What's happening with the forensic accountant?"

"He's making progress, but it'll be another few weeks before he has anything for us."

"Okay. Hopefully he'll be able to figure out how they padded the invoices." Dani knew that finding concrete proof of excess billing for the jail was essential, but only a start. They'd need more to get a new trial.

"Can Ellen Michaels testify about the bank account?" Melanie asked. "Is the spousal privilege still in effect?"

"I hate to say someone's death is fortunate, but in this case the spousal privilege died along with her ex."

"If Ellen can testify and the accountant finds proof of billing fraud, will that be enough for a new trial?" Melanie asked.

HIPP represented clients throughout the country, and Dani realized this was Melanie's first case in New York. Law schools didn't teach students the ins and outs of court procedure. Most didn't even teach students the specific laws of each state. It taught students the "how," not the "what." How to read the law, how to analyze cases, how to think like a lawyer. But the nuts and bolts—that was something lawyers learned on the job.

"We'll file a motion under section 440 of the criminal procedure law to vacate the judgment on the grounds of new evidence. We have to show that if the new evidence had been heard at Molly's trial, it's probable that she wouldn't have been convicted. We need to convince the judge that others had a greater motive to murder the Singers and, if the jury had known that, they wouldn't have convicted Molly. We're not there yet. At the least, we need to show that Singer knew about the skimming. If we can show that, we can argue he was killed to quiet him. And Sarah Singer was just collateral damage."

As they finished their discussion and rose to leave, Tommy noted, "You know, even though Quince Michaels's death paved the way for his ex-wife to testify, he may have been the only chance we had to find out who else was in on the scheme."

"Unless he told his new wife and she's willing to admit it," Dani said. "Tommy, I think you need to go back to Miami."

It was parent-teacher conference night at Jonah's school, and Dani left work early to make sure she wouldn't miss it. Traffic on the FDR Drive moved steadily north to Westchester County, and she arrived home in time to have a leisurely dinner with her family. Katie had agreed to stay until they returned from their meeting, and so she joined them for dinner.

"Katie, how come everything you cook tastes so delicious, and when I make something, it's barely edible?"

"It's because she's acknowledged, Mommy."

Usually Dani understood Jonah's meaning, even though he often mixed up words. Now she was at a loss. Doug had cocked his head, too. "How is she acknowledged, Jonah?" she asked.

"Well, she went to school and studied cooking, so now she's efficient at it."

"I see."

"Like I'm acknowledged as a composer."

"Yes, although I'd say you're more than an efficient composer. You're quite brilliant at it." Jonah beamed at the compliment.

Dinner over, Dani helped Katie clean up, changed out of her work clothes, and then she and Doug headed over to Jonah's school. It was a private school geared toward children with developmental disabilities. Jonah was one of several Williams syndrome kids there.

Dani and Doug passed corridor walls adorned with drawings and projects by the students, just as in any public school, and then waited on chairs outside his classroom until their turn came.

Mrs. Radler called them in and they sat in two chairs in front of her desk. Dani understood why Jonah gushed over his teacher. She appeared to be in her early thirties, and with shoulder-length brunette hair, porcelain skin, and thickly lashed eyes, she was quite pretty. More important, though, she had a smile that made them feel welcomed.

"I've been looking forward to meeting you," Mrs. Radler said. "Jonah is one of my favorite students."

"Thank you. We're happy to hear that," Doug said.

They discussed Jonah's progress in class, and then his teacher asked, "Have you made future plans for Jonah?"

Dani understood the question. That's just what it was: *the* question. It was one they, and all parents of Williams syndrome kids, knew had to be dealt with at some point, but Dani and Doug had kept pushing that point further away, unwilling to face the inevitable. It was unlikely that Jonah would be a self-sufficient adult, one who could live on his own and be responsible for his basic needs. At some time, hopefully in the distant future, she and Doug would no longer be around to care for him. Plans needed to be made, but not yet. She wasn't prepared to face that future. "There's still plenty of time for that," Dani answered.

"That's true. But we like to start transition planning with parents when their child is Jonah's age. We think it's best to start the process early."

Dani nodded. "I appreciate that. But it's too soon for us." She stood to leave and motioned to Doug to follow.

"Mrs. Trumball, I think it's especially important in Jonah's case to start the planning early."

Dani slowly sat down again. "Why is that?"

"Well, he's so talented musically. I think he would do well at a college specializing in music."

Dani was stunned, unsure that she'd heard his teacher correctly.

"We've never thought of college as a possibility for Jonah," Doug said.

"Well, of course it would need to be a school that provided support services," Mrs. Radler said. "Jonah is at the high end of functioning for Williams syndrome students. Many of our students do go on to college. Usually a community college. More and more schools now have programs that teach students practical academics."

"What does that mean?" Dani asked.

"Well, they might teach skills such as check balancing and money management. Or offer courses that prepare the students for independent-living skills. Much more is being done now to reach out to developmentally disabled persons so they can maximize their potential."

A smile had erupted on Dani's face. When she looked at Doug, she found the same smile engulfing his. It was a smile of relief, a smile of happiness, a smile for her son's future. She'd worried so much about what would happen to him. Now this angel of a teacher was telling them that Jonah might have a much more independent future to look forward to than they'd allowed themselves to dream of for him. Without even realizing it had been there, Dani felt a heaviness lift from her body and float away.

"But I wanted to focus on his musical ability with you," Mrs. Radler continued. "I think you should think beyond community college for him. Many of our students hold responsible jobs after they finish their studies, but usually lower-level positions. I think Jonah could make a living as a composer. He's shown remarkable potential in that area. And there are a lot of opportunities composing music for all sorts of things—advertising, TV, even sound tracks and scores for movies."

Dani looked over at Doug. He, too, seemed shaken.

"But where would he live?" Doug asked. "Wouldn't he be ostracized in a college dorm?"

"That's why I think we should start the process of exploring possibilities early. To me, the ideal solution would be a music college, such as the Berklee College of Music in Boston, or a four-year college with a strong music program, and where there's a group home nearby where he could live off campus."

Dani wanted to stand up and hug Mrs. Radler. She wanted to run home and hug Jonah. Neither of those things was possible, but there was no stopping herself from throwing her arms around her husband.

CHAPTER
26

The last time Molly had been this nervous was when she'd awaited the jury verdict. It had taken days. Days of unspeakable agony, not knowing whether she would emerge from the nightmare of the previous five months. And knowing that if she did somehow escape the hell she'd been through, she would return to an empty home. After the jury found her guilty, she'd been too numb to worry about her sentence. Nothing mattered anymore. Nothing except the baby growing inside her.

Finn's letter had taken her by surprise. Sophie wanted to visit her. Sophie. Her daughter. Molly had named Sophie after her grandmother, and she still smiled at the memory of getting a bear hug from her nana every time she'd visited her. It had been ten years, seven months, and six days since Molly had stopped caring for Sophie in the mother's ward of the prison. Ten years, seven months, and six days since she'd last held her in her arms, fed her meals, rocked her to sleep. She'd counted every day since the guard came and pulled her daughter from her arms, mother and child both wailing as they were torn apart. She'd agreed when Finn said he should stop bringing

Sophie for the weekly visits, that it was too traumatic for Sophie when she had to leave. In truth, it was too hard for Molly. She'd return to her cell on those Saturdays and sob for hours.

Now Sophie waited in the visitors' room. Each step Molly took alongside the guard brought her closer to her daughter. Her hands shook, and as the guard opened the door to the long room lined with chairs, a Plexiglas partition separating the prisoners from the visitors, she stopped, afraid to move forward.

"Move it, Singer," the guard said.

Cautiously, Molly stepped into the room. The fluorescent lights shone brighter than the dull lights lining the prison cells and cast an artificial glow over the space. The hum of murmured conversations filled the air. She looked down the row of visitors, some sitting opposite a prisoner, telephones in their hands, others sitting alone, waiting for the women they'd come to see. Their wives, their mothers, their sisters. Maybe just their friends. Whatever the relationship, they were a window to the outside world for the women inside.

Molly scanned the room until she glimpsed a young girl sitting alone, and gasped. Her silky blonde hair hung straight to her shoulders, and her eyes were half closed, as though she could shut out the nastiness of her surroundings. Her slim frame sat slumped in the seat and her arms were folded across her chest. *She looks like me. Like I once looked, when I was still a child.* Molly could barely breathe as she moved closer.

"Right here, Singer," the guard said as she pushed her into the chair opposite Sophie.

Sophie's eyes opened and she stared at her mother. She picked up the phone next to her and Molly did the same.

"Hello," Sophie said in a child's high-pitched voice, though Molly could see she was beginning to mature.

"Hello, Sophie."

"Um, I don't know what to call you."

"Why don't you call me Molly." She wanted to cry out, *I'm your mother! I nursed you and loved you and would have cared for you if I'd been allowed to. Call me Mommy, or Mom, or anything but Molly.* But she was no longer her mother. Another woman was.

"Daddy said it was time for us to meet."

"I'm glad."

"He said you didn't murder your parents. Is that true?"

It was as though Sophie had reached through the glass and stolen the air from her lungs. These awful words, coming from her daughter. But Molly forced herself to answer simply, directly. "No, I didn't."

"But you confessed. That's what the newspaper said."

"Did you look up the stories from back then?" Molly asked.

"Yeah. Well, now you don't have to look anything up, like in a library or something. Everything is online."

"Of course. I keep forgetting."

"So why did you? Confess."

Molly sighed. How could she explain something she didn't fully understand herself? "The police officer who questioned me said I didn't remember doing it because I'd taken sleeping pills. He told me they found evidence that proved I'd killed them. I didn't think he would lie to me, so I thought I must have."

"But you didn't?"

"*No,* Sophie. I loved my parents. I don't believe it was in me to ever hurt them. Later, I found out there was no evidence I'd murdered them."

Sophie scrunched up her face. "Can they do that?"

"What?"

"Lie to you?"

"Unfortunately, yes. That's something you should always remember."

"It doesn't seem fair."

"No, I don't think it is."

Sophie squirmed. She still held the phone to her ear, but cast her eyes downward.

"Is there something you want to ask me?" Molly said.

"Um, I just wondered—never mind. Forget it."

"It's okay, Sophie. You can ask me anything."

"It's just, I wondered . . ." She brought her eyes up and looked at Molly. "Why did you give me up?"

Molly struggled to keep her breathing under control despite her racing heart. Just looking at Sophie, so grown up, so beautiful, so hurt, made her ache. "I didn't give you up. You're my daughter. You always will be."

"But you told Dad to stop bringing me here for visits."

Molly shook her head vigorously. "No. I didn't. I always wanted to see you. But your dad thought it would be easier for you if you stopped coming here. It made sense to me then."

"Kim told me you didn't want to see me. Because I was so bratty."

Molly struggled to hold back her tears. "Oh, no, sweetheart. You were never bratty. I loved seeing you every week. It broke my heart to give you up."

"Kim hates me."

Molly didn't know what to say. If only she could reach through the Plexiglas and wrap Sophie in her arms, tell her she wasn't hated, by Kim or anyone else. Tell her that things would get better, even if it didn't seem so. But all she could do was tell her she was sorry.

Their time together was, of course, too short. In what felt like seconds, the guard was tapping her on her shoulder.

"Time."

What an awful word.

Molly turned back to Sophie. "Will you come again?"

Sophie shrugged. "I don't know—I guess so."

It had been many years since Molly had given up hope of ever getting out. Now, as her daughter walked away, her only thought was a desperate longing for HIPP to uncover the truth behind her parents' murders and unlock the door that kept her from her girl.

27

This time, the Miami air felt less heavy. Dark clouds overhead kept the temperature lower, and Tommy hoped he'd be on his way home before the predicted thunderstorms arrived. Once again, he'd picked up a rental car and made his way to the home of Lisa Michaels. It had been only a little more than a week since Quince Michaels's death, but his widow had agreed to meet with him.

He pulled up to Michaels's home and rang the bell. After a short wait, Mrs. Michaels opened the door. Instead of the jogging shorts she'd worn when he first met her, she was now dressed in a black pencil skirt with a simple white blouse and a string of pearls around her neck.

"I appreciate you meeting with me," Tommy said. "I'm so sorry for your loss."

"Thank you." She led him into the living room, then said, "Quince told me the reason for your last visit. I assume you're here again about Molly?"

"For Molly. But about Quince."

Mrs. Michaels nodded, as though she expected the response.

"I wish I didn't have to bother you at a time like this, and I'm afraid my questions may disturb you." He felt like an intruder, imposing himself on this woman at a time so close to her husband's death. He rubbed at the knotted muscles at the back of his neck.

"It's about the money, right?"

It took a lot to surprise Tommy, but that stopped him in his tracks. The last thing he expected to discover was that Lisa Michaels knew about the money. He'd come down to Miami to ask her to search Quince's records, to try to uncover some information about the bank account in Belize.

"Yes," he said. "I'm here to find out what you know about it."

Mrs. Michaels's shoulders had drooped, and her lips clenched as though trying to hold back tears. "You know," she said, "most people assume I married Quince because he was wealthy. That couldn't be further from the truth. I fell in love with him because I'd never met anyone else as warm and funny and caring as him—or, frankly, as handsome. He treated me like I was the most important person in the world. And not just because I have money of my own. He didn't know I was wealthy until we'd already become a couple."

Tommy cocked his head at her.

"My best friend and I started an Internet company straight out of college and built it up to a multimillion-dollar operation."

Two surprises in as many minutes. It must have shown on his face, because Mrs. Michaels laughed and said, "Yes, not all pretty, tennis-playing women married to rich men are bimbos. Some of us actually have a brain."

"I'm sorry. I never meant to imply you didn't—have a brain, that is."

"Relax. I'm used to your reaction when I talk about my business. We sold it seven years ago, fortunately before the economic bust, and made a killing on it." As soon as she finished, her face reddened. "Oh, how awful of me. What a horrible choice of words."

"It's okay. It's hard to think straight at a time like this." *Beautiful, smart, and rich. How lucky could one man get? Not so lucky, I guess. He's dead.* Tommy shook off his ruminations. There was work to do. "So, your money paid for this house?"

"No. Quince already had the house when I met him."

"You said you knew I was here about the money. What did you mean by that?"

"Quince was very nervous after you left, but wouldn't tell me why. We left shortly after you, for our tennis match. We played a foursome, with good friends, then went out for lunch and drinks afterward. I figured whatever was bothering him had passed. When we got home, though, he was still fidgety."

"So he told you?"

"Not right away. But I didn't let up. Finally, he told me about the jail. How he'd stolen money from the county by beefing up the bills."

Tommy restrained the smile that threatened to erupt. Finally, confirmation. Not just from an ex-wife who might have been bitter toward her husband, but from a grieving widow. Tommy was certain Dani could use her testimony, assuming she agreed to come to New York for a hearing.

He felt himself relax and his eyes wandered over to the pool outside, the open water just beyond it. After a few moments, he turned back to Mrs. Michaels. "Did Quince tell you whether his partner was part of it? The scam?"

Lisa Michaels nodded. "Not at first. But, again, I pushed. He told me they were in it together. It was meant to be the big payoff after decades of hard work. Pay for a retirement in style when the time came."

Now came the key question, the one that could lead to freedom for Molly. "Did your husband have any documents that showed Joe Singer was in on it?"

"Wait. I'll be right back." She got up from her chair and left the room. Tommy stood up as well and walked over to the French doors leading to the pool. He watched the boats glide by, small sailboats and large cabin cruisers and everything in between.

"I'm back."

Tommy turned around and returned to the sofa where Lisa Michaels again sat, now with a collection of documents spread before her on the glass-topped table.

"What are these?" he asked.

"The proof you needed. After Quince died, I rummaged through his files. I've pieced together what they are." Mrs. Michaels picked up one document. "This is a partnership agreement for a new company they set up while they built the jail. They called it MS Assets. It's a dummy company—it didn't do any work, just held they money they poured into it. You can see from reading it over that Quince and Joe were the only partners. If one died, the assets went to the survivor."

She held up another set of papers. "These are the bank records from Allegiance Bank in Belize. The account was in the name of the partnership. It shows the signatories were Quince and Joe and lists each as the beneficiary of the other. It also shows when the deposits were made—all between twelve and fourteen years ago. A total of fourteen million dollars." She sat back with a smile on her face. "I assume these will help free Molly Singer."

Now it was impossible to hold back a smile. He was ecstatic. It was just what Dani said they needed to prove someone else had a motive for murdering the Singers. And then it hit him. It all pointed to Quince Michaels as the murderer. He was the one who'd benefit if Joe Singer died. He'd collect double the bounty, his own and Joe's.

"Mrs. Michaels. I appreciate you sharing this with me. I have to say, though, it raises questions about your husband's role in the Singers' murders."

"No, you don't get it. Until you came last week, Quince never linked their murders to the jail money. He always hoped it wasn't Molly but, after she'd been convicted, assumed it was. When I pushed him on the nature of your visit, and he told me about the possible connection with the jail money, he was scared. More frightened than I'd ever seen him."

"Well, he was probably afraid that it would all come out and he'd be arrested."

"No, that wasn't it at all. He was afraid of the others."

Tommy did a quick calculation in his head. If Quince and Joe together pocketed fourteen million dollars, and everyone in on the scam took equal amounts, that meant three other people were involved. "The others? Did he tell you who?"

"He refused. Said it was too dangerous for me to know."

Lisa's testimony would guarantee Molly a new trial. Tommy spun the wedding band on his left hand, nervously preparing to ask his final question.

"Would you be willing to come to New York and testify in court about everything you've told me today?"

"Absolutely."

Relieved, Tommy said, "You're very brave."

"No. I'm very angry." She took one more piece of paper from the pile on the table. "This came yesterday. It's the coast guard report of the explosion on Quince's boat. It wasn't an accident. Someone tampered with the gas line."

Dani needed more. Lisa Michaels's testimony would help a great deal, but was it enough? She wished she could demonstrate actual innocence. Go into court with the name of the real killers, wrap it all up with a nice bow. But who? Quince Michaels? He would have been the logical culprit. After all, since Quince benefitted financially from Joe's death, he had a motive for murdering the Singers. Lisa Michaels was adamant, though, that Quince was afraid of someone himself. And now the coast guard had ruled his death a homicide. No, it seemed more likely that the same person who killed the Singers murdered Quince Michaels as well. And tried to kill her.

She took out a yellow pad and wrote on it a list of witnesses against Molly. A few classmates from school and her boyfriend, Finn. He'd seemed surprised when Dani suggested his father had been involved in a theft. As far as she could tell from her interview, he'd only been a scared teenager doing what he thought was right. The medical examiner testified as to the cause of death. Nothing to attack there. The assistant sheriff on the case described the scene. Bob MacDonald had questioned him thoroughly on the lack of forensic evidence tying

Molly to the murders. No place to go with that. And then the most damning evidence of all—Molly's confession. It didn't matter that she'd recanted the next day. The jurors had glommed on to her admission and decided that an innocent person wouldn't confess no matter what deprivations she'd been put through.

Dani turned to her computer. A few years back HIPP computerized its records and now, with a few clicks, Dani could research all the cases the office had handled. She typed in "false confessions" and spent the next hour reading. When she finished, she put in a call to Derek Deegan, an expert witness.

As soon as she hung up, Tommy stepped into her office. "Hot off the press," he announced.

"What's that?"

"The report of the forensic accountant."

Dani felt a sense of excitement. This could be the missing piece they were waiting for. They already had testimony that showed Quince Michaels and Joe Singer pocketed far more than they should have for the jail. But Ellen Michaels's testimony could be discredited as that of a bitter ex-wife. And although Quince Michaels told his widow that he'd skimmed money from the jail project, it was possible the judge could exclude it as hearsay. Even though they had records of the dummy company and bank records, they needed more to prove the money in that account came from the jail and not something else. Dani prayed the accountant found that proof.

"What's it say?" she asked.

Tommy sat down at her desk and passed over the report. "Our guy didn't just match up each contractor's invoice to the bill submitted to the county. He went back to each of the contractors and subcontractors to confirm the invoices. In many cases, when he showed the owner the bill, he scratched his head and said it wasn't the bill he'd submitted to Quince and Joe. In at least thirty instances the original bill was doubled, even tripled, by Quince and Joe before they submitted it to the county."

"How did they get away with that?"

"It was even hard for our accountant to spot the changes on the invoice, and he was looking for it. They did a damn good job."

"That's great. It's just what we need. And they were able to charge an extra thirty-five million by doing that?"

"There's more." Tommy smiled his Cheshire cat grin, the one that always signaled to Dani he'd hit the jackpot. "That accounted for close to ten million, but he couldn't find four of the subcontractors. He searched every state record and came up with zilch. And those four contractors accounted for payments of over twenty-five million dollars."

"Maybe they'd gone out of business. It's been twelve years, and the building industry has suffered in the last four or five."

"Yeah, that's what he thought at first, but when he combed through back records for the ownership of those companies, in each case they were owned by a different company."

"So. Isn't that fairly common?"

"Maybe. But in this case it was done to make it harder to track down the true owner of the company. He hasn't been able to track down three of them, but the fourth company is owned by MS Assets, and we know through Lisa Michaels that Joe and Quince were the owners. It's the very same company that had a Belize bank account with deposits of fourteen million dollars."

Dani took in Tommy's information. "Wouldn't the state have discovered the phony companies?"

"They were clever. The state auditors flag a company as suspicious if it has a residential address, or a PO box for receipt of payments, instead of a commercial address. Each of the dummy companies rented commercial space for the period of the build, hired a receptionist to receive mail, then closed the doors after the audit was complete. Since there was nothing suspicious about them, the auditors didn't check further.

"One other thing," Tommy continued. "Our accountant spoke to someone at the state comptroller's office—they do the audits—and he said it's easier to get away with a fraud if they have someone at the county who's in on the scheme."

"Like Reynolds," Melanie said.

"Yep."

On its face, the information was great. It validated the testimony they had. Slam-dunk grounds for a new trial. Yet Dani wasn't ready to celebrate.

Tommy sighed. "Okay, Dani. Why don't you look happy?"

"Because it probably means there are at least three other people who owned the other phantom companies, and they were stealing money as well. And if we introduce this information at trial, those people will know we're on to them. Or at least on their trail. It'll send them hiding for cover, and then we'll have no chance of identifying the real killers."

Dani felt torn. Her goal—HIPP's goal—was to free wrongfully convicted clients. Finding the real perpetrators in the process was gratifying, but not their job. With DNA evidence, they rarely found the real culprit, but at least when DNA from the crime didn't match their client, exoneration routinely followed. But here, there was no DNA to exonerate Molly. They had evidence that Joe Singer and Quince Michaels, and likely three others, fraudulently benefitted from the construction of the Hudson County jail, which created a motive for one of those others to murder the Singers, but the jury would need to believe that Joe Singer was about to tell the authorities of the crime and he was murdered to silence him. The evidence they'd uncovered so far should be enough to get them a new trial. But was it enough to get Molly acquitted?

"I think we need to turn this information over to the US Attorney's Office," Dani said. "We have evidence of a crime, and at least some of the monies were moved overseas. That should give them jurisdiction to investigate."

Tommy nodded. "Okay, but I still have concerns about Frank Reynolds's involvement, and since he's the county executive, won't an investigation into a crime against the county alert him anyway?"

"I still know people there. I think I can convince them to keep the investigation secret—at least until they know the other people involved."

"And in the meantime?"

"We have to go ahead and file a motion for a 440 hearing. There should be enough here to grant a new trial, and hopefully by the time it starts, the feds will have something for us."

"Why not wait until they do?"

"Because the bodies keep stacking up. And I don't want one of them to be someone from HIPP."

Sitting in the spacious office of Senior Assistant US Attorney Joshua Cosgrove, Dani felt a wave of nostalgia wash over her. She'd started her career in this building, one of dozens of Ivy League law school graduates who'd turned down positions with prestigious Wall Street firms to devote themselves to public service. It was only blocks away from HIPP's office, yet it felt like a world away. She'd met her husband in these halls. Now both had embarked on different career paths.

Josh swept into the office with apologies for being late. He brushed back his golden hair, loosened his tie, and plopped into his chair.

"Whew. Judge Edsel just put me through the wringer. I couldn't get out of there. These bleeding-heart liberal judges are going to be the death of me."

Dani smiled. Josh would probably consider the attorneys at HIPP to be bleeding hearts as well, although they ran the gamut from right-wing conservatives to left-wing liberals. The one thing they held in common was the belief that innocent men and women shouldn't be incarcerated for crimes they didn't commit. When she was a prosecutor, she considered all defense attorneys to be misguided, fooled by their clients into believing their lies. Now she knew differently. Funny how things change, she thought. Once, she'd wanted to make a career as a federal prosecutor, maybe aspire to a federal judgeship. She believed she had the temperament to make a good judge. Fair but strict. And in her most closely held dreams, those she hadn't even shared with Doug, she'd fantasized an appointment to the United States Supreme Court. She'd pushed those notions away after Jonah was born, after his Williams syndrome diagnosis. Now her dreams were for him to grow into a self-sufficient, happy adult.

"So, what's up?" Josh asked. "It's been ages since we spoke."

"I'm here for a favor."

"Spill. If I can help, I will."

Dani told him about the anonymous letters, the discovery of an offshore account opened by Joe Singer and Quince Michaels, and the results of their forensic accountant's investigation.

"Shouldn't this go to the DA's office in Hudson County?"

"We don't know who else was on the take. We're suspicious of the county executive. For all we know, the DA or a top assistant in that office was part of the scheme as well."

"Then how about the state attorney general?"

"I suppose. But the state did an audit of the jail finances and okayed it. I'm worried that they'd be embarrassed that they missed what really went on. Or, worse, that someone in that department deliberately covered it up."

Josh glanced over the documents Dani had given him. "Hold on. Let me check something." He turned to his computer and punched a few keys, then read the chart on the screen. After a few more clicks, he turned back to Dani. "You're in luck. The federal government had a grant program between 1997 and 2002 for construction of local jails and prisons. New York State received some of that grant money, and it looks like a piece of it was allocated to Hudson County when it built its jail. Since they used money from the federal government, we have jurisdiction to investigate any funny business. I'll assign someone to look into this. I can't promise that we'll have something for you quickly, but I'll keep you in the loop if we find anything."

"Thanks, Josh. You're a prince. Just one other thing."

Josh raised his eyebrows.

"It's important your inquiry remain secret. The others, the ones who stole money as well—they can't know we're sniffing around until we know for sure who they are."

"Understood."

Before leaving the building, Dani made the rounds of the other offices to say hello to her former colleagues. She then headed back to HIPP, ready to start work on a motion for a new hearing for Molly Singer—the first step in her quest for freedom.

Dani and Melanie had spent the week putting together the motion papers. When they were satisfied with their product, it was electronically filed with the County Court in Hudson County and a copy was served on the district attorney's office. Now they needed to wait for the court to assign a hearing date.

Dani decided to leave the office early. It had been only three weeks since she'd come out of her coma. Although her ribs were healing, fatigue hit her each day as the hours wore on. She retrieved her car from the parking lot, then headed east to pick up the FDR Drive northbound. She exited for the Triboro Bridge toward the Bronx, the route she took to her home in Bronxville, a leafy Westchester County suburb an easy commute from Manhattan. She meant to get off the Sprain Brook Parkway at her exit, but somehow she drifted past it and kept driving until she realized she was near the Bedford Hills Correctional Facility. She left the highway and drove over to the prison, showed her attorney's credentials, then waited. Before long, she was escorted to an interview room.

"I didn't expect you today," Molly said when she was brought into the room.

Dani smiled. "I didn't expect to be here today. But I was nearby and thought I'd drop in to see how you're doing."

Suddenly, tears welled up and some escaped down Molly's cheeks.

"What's wrong?"

"Noth-nothing. "She wiped the drops away with the back of her hand. "I'm happy, really, I am."

"Tell me, what's going on?"

"Sophie came to visit me."

Now Dani understood. Molly had to feel overwhelmed by conflicting emotions. Joy at seeing her daughter, heartsick at her absence.

"She's so beautiful," Molly continued. "And she seemed so sad. I wanted to put my arms around her and hug her, but of course I couldn't. I couldn't even hold her hand." Molly began crying, copiously now. Dani searched through her purse and handed her a tissue.

"Th-thank you," she said between sobs.

When she'd finally cried herself out, Dani asked, "Why did she come? I mean, she hasn't seen you since she was a toddler."

"Finn brought her. Oh, it was horrible. I thought it was the right thing to give her up, let Kim be her mother. Wasn't that better than having a mother in prison? But she told me things Kim said to her that were so mean. I hate that woman."

"I'm sorry. Can you speak to Finn about it?"

"If Finn cared, he would have come himself."

"Maybe he brought Sophie here because he does care."

"Maybe. There's no way for me to know. I'm so cut off from everyone and everything. I've gotten used to it. I go about my work and don't bother anyone. I stopped wanting more a long time ago. But now, with you here and trying to open my case, with Sophie so unhappy, it's changed. I want to be free. I want to have a life. I want my daughter."

Driving home, Dani understood why she'd absentmindedly drifted toward the women's prison. Ever since leaving the US Attorney's Office, her workplace for so many years, she'd pushed aside gnawing feelings of regret. If, once she'd returned to work after her years at home with Jonah, she'd gone back to that office, she'd be in a senior position now. She'd have all the resources of the United States government at her disposal. She'd prosecute criminals that wreaked havoc on the populace, and she'd have automatic respect in courtrooms and among friends and acquaintances. As a lawyer for HIPP, she was often held in disrepute. She was a lawyer trying to free criminals, putting them back on the street to kill and rape and pillage once again. No matter how often she tried to explain that she represented people she believed to be innocent, whom further investigation or DNA proved were innocent, beyond any doubt, there lingered a sense that she relied on legal technicalities to overturn convictions. Police didn't make mistakes. And if they did, jurors corrected those mistakes. Twelve men and women who found guilt beyond a reasonable doubt couldn't be wrong.

Dani knew they were mistaken. Jurors only heard evidence that the prosecuting and defense attorneys offered and the judge permitted. Many times other evidence wasn't known to the parties, or allowed by the judge. Like with Molly's case. No one knew then that Joe Singer had stolen money from the jail project. No one knew that others wanted to keep him quiet about it. If jurors had heard about it, Dani felt certain they would have had reasonable doubt that Molly Singer, barely eighteen and pregnant, had ruthlessly murdered her parents.

Sitting with Molly today, all her lingering regrets that she hadn't returned to work at the US Attorney's Office vanished, replaced with a renewed desire to grant this mother's wish. Dani would do everything she could to free her from prison and reunite her with her daughter.

CHAPTER 30

Dani and Melanie had been summoned to Bruce's office. "We have a hearing date for the Singer case," he told them when they arrived. "It's in three weeks."

"Who's the judge?" Dani asked.

"Bryson. He's the chief judge there. I don't know whether he was next on rotation or he took it out of rotation." In courts throughout the country, cases were typically assigned to judges on a rotating basis. However, the chief justice of the court always had the option to assign the case to a justice other than the one next up.

"Is that good or bad?" Melanie asked.

"He was the trial judge on Molly's case," Dani said. "Sometimes the trial judge will want to stick with a case that's returned because he believes the defendant got a raw deal from the jury. Other times it's because he wants to make sure the defendant remains behind bars."

Melanie looked over at Dani. "What do you think the case is with this judge?"

"Well, he sentenced Molly to two consecutive life terms instead of concurrent terms. That's pretty unusual, especially with someone who has no criminal record. And many of his rulings went against Molly. So, I'm inclined to think he falls into the latter category."

"Ugh! That's not good."

"Where's the US attorney on this?" Bruce asked.

"Nothing back from them yet. They're trying to track down the owners of the three other companies. Whoever they are, they've set up quite a labyrinth. Each company is owned by several other companies. They haven't gotten any further than that."

"Let them know the trial date," Bruce said. "If we can learn something before then, it'll be a big help. Your case is pretty skimpy so far."

"Well, skimpy for a trial on her guilt or innocence, maybe," Dani said. "I think it's pretty solid on showing grounds for a new trial."

"It's suggestive, certainly. But you have to show that, had this evidence been introduced at her trial, there's a probability that the verdict would have been different. I just don't know that it rises to that level. Possibility—yes. Probability? I'm not sure."

"Why do you say that?" Melanie asked. "They had no real motive for Molly killing her parents. We're presenting evidence of a powerful motive for someone else to have killed them."

Bruce leaned back in his seat and put his arms behind his head, a gesture he often made when he knew he was right. "Because of her confession. Jurors have a hard time overlooking a confession. Even when it's recanted, it's still out there."

"Five of our overturned convictions were based on false confessions," Dani pointed out. "Why do you think this is different?"

"Because we had DNA evidence in those cases that proved our client was innocent. I told you at the outset this would be a difficult case."

Dani knew Bruce was right. They had a huge hurdle to overcome. In the eyes of jurors, a confession trumped all other evidence, including lack of evidence. "I think I've got that aspect covered, but I just had another idea. I don't know if it'll work. I need to call Molly's lawyer first."

Their meeting over, Dani headed back to her office and telephoned Bob McDonald. When he got on the phone, she asked, "Bob, how long were the jurors out on Molly's case?"

"If I remember correctly, it was quite a while. Hold on a sec. Let me grab her file." A few minutes later, he returned to the phone. "Just what I thought. It took them five days to come back with a verdict."

"Did you poll the jurors afterwards?"

"Sure. It was her confession that swayed them."

"But why, then, did it take them five days?"

"There were four people on the jury who had a hard time believing this girl, who'd never been in trouble before, suddenly went psycho. They had teenagers themselves and knew that complaining about parents was common behavior. Gradually, they just got worn down by the others."

"Do you have the names of those four?"

"Let me see." Dani could hear pages in the file being turned. "Yep. Do you need them?"

Dani felt a surge of excitement. If this panned out, it could be just the testimony she'd need to lock up her motion. "E-mail it to me, okay? And their addresses, too, if you have it."

"Consider it done."

Dani thanked him and got off the phone. Fifteen minutes later her in-box held the e-mail from Bob. She opened it up, then buzzed Tommy's desk with her intercom.

"What's up, boss?"

"I need you to try and track down four people. I'm forwarding an e-mail to you with their names."

"Got it."

Dani hung up, then smiled. Things were coming together nicely. She felt cautiously optimistic that she'd get a new trial for Molly Singer.

31

The county court building in Andersonville was a plain brick building without any distinguishing features, sandwiched in between nondescript retail stores and restaurants. Dani and Melanie had already introduced themselves to Eric Murdoch, the assistant district attorney opposing their motion for a new trial, and were now seated at the defendant's table in the front of the courtroom. Molly had been brought up from the state prison and sat in the prisoner's box, an armed guard next to her. She remained in her orange jumpsuit, shackles still binding her hands and feet.

The bailiff announced the entry of Chief Judge Alan Bryson. The parties stood as he walked, his shoulders thrust back and head erect, to his place behind the massive desk on a raised platform, then sat once the judge had taken his chair. Dani knew from her research that he was fifty-two, but he looked older, with his silver-white hair and deeply lined face. He couldn't have been mistaken for someone's jolly grandfather, though. His eyes were a steely gray that seemed to bore into her. There was no jury. It was solely Judge Bryson who would decide whether Molly's conviction should be vacated.

"The People of the State of New York versus Molly Singer," called out the bailiff in a loud voice, even though he knew the only people in the courtroom were the ones assembled for that case.

Dani stood up. "Dani Trumball for the defendant."

"Eric Murdoch for the State."

"I want to remind you, Ms. Trumball, that what you're seeking under section 440 is extraordinary relief, and you have a high burden. I hope you're not here to waste my time."

Okay, Dani thought. If she'd had any doubts, it was now clear he wasn't going to be sympathetic to her defendant. "Understood, Your Honor. We believe a grave miscarriage of justice has occurred, and new evidence that only recently came to light will confirm that."

"Enough of the grandstanding. Call your first witness."

"I call Ellen Michaels to the stand."

Ellen Michaels walked slowly from the back of the courtroom, as though she were on a funeral march. Dani knew she was uncomfortable testifying about something that would subject her to humiliation in the community in which she'd grown up. But she loved Molly Singer. If her testimony helped Molly win a new trial, she would bear the embarrassment.

After Ellen was seated in the witness chair and sworn in by the bailiff, Dani approached the witness box. "Would you state your relationship to Quince Michaels?"

"He was my husband. We divorced eleven years ago."

"And how long were you married?"

"Twenty-two years."

"Are you familiar with Molly Singer?"

"Yes. Quince and Joe Singer were partners in a construction business. I've known Molly her whole life."

"What was the name of their business?"

"Building Pros Inc."

"Was Building Pros awarded the jail construction project by Hudson County, about fourteen years ago?"

"Objection, Your Honor," Eric Murdoch said as he slowly arose from his chair. "I fail to see the relevance of this line of questioning."

"Ms. Trumball?" asked the judge.

"It will become clear very soon, Your Honor. If you'll indulge me just a bit more."

"Okay, but make your point soon."

Dani turned back to Ellen Michaels. "Please answer the question."

"Yes. They built the Hudson County jail."

"And did there come a time when you learned from your husband that he defrauded the county by overcharging for the jail?"

Murdoch shot back out of his chair. "Objection! This witness can't testify to something told her by her husband. It's barred by marital privilege."

Dani turned to the judge. "Mr. Michaels is now deceased and so marital privilege is no longer applicable."

"My objection stands. It's also hearsay."

Both attorneys looked to the judge for his ruling.

"The marital privilege doesn't apply here. I'll rule on the hearsay objection after I hear what she has to say."

Dani nodded at Ellen to answer.

"Yes. I found a statement from a bank in Belize addressed to him. There was fourteen million dollars in the account. I confronted Quince, and he told me the money was from the jail."

"Did he say this was the profit he'd expected to earn from building the jail?"

"No. He told me he'd deliberately overcharged the county."

Murdoch stood up. "I renew my objection to this testimony. It's clearly hearsay. Mr. Michaels isn't here to confirm he made these remarks and to be cross-examined on them."

"Your Honor, this falls within an exception to the hearsay rule. The—"

Judge Bryson held up his hand. "Don't waste time on arguments now. Both of you give me briefs on it, and I'll decide after the hearing."

"Do you have a copy of that bank statement?"

"No, when we divorced, Quince took all of his business records."

"Thank you. I have no further questions."

"Your witness," Judge Bryson said to Murdoch.

Murdoch stood up and strode over to the bench. Despite his small stature and loosely fitted suit, his deep voice lent him an air of authority.

"Mrs. Michaels, upon your divorce, were the assets acquired during the marriage divided between you?"

Ellen shifted in her seat. "What do you mean?"

"The house, the cars, the bank accounts, the value of the construction business, anything else of any worth. Were they divided equally between you and Mr. Michaels?"

"Well, I got the house and the BMW. Quince paid me five thousand a month for two years. And I got some money."

"How much money?"

"Seven hundred and fifty thousand."

Murdoch walked closer to Ellen. "And excluding this alleged bank account in Belize, how much money did you and your husband have in all other bank accounts?"

"Two million, maybe a little more."

"Now, you said you got the house. How much was that worth when you divorced?"

"I'm not sure."

"Take a guess."

"Maybe seven hundred thousand."

"So, you had a house worth seven hundred thousand, and bank accounts with at least two million, and you left the marriage with approximately half of that, isn't that correct?"

"I suppose."

"So who got the fourteen million in the Belize bank?"

"Quince."

"Mrs. Michaels, you got half of everything else. Do you expect us to believe you walked away from seven million dollars?"

Ellen sat up straighter and narrowed her eyes at Murdoch. "I didn't want any of that money."

"Very noble of you. By the way, you're very fond of Molly Singer, aren't you?"

"Yes."

"In fact, aren't you her godmother?"

"Yes."

"You'd like to see her free, wouldn't you?"

"Of course. I don't believe she killed her parents. But I'm not lying. Quince did have that back account."

"So you say. No other questions. You can step down."

"Call your next witness," Judge Bryson said.

"I call Lisa Michaels."

A court officer stationed by the back door opened it and called her name. Lisa Michaels sauntered into the courtroom. Her skintight black dress was in stark contrast to the matronly flowered dress worn by Quince's first wife. Large gold hoops hung from her ears, and a gold necklace with a diamond pendant was draped around her neck. Dani saw Murdoch's mouth drop open as Lisa sashayed by, and stifled a smile.

"State your name for the record please," Dani said.

"Lisa Michaels."

"And are you any relation to Quince Michaels?"

"I was his second wife and, as of six weeks ago, his widow."

"When did you marry?"

"Seven years ago."

"Where did you live when you married Mr. Michaels?"

"I moved into his house."

"And where is that?"

"Miami Beach."

"Would you describe that house?"

"Sure. Four bedrooms, four bathrooms, living room, dining room, media room, exercise room. Oh, and a kitchen."

Dani smiled at the mention of a kitchen. She doubted that Lisa Michaels spent much time cooking meals. "Would you describe the plot of land it's on?"

"A half acre on the intercoastal."

"Do you know the value of the property?"

"I would guess seven or eight million."

"Did Mr. Michaels ever discuss with you how he paid for it?"

As expected, Murdoch popped up with the same "hearsay" objection, and once again the judge reserved decision until after briefs were filed.

"I never questioned him about it, until a few weeks ago, after your investigator, Tom Noorland, met with him." Lisa went on to describe her conversation with Quince and his admission that he and Joe defrauded Hudson County out of the money.

Dani marked a copy of the partnership agreement for MS Assets, as well as the bank records from Allegiance Bank in Belize, as exhibits and submitted them. "Were these records obtained from your husband's file cabinets in your house?"

"Yes. After his death, I went through all his records."

"Just one more question. How did your husband die?"

"He was murdered."

Dani thanked Lisa Michaels then walked back to her table.

"Just a few questions," Murdoch said as he stood and walked toward the witness. "You said that your husband was murdered. How did he die?"

"He was on his boat and it exploded."

"Did the coast guard investigate that explosion?"

"Yes. They said that someone tampered with the gas line and that's why it exploded."

"And did their report conclude that it was a homicide?"

Lisa bent her head down, then said softly, "They said his death was suspicious. Because they couldn't rule out he'd tampered with it himself." She lifted her head and spoke with a firm voice. "But he wasn't suicidal. Someone did this to kill him."

"Was anyone arrested in connection with his death?"

"No."

"Did you and your husband usually keep secrets from each other?"

"I didn't have any secrets. And I never thought Quince did."

"Prior to Mr. Noorland's visit to your husband, did he ever tell you about this alleged theft?"

"No."

"And wasn't your husband Molly's godfather?"

"I believe so."

"Isn't it possible that Mr. Noorland convinced him to make up this story to free Molly from prison?"

"I doubt it."

"But you don't know with absolute certainty, do you?"

Lisa looked directly into Murdoch's eyes. With a clear voice, she answered, "What I know with absolute certainty is that my husband was frightened, and a week later he was dead."

"Nonresponsive," Murdoch muttered, then, "I have no further questions of this witness." As Lisa left the witness chair Murdoch said, "Your Honor, I move to strike the testimony of the previous two witnesses. The State of New York did a thorough audit of the jail finances and found no wrongdoing. These witnesses have no direct knowledge other than what was purportedly told them by the defendant's godfather. It's not only hearsay, but this court must give deference to the findings of the State."

Dani stood up. "I believe my next witness will answer the objections of Mr. Murdoch."

Bryson nodded. "Go ahead and call him."

"Saul Delinsky."

Once again, the routine was followed. The court officer opened the door to the hallway and called his name. The sound of footsteps and conversations from outside intruded on the silence of the courtroom. Delinsky stepped inside, the door closed behind him, and quiet returned. He lumbered up to the witness chair and was sworn in.

"Mr. Delinsky, please state your profession," Dani said.

"I'm a forensic accountant."

"By whom are you employed?"

"I'm semiretired now. I work for myself."

"And before you retired?"

"I worked for the FBI for thirty years as a forensic accountant."

"Please describe your duties."

"I would go over accounting records and look for evidence of illegal financial activity. I worked as part of an investigation team. My specific expertise was in matters of fraud."

"And during the course of your thirty years with the FBI, how many investigations were you part of?"

"Over three hundred."

"Were you asked to review the financial records relating to the construction of the Hudson County jail?"

"Yes. By a member of your office."

"And how did you obtain those records?"

"They were provided to me by the State of New York. They gave me copies of all the materials they had for their own audit of the jail finances."

"And did you reach a conclusion as to whether there had been any illegal financial activity?"

"I did." Delinsky went on to describe the methods used to overbill the county by $35.3 million.

"The state audit didn't uncover any discrepancies. Can you explain that?"

"Their auditors aren't trained in forensic accounting. And the perpetrators were extremely skillful in covering their fraud."

"Thank you. I have no more questions. At this time, Your Honor, I'd like to submit as an exhibit Mr. Delinsky's report."

Murdoch stood up. "I have no questions of this witness, but I reserve the right to call him later."

Dani wasn't surprised. Delinsky's credentials were impeccable and his report thorough. Murdoch would be hard pressed to find any holes in it.

"Counselors, this seems like a good time for a lunch break," Judge Bryson said. "We'll reconvene in ninety minutes."

Dani and Melanie found a luncheonette a few doors away from the courthouse. "I think it's going well," Melanie said.

"I do, too. We got in everything we needed." Dani surprised herself. Usually, she came away from court proceedings filled with doubt about the outcome. Now she was eager to get back in the afternoon and continue with her witnesses.

"What do you think he'll do on the hearsay exception?"

"I don't know. The law is on our side, and so far he's seemed fair. Having heard the testimony, I think it'll be hard for him to throw it out."

They finished their lunch, the food more gourmet than they'd expected from the barren decor. Dani knew, though, that the Culinary Institute of America, which trained student chefs, wasn't far away. She suspected the owner of the little restaurant was a graduate.

They strolled down the street, gazing into the storefront windows of antique and art shops until it was time to head back to the court. Their next witness was waiting for them in the courthouse lobby.

"You'll be the first one up when we reconvene," Dani told him. "I really appreciate you coming here."

"I feel it's my duty," the white-haired man said. "I've been troubled by my role for twelve years."

Dani patted his arm. "Then I'm glad you'll have the chance to help."

The three headed into the courtroom and waited for the judge to return. Once he retook the bench and told Dani to proceed, she called Tony Winslow to the witness chair.

After the preliminary questions—name, address, occupation—Dani asked, "Were you a juror for the trial of Molly Singer twelve years ago?"

Murdoch shot out of his seat and shouted, "Objection."

"Grounds?" Bryson asked.

"Relevance. Anything a juror from Singer's trial has to say bears no relation to whether there are grounds for a new trial."

"On the contrary," Dani said. "It's directly on point as to whether the new evidence we submitted had the probability to change the outcome of that trial. Who better to answer that question than a juror from that trial?"

Bryson rubbed his chin. "This is a new one for me. I'll allow the testimony subject to a ruling later on the objection."

Dani turned back to the witness. "Please answer the question."

"Yes, I was a juror."

"Would you describe the deliberations in the jury room?"

"Well, on the first vote, it was eight guilty and four not guilty. I was one of the four. I voted that way because I thought we needed more discussion."

"And did a discussion ensue?"

"More like an argument. Most of the jurors thought there was no need to go beyond the confession. I mean, why would someone confess to a crime they didn't commit?"

"And did you feel that way?"

"I have to admit, that confession was pretty persuasive. But she was just a kid. That bothered me. And I didn't really see any motive for her killing her parents."

"How long did the deliberations last?"

"Five hellish days, pardon the language. By the end, everyone just wanted to get out of there. Finally, those of us still holding out—and it was down to three at that point—figured if she confessed, she was guilty of something. So we went along. It's bothered me all these years, though, her being so young, and pregnant on top of that."

"If you heard evidence that her father had defrauded the county out of seven million dollars, that others had done the same, for a total of thirty-five million dollars, and if you heard that Joe Singer had been thinking of telling the authorities about his and the others' theft, would that have changed your vote?"

Winslow sat up straight in his seat. With a loud voice, he answered, "You bet it would have. That would be a powerful motive for someone to kill him, to shut him up. I never would have changed my vote if I'd heard about that."

"Thank you. I have no other questions."

Murdoch walked slowly up to the witness.

"You said you've been bothered since the trial about your vote."

"Sure have."

"I'm sure all of us wish we had do-overs in life. Aren't you here today to give yourself a do-over?"

"What do you mean?"

"Well, isn't it true that even if no other motive were presented, you'd still wish you'd voted differently?"

"I suppose that's true."

Murdoch turned to Judge Bryson. "Your Honor, I repeat my objection as to relevance. Many jurors regret their decision afterwards, both those who choose to convict and those who choose to acquit. It's pure speculation for this juror to now say his position would have been different with new information about the jail. Faced with the defendant's confession, it's likely he would have done the same. I move to strike his testimony."

"Your Honor," Dani countered, "what greater proof can there be that had this evidence been available at trial, the result would have been more favorable to the defendant. It's highly relevant."

Judge Bryson looked at both advocates, scribbled something on a piece of paper, then said, "I have to agree with the State. The statute looks at what a reasonable person would think, not a specific juror. This witness brings baggage with him that may be clouding his judgment. His testimony is stricken."

Dani fumed. How could the judge have dismissed the testimony so cavalierly? Shouldn't she at least have been given the opportunity to brief the issue? "Preserve for appeal," she muttered to the court reporter.

Murdoch smiled broadly, then moved closer to the bench. "It's clear to me that, unless Ms. Trumball is prepared to offer definitive proof that a specific individual or individuals has committed the crime, everything we've heard so far is too nebulous to overcome the weight of the defendant's confession. I move that the hearing be concluded and defendant's motion denied."

Dani turned from glaring at Murdoch to face the judge. "Your Honor, I'm not finished with my witnesses. I promise it won't take much longer."

Bryson sighed. "Go ahead, then."

"I call Derek Deegan."

The door to the hallway opened and a heavy man in his mid-forties, with coal-black hair and a handlebar mustache, slowly walked to the witness box.

"What is your profession Mr. Deegan?"

"I am a professor of law at Harvard Law School, where I teach criminal law. I have studied, and published numerous papers on, the issue of wrongful convictions. My research has included the phenomenon of false confessions."

"Have you reviewed the files, including the confession, in Miss Singer's case?"

"I have."

"And have you reached any conclusions?"

"First, let me explain that since Ms. Singer's conviction, a great deal has been learned about false confessions. Through examining those individuals whose convictions have been overturned as a result of DNA evidence, and who had confessed to the crime, studies have shown that the police telling a suspect false evidence exists is a common thread."

"And was such a tactic used with Ms. Singer?"

"Yes. The police informed her that they had conclusive evidence tying her to the crime."

"And that was sufficient to induce a false confession?"

"That's the first step. The second is to provide the defendant with a reason why they don't remember committing the crime. In Ms. Singer's case, she had taken Ambien the night of the murders. The police convinced her that she didn't remember murdering her parents because of the drug."

"Ms. Singer recanted soon after. Is that common?"

"Yes, most defendants who have been persuaded to confess through the use of such tactics recant once they're away from the interrogators."

"Thank you, Mr. Deegan." Dani turned to Murdoch. "Your witness."

Murdoch stood but stayed by his table. "To your knowledge, do police often tell a defendant they have incriminating evidence when they don't?"

"Yes, that's fairly common."

"And does that always result in the suspect admitting to a crime he didn't commit?"

"Of course not."

"And do criminals who confess to a crime and are truly guilty sometimes recant afterwards?"

"Yes."

"Thank you. I have no further questions."

"Is that it, Ms. Trumball?" Judge Bryson asked.

"Yes, Your Honor."

"Mr. Murdoch, do you have any witnesses?" Judge Bryson asked.

"No, Your Honor. I'm satisfied that the defendant has failed to meet the heavy burden she has to show entitlement to a new trial."

"Okay, then. Ms. Trumball, file your brief on why you think a hearsay exception applies by one week from today, and Mr. Murdoch, yours will be due a week after that. Include in your briefs any other arguments you wish to make about the evidence heard here today."

"Yes, Your Honor," they both said in unison. And with that, the hearing was over.

By the time Melanie and Dani left the courthouse, it was dark. Daylight savings time had ended a week earlier and the cool chill signaled that winter wasn't far away. They walked in silence to the municipal parking lot two blocks away, the only sounds the clicking of their heels on the sidewalk. The confidence Dani felt over lunch had dissipated. Left was an uneasy feeling that she had failed her client.

Judge Bryson hadn't asked for a summation—a marshaling of the evidence that favored granting their client a new trial—at the end of the hearing. "Put it in your brief," he'd said. Dani knew that was never as effective as standing before a judge and describing why all the evidence she'd presented led to only one conclusion. The written word didn't carry the same emotional punch.

The Catskill Mountains, which ringed the town, had disappeared in the dark. Only a few cars were still parked in the lot, and the sidewalks were devoid of pedestrians. The desolation of the town settled over Dani and magnified her own sense of unease. She was missing something. She knew it. People didn't steal millions of dollars and go on as though nothing had happened. Yet it seemed as though they had.

Was it Frank Reynolds? He still lived in the same house he'd owned for thirty years. He hadn't taken any elaborate vacations, purchased any expensive cars or boats. Tommy had scoured the public records and found nothing. Still, for Joe and Quince's scheme to work, they must have had people on the inside. Frank Reynolds approved the invoices from Building Pros. Was it incompetence? Even the state thought the invoices were legitimate. Still, it was Reynolds's job to scrutinize each expense. Reynolds and—

Dani stopped. "We never spoke to the nun's husband," she said to Melanie.

"Huh?"

"The nun. I don't remember her name. The one who was responsible for approving the construction bills along with Reynolds."

"Mary Jane Olivetti. And she wasn't a nun any longer."

"Yes, I know. Tommy said she was married. He never spoke to her husband, though."

They reached their cars, parked next to each other, and stopped. Melanie leaned against her Acura sedan and asked, "Do you think she was in on the scam?"

"I don't know. But we have to find out. Tomorrow. It's late now. Go home and get some rest."

They got into their respective cars and drove off.

Was greed so pervasive that even a former nun would succumb to it? Dani wondered as she headed toward the thruway. Was there ever a point at which a person would be satisfied with the money he had? Joe Singer and Quince Michaels were living comfortable lives, with expensive homes and fancy cars. Why did they need to steal from the county? Taxpayers footed the bill for their avarice. People barely holding on to their homes as property taxes escalated paid more so Quince Michaels could have a mansion on the intercoastal and a boat to navigate the waterways. It sickened Dani.

She thought back to a trip she and Doug had made to South Africa, before Jonah was born. While in Cape Town, they visited the shanties of the poorest of the poor, one-room homes minimally constructed with colorful sheets of metal, barely standing upright. Yet, so many years later, she still remembered the faces of the children she met there, their happiness exploding in their smiles and playful energy. The people who stole from Hudson County had so much more, yet it wasn't enough. Their greed led to the murders of Joe and Sarah Singer and Quince Michaels and placed eighteen-year-old Molly Singer, pregnant and an orphan, in jail for the rest of her life.

It was after seven o'clock and all the government workers had left for the day. Only Frank Reynolds remained in his office, along with Sheriff John Engles.

"How did it go?" Reynolds asked.

Engles had sat through the day's court proceedings. "They know about Joe and Quince. Some expert—I think he said he was a forensic accountant—figured it all out. But only them. He knows there are others but doesn't know who."

"But what about Molly?" Frank asked. "Do you think he'll give her a new trial?"

"Nah. Too risky."

Frank felt a weight in his chest. It didn't matter what the judge had said. Once Quince was found dead, Frank knew Molly was innocent. He'd never for a moment believed the boat explosion had been an accident. She didn't belong in jail. She shouldn't have spent twelve years there, her daughter taken away from her.

He could change her fate. He knew enough to blow open the whole case. Only doing so would put his own life at risk. And maybe Finn's as well.

The next night, Tommy rang the bell of Burtram Olivetti. When the door opened, he saw a tall man, well over six feet, and rail thin. Olivetti held out his bony hand to shake Tommy's, then welcomed him inside.

"I wondered when you'd get around to speaking to me," he said.

"Why?"

"Because of Mary Jane. Her role approving the payments for the jail project."

Tommy nodded. "Yeah. That's why I'm here."

Olivetti led Tommy into the living room. The home was a modest ranch house, identical to the others crowded together on the block. The sofa had started to show signs of wear, and the rug underneath it was threadbare. The Subaru parked in the driveway was at least six years old. It didn't seem to Tommy like the home of someone who'd pocketed money from the jail project.

"First, let me say I'm sorry for your loss."

"Thank you. It's been twelve years, but it seems like yesterday."

"Do you mind my asking, how did the accident occur?"

Olivetti quickly responded, "It wasn't an accident."

Tommy looked at him quizzically and waited for an explanation.

"The police said it was, of course. The roads were slippery. They claimed she'd lost control of the car. But Mary Jane was a very cautious driver. Always had been, even in the best conditions."

"Was there an investigation into the accident?" Tommy asked. "Maybe to see if there had been any tampering with the car?"

"The car was destroyed. Even if they took my concerns seriously, it would have been hard to tell."

"Other than how cautious she was as a driver, is there any other reason you're so sure it wasn't an accident?"

Olivetti grew silent. Outside, the wind rustled through the trees. Tommy could see through the window that it was blowing up. The storm that had been forecast was getting closer. He hoped to be back home before it hit full blast, but he didn't want to rush the man sitting opposite him.

Finally, Olivetti spoke. "I've never told this to anyone before. My failure to speak up has weighed heavily on me these years. When I saw there was going to be a hearing on Molly Singer's case, I knew it was time."

"I'm listening."

"This is difficult. Please be patient with me."

"Take all the time you need."

Olivetti swallowed deeply, then began. "Mary Jane hadn't planned on going into politics. I mean, she'd been active behind the scenes for a while, but never wanted political office for herself. But she didn't like the way things were going, and someone, I don't want to say who, urged her to run. He was in the county legislature himself. This man, he became Mary Jane's mentor, and she grew very close to him. Mary Jane was a good legislator. She listened to her constituents, and every two years they re-elected her. She got to a senior position on the appropriations committee, and that's when it happened."

"What's that?"

"She had opposed building a new county jail, like most of the Democrats. But they were in the minority, and it got approved. After the contract was awarded, Paul Scoby asked for a meeting with her."

Tommy remembered that Scoby was leader of the Democratic Party in Hudson County.

"He told her he wanted her to approve the bills that came in for the jail. She said she'd look each one over, and if it was in order, she'd approve it. He said no. She had to approve them even if she thought something was wrong. Mary Jane laughed at him. 'Why would I do that?' she said. Scoby told her if she didn't do as he said, he would reveal some personal information about her mentor. Information he didn't want known."

"Did he tell her what that was?"

Olivetti nodded. "He told Mary Jane that her mentor was carrying on an affair with another man. He showed her pictures of them together. Explicit pictures."

"This is a pretty progressive county. His constituents probably wouldn't have cared."

Olivetti shook his head. "He's married, had been for almost twenty years back then. He had children in the schools here. It would have devastated his wife and kids. And you have to remember—even just that long ago, people weren't as accepting of homosexuality."

"So, Mary Jane agreed?"

"It was the hardest decision she'd ever had to make. Harder than the decision to leave the church. She knew she had a duty to her constituents. But she'd come to love her mentor. He was like a father to her. She went to see him, told him what Scoby said, what he threatened to do. He begged her to keep his secret. She did."

"Then why was she killed?"

"At first, when the Singers were murdered, she didn't think it was related. Then they arrested the daughter. She followed the case closely, saw they didn't have any real evidence against the girl. She began to think maybe it had to do with the money Joe Singer had skimmed. So, she called her mentor and said she had to tell the authorities about it. She'd wanted to give him a heads up, so he wouldn't be blindsided. She was on her way to the police when the accident happened."

Olivetti sank down onto a chair and buried his head in his hands. Moments passed, and when he lifted his head, his cheeks were tear stained. "For a long time, I harbored an intense hatred toward her mentor. He had to have called someone, alerted them to Mary Jane's intentions. Maybe Scoby. Maybe someone else. I don't know. But I realized Mary Jane would have forgiven him, and I needed to for her."

"After the accident, why didn't you tell the police about this?"

Olivetti looked downcast. "Because I was a coward. I was afraid they'd kill me, too."

"Why are you telling me now?"

"I have stage-four liver cancer. In a few months I'll be dead. They can't hurt me anymore."

CHAPTER 33

"I guess for once Republicans and Democrats agreed on something," Dani said. "They teamed up to bilk the county." Tommy had just filled her and Melanie in on his meeting with Burtram Olivetti.

"You're assuming Frank Reynolds was in on it, too?" Melanie asked.

"Had to be. They couldn't have approved the payments without him. Whether he was coerced, like Mary Jane, or participated voluntarily, I don't know. But he had to be in on it."

"So what now?" Tommy asked.

Dani wasn't sure what to do with the information, other than turn it over to the US attorney. Josh Cosgrove would have one more name to investigate. Paul Scoby had to be one of the three others who profited from the jail. Why else would he have strong-armed Mary Jane? Dani considered making a request that the hearing be reopened to add Olivetti's testimony—but to what end? They already had put in substantial evidence that five people illegally benefitted from the construction of the jail—including Joe Singer. But there was still a missing link—something that tied the fraud to the murders. Dani firmly believed Joe Singer was killed to silence him, quickly followed by Mary Jane Olivetti and now Quince Michaels. Could she convince a jury of that?

At Molly's first trial, her confession had trumped the lack of evidence. Now, in addition to her expert, Dani could trot before the jury a slew of wrongfully convicted men and women who'd confessed to crimes only to be later absolved with DNA evidence. She'd suggest someone else had had a powerful motive to kill Joe Singer, but Murdoch would undoubtedly point out that it was speculation. No one could know for certain that Joe Singer was about to come forward about the theft when he was killed. Molly overhearing her father's increasingly heated arguments with Quince Michaels wasn't nearly enough.

Dani wanted to find the murderer. That was the equivalent of DNA—absolute proof of innocence. Whoever had been sending the anonymous letters knew who it was. But she had no clue as to how she could find him or her.

Dani turned to Tommy. "Two people approved the payments— Mary Jane Olivetti and Frank Reynolds. One is now dead. Let's put more pressure on Reynolds. He has to have been in on it."

Tommy nodded. "I'll make another trip up there."

The meeting over, Dani turned her attention to the brief Judge Bryson wanted. The law and the facts were on her side. The outcome of the hearing should be clear—a new trial for Molly. Still, she had a feeling of unease. Especially with Judge Bryson. He'd sentenced Molly to two life terms, unusual even with hardened criminals. Was he simply a tough-on-crime judge? Or did he have some reason to keep Molly behind bars?

Frank Reynolds stood outside his house, his hand on the doorknob, unable to move. It had been impossible to get any work done at the office today. All he could think about was Molly and the hearing.

Inside, Betsy waited with dinner in the oven. Like most husbands, he kept few secrets from his wife. They shared the daily tidbits of their lives, how they'd spent their day, who they'd spoken to, what they'd accomplished. They shared their hopes and dreams; they shared their disappointments. But he had kept one secret from his wife—what he had done to become county executive. That secret now felt like a two-ton burden he carried on his back, dragging him down with every step he took.

Suddenly, the door opened from inside. "What are you doing out here?" Betsy asked. "I heard you pull into the driveway ten minutes ago."

Frank put on a smile. "Just checking for any cracks in the foundation. Winter's not too far away." Their house was almost eighty years old, as were most in this section of Andersonville. It was a saltbox cape, with two bedrooms on the main floor and two rooms upstairs.

"Well, come on in. Supper's almost ready."

Frank stepped inside, hung his coat in the closet, then headed for the pantry, where he kept the liquor. He brought a bottle of scotch into the kitchen, retrieved a glass from a cabinet, and poured himself a double. It would make his headache worse, but he needed to numb himself. He massaged his temples, hoping to rub away the pain.

"What's going on?"

Frank turned and found Betsy staring at him. They'd been married close to thirty-five years, and she still looked beautiful to him. Despite the fifteen pounds she'd added over the years, she looked like the teenager he'd fallen in love with so long ago.

"Nothing. Why?"

"Come on, Frank. You haven't been yourself for two days. Something's bothering you."

"Just work," he mumbled.

"What about work?"

Frank shook his head, but Betsy wouldn't let it lie.

"And frankly, it's not just the past two days. Something's got you tied up in knots the last two months."

He ached to tell her, to confess his sins and seek absolution. His desire for her to guide him, tell him what to do, welled up in him, and he was about to speak when the phone rang. He lunged to pick it up, relieved at the interruption.

"Hello."

"Frank, it's Alan. Just wanted to let you know. I'm letting the others know, too. I'm denying the motion for a new hearing. It's over."

Frank got off the phone and sank down into a kitchen chair, then dropped his head into his hands and cried.

Frank didn't know why that investigator was still bothering him. He'd considered brushing him off, saying he was too busy to see him. But Frank knew the type—the pushy, aggressive, can't-take-no type. He figured he'd see him one more time and get it over with. When his secretary buzzed, he told her to send him right in.

"Mr. Noorland," he said, "I've already told you everything I know."

Noorland stared straight at him, his eyes unblinking. "No, I don't think you have."

Frank took a breath. No need to be nervous, he reassured himself. He's just fishing. "I don't know what you're talking about. Get to the point or leave. I'm too busy for games."

"We know about Mary Jane Olivetti."

It felt like his heart had stopped. He forced himself to breathe again, to get control of himself. "I don't know what you're talking about."

Noorland smiled as though he'd seen right through him and felt the panic emanating from his pores. "Sure you do. Do you want me to spell it out?"

"I guess you'd better, 'cause I'm in the dark."

Noorland stepped closer and leaned across the desk. "We know Scoby blackmailed her into overlooking the excess payments. So tell me, who blackmailed you? Or were you an equal partner?"

Frank could feel his face go hot. He stood up, pointed his finger at the investigator, and, with his voice raised, said, "Get out of here."

Instead, Noorland helped himself to a seat. He stared into Frank's eyes so long, Frank had to turn away. Finally, he spoke. "I can help you. I know you're worried if you talk you'll end up like Singer and Michaels. But there are people who can keep you safe."

Frank wanted to believe him. He wanted to unburden himself to this stranger, explain that he hadn't meant for any of this to happen. He wanted him to know that he hadn't taken any money for himself. He wanted him to know that he prayed Molly would go free, but he didn't want to go to jail himself. He wanted to return to the day fourteen years ago when Bryson promised him the position of county executive. All he had to do was one thing, one small thing. He wanted this stranger to understand that he'd known he'd be a good county executive and that he'd lived up to that belief. He'd cut back taxes and reduced expenses. He'd lowered crime. He'd expanded low-income housing. Yes, he'd been good for the county. And still, if he could go back to that day, if he could do it all over, he would say to the judge, "No." Even if it meant the end of his life in public service.

This stranger promised to keep him safe, but Frank knew no one could. Not from the judge. "I'm sorry. You're misinformed. And now you really must leave."

After Noorland left, Frank stared at the phone. He had a decision to make—call the judge and alert him to this new development, or keep quiet and see what happened. He reached for the receiver, then stopped.

If Noorland knew about Scoby, then Bryson might think Scoby was a weak link—a portal into their scheme—just as Quince had become when his ex-wife squealed to Noorland. Four dead people were enough. Paul Scoby didn't need to be added to the list.

34

D ani's hands trembled as she read the decision.

The defendant filed a motion pursuant to section 440 of the criminal procedure law seeking a new trial based on a claim of newly discovered evidence. This newly discovered evidence consists of claims that the defendant's father, Joseph Singer, along with his partner, Quince Michaels, fraudulently obtained millions of dollars from Hudson County in connection with their company's construction of the Hudson County jail. The defendant's motion is denied, for the reasons set forth below. For the judgment to be vacated and a new trial held, (1) the evidence must not have been discoverable before trial by due diligence, (2) it must be admissible at trial, (3) it must be worthy of belief, and (4) it must be such that if the jury heard this evidence, it is probable that the verdict would be changed. Because the State of New York conducted an audit of the jail finances and did not discover a discrepancy, I conclude that defendant met the first prong of the test. With respect to the second prong, the testimony of Ellen Michaels as to conversations with her then husband concerning a bank account in Belize is excluded as hearsay and therefore would not be admissible at trial. However, the testimony of Lisa Michaels, solely with respect to the documents concerning the partnership agreement between Quince Michaels and Joe Singer and the Belize bank-account records, is not hearsay and is admissible. The testimony of Saul Delinsky, which identifies irregularities in the payments for the jail, is also relevant and admissible at trial. However, assuming it is true that Singer and Michaels purposefully overcharged the county, there is no evidence of worth to connect those acts to the murder of Joseph and Sarah Singer. Accordingly, it is not probable that the jury verdict would be changed as a result of the newly discovered evidence. Motion denied.

At the end of the decision, a footnote was added.

Defendant contends that her confession was obtained through methods that lead to false confessions, and had the jurors heard expert testimony on the nature of false confessions, she would not have been convicted. I do not believe that the tactics used by the police, namely lying about her fingerprints on the weapon, and other evidence tying her to the crime, were likely to lead to a false confession. Accordingly, the testimony of Derek Deegan concerning false confessions would not have resulted in a different verdict.

Dani put down the decision. If she'd been a cartoon character, she would have had steam emanating from every pore. *How could he be so misguided?* She'd brought in a juror from that very trial who said he wouldn't have voted to convict Molly if he'd known her father was involved with others in a massive theft. The judge didn't even acknowledge his testimony. She stormed out of her office and into Melanie's, threw the decision down on her desk and announced, "He denied the motion."

Melanie looked up, startled. "Molly Singer's motion?"

"Yep."

"I thought we had that in the bag."

"So did I."

"I guess we appeal," Melanie said.

"I want to get started on it right away."

They buckled down to work, dividing the issues that each would research and then write in their brief to the Appellate Division. Dani was happy to be doing something productive. By burying herself in the work, she avoided, at least for the time being, sharing the news with Molly. Early tomorrow morning, before Molly had a chance to read the newspaper, Dani would drive up to Bedford Hills and let her know that her chance for a new trial had grown considerably slimmer.

The first snow of the season fell as Dani drove cautiously to Bedford Hills Correctional Facility. It was early this year, perhaps a harbinger of a difficult winter ahead. It had once been one of her favorite seasons, when she and Doug would head for the slopes after the first large snowfall. Vermont didn't get the deep powder of Colorado or Idaho, but they could drive there in half a day and be on the slopes by the afternoon. They hadn't gone since Jonah was born. As she watched the plump drops of white hit her windshield, she thought perhaps this was the winter they'd introduce Jonah to the thrill of schussing down a mountain. After all, he was no longer a little child, a fact made clear to Dani every day as she watched him get ready for school and handle more and more activities on his own. He'd wash up, dress himself—usually in a reasonable facsimile of matching clothes—and make a sandwich for his lunch, all without Dani's help. At times, she missed having a baby in the house. Now and then she'd think about having another child. Then she'd remember her age and shake her head. That time had passed for her. She couldn't go back.

It wasn't too late for Molly. Her daughter had been ripped from her arms eleven years earlier and now was a virtual stranger to her. If she were freed, perhaps she could reconnect with Sophie. If she were freed, perhaps she could fall in love again. She'd be young enough to have another child, one she could raise and nurture. If. A big *if.* Dani had been confident she'd get another trial for Molly. What had gone wrong? Her evidence was solid, her witnesses strong. How could the judge not see what a difference it would have made to the jurors if they'd known someone else had a motive for murdering Joe Singer? Unless the judge was part of the jail scheme. Everyone had become a suspect to her. She was starting to doubt her own rationality, imagining everyone a conspirator.

She turned into the prison and parked in the visitors' lot, then trudged to the entrance. Once again, she waited in the attorney's lounge until they motioned for her to follow a guard. The stale air of the hallways pinched her nose as she walked to the interview room. Once settled in the barren space, she waited for Molly to arrive. It was a meeting she'd dreaded since reading the court's decision.

After a short wait, the guard escorted Molly into the room, then exited to wait outside the door. Unlike the guard escorting Molly on Dani's previous visit—who seemed to have a grimace permanently etched on her face—this guard actually seemed human. "Just knock on the door when you're finished," she said with a smile before closing the door behind her.

Molly beamed on seeing Dani. "Is there any news?"

"I'm afraid so. It's not good."

"I'm not getting a new trial?"

"Not yet. But we're going to appeal. I think we still have a shot at it." Dani knew she was being optimistic. Appellate courts gave great deference to trial court judges.

Molly's body seemed to deflate, as though it were made up of air and someone had stuck a pin in her. "I'd accepted that this is my life, that I would never be free. Sophie's visit changed that." Her voice was husky with emotion. "I want my daughter. I want to hold her and kiss her and protect her. I want to watch her grow into a woman. I want to teach her to treasure every moment, because you never know what's going to happen." Molly sank into her chair, then buried her head in her hands.

Dani reached over and wrapped her hands around Molly's. "Don't give up. We're not. We'll keep fighting until we get you another trial."

Molly lifted her head. "You're very kind. But if nothing else, the one thing you learn in here is to face reality. I let myself hope for a bit. I can't do that any longer. It's too painful."

There was nothing more Dani could say. She left Molly without making any promises, but more determined than ever to fight for her freedom.

Finn opened the front door and found his father standing on the welcome mat. Frank rarely visited during the week, and never unannounced.

"What's wrong?" Finn asked.

Frank stepped past him with the morning's newspaper in his hand, still wrapped in plastic, retrieved from Finn's driveway. He handed it over to Finn, then said, "Look at page three."

"Just tell me what it says."

"Molly's bid for a new trial was denied."

Finn said nothing, but the look on his face told his father he felt devastated.

"I'm sorry, Son. I'd hoped for a new trial, too."

"What now?"

"I suppose her attorney will appeal."

"What do you think her chances are?"

Frank hoped they were good. He wanted his granddaughter's mother out of jail. It wouldn't rectify twelve years of incarceration for a crime he now felt certain she hadn't committed, but it was a first step. "I don't know. At least there are five judges who'll make the decision, not just one."

"And if they don't give her a new trial, then what?"

Frank knew what Finn was asking. What would Frank do? Would he come forward with what he knew? Or would he continue to mask his own involvement and deny Molly vital information? "I don't know. I hope I don't have to decide."

CHAPTER 35

By the next morning, eighteen inches of snow had fallen in New York City, with the northern suburbs getting four to six inches more. Jonah had woken up elated that school was closed for the day. Even Doug's classes at Columbia Law had been cancelled. Only Dani was expected at work. HIPP never closed down. The inmates they represented, in states all throughout the country, needed their efforts to free them every day of the year. Looking out at the pristine snow piled high in their driveway, and the cloud-free deep-blue sky, Dani nonetheless decided to play hooky herself. Stashed in the garage was a Flexible Flyer wooden sled handed down from her mother to her and now to Jonah. Three blocks away was a park with a hillside that seemed to have been created solely for the purpose of winter sledding.

After a leisurely breakfast, Dani, Doug, and Jonah bundled up in their warmest coats, hats, and gloves, pulled on their fleece-lined winter boots, and headed over to the park with the Flexible Flyer. They entered the white expanse and walked past the lake. In the depth of winter, after weeks of below-freezing temperatures, the lake would freeze and skaters flocked to it. The past few winters had been mild, though, and it remained a haven for the few ducks that hadn't yet flown south. The family stopped and Dani pulled out a bag of torn-up bread, which Jonah threw to the ducks. When the bag was empty, they continued walking to the hill, already filled with children, from toddlers to teenagers, all enjoying their unexpected day of freedom.

They all trudged to the top of the hill, then Dani and Doug watched as Jonah rode the sled down the slope. It was a long, easy decline, not too steep and not too flat. Just the perfect pitch for sledding, with no trees along the way to maneuver past. Jonah called out gleefully as it sped down the hill, then climbed up to do it again.

When he climbed up a second time, Dani opened a thermos she'd brought to the park and poured everyone a cup of steaming hot chocolate. As she sipped hers and looked around at the assembled children and their parents, she glimpsed, out of the corner of her eye, a man leaning against a tree, seemingly alone. He was tall and huskily built and wore a wool hat pulled low over his forehead. Dark sunglasses covered his eyes, and a cigarette dangled from his mouth. Dani quickly looked away, unnerved by him for a reason she couldn't name.

After a few more runs, it was time to head home. Dani looked around once more. The strange man had moved to a tree closer to her family, and this time it was clear that he was staring straight at them. Dani could feel the muscles in her neck tighten. She slipped her hand into Doug's, wrapped her other arm around Jonah, and they headed out of the park. She wondered if she should tell Doug about the man and dismissed that thought as soon as it entered her mind. Since the accident, she'd become easily spooked. Just nerves, she told herself.

They left the park, and as they turned the corner to their block, Dani saw the man again, about fifty paces back. His hands were in his coat pockets, and his head was down. She leaned over to Doug and, careful that Jonah wouldn't hear, whispered into his ear, "I think that man behind us is following me."

Doug stopped and looked back, then asked, "Why do you think so?"

"Because he was in the park, by the sledding hill. He was by himself, and he kept staring at me."

"Wait here." Doug dropped Dani's hand and walked back to the man. Dani saw them speak, then Doug nodded. Moments later, they both walked up to Dani and Jonah.

"He kept staring at you in the park because he thought you looked like the lawyer that helped his brother," Doug said.

The man held out his hand. "Sorry if I frightened you. I'm Johnny Dunbar. You got my brother freed from prison. Eddie Dunbar. You look different in your everyday clothes, so I wasn't sure. But if it was you, I wanted to thank you. Eddie's doing real good now. We're very grateful to you."

The tension emptied from Dani's body in a rush. He wasn't a killer looking for a second chance at her. Just an appreciative family member.

Just one day after a massive snowfall and the streets of Manhattan were clear. Piles of snow, already brown from soot, were lined up against the curb, but cars moved freely through the streets. Back in her office, Dani had Molly's folder open on her desk. Melanie and Tommy sat opposite her.

"Look," Dani said, "I don't think we should sit by and wait for the appeal. Even if they reverse the trial judge, we still need more if it gets to a jury."

"Yeah, we need the scum that did it," Tommy said.

"That would be nice, but we're not the police. We don't have to prove someone else did it, just create reasonable doubt that Molly did."

"Bob McDonald didn't bring in an expert on the effects of Ambien," Melanie said. "One of the things that hurt her at trial was that she didn't hear anything that night. We know that the intruders woke her parents. At least one of them must've cried out when they knew what was happening. The prosecutors claimed she didn't hear anything because she had killed them herself. And then didn't remember doing it because of Ambien."

"So, what are you thinking?"

"Well, maybe we get a doctor to testify that with twenty milligrams in her she would have slept too soundly to hear anything. Or do anything. And that there's no evidence of anyone committing a violent act while on Ambien."

Tommy shook his head. "Gotta stay away from that. I know of a couple of cases where people on Ambien committed violent acts and claimed to have no memory of it. And they had no history of aggressive behavior beforehand."

Dani was silent. Was it possible Molly *had* murdered her parents and Ambien wiped out her memory of it? She'd been so sure Molly was innocent. Molly was so certain she was innocent. Could it be otherwise? No, her gut said Molly was innocent, and a few whacko claims didn't change how she felt.

"Where are the feds on the Scoby lead?" Tommy asked.

"I don't know. I'm meeting with them this afternoon for an update."

Dani spread out the papers from Molly's folder and rifled through them. "I keep thinking we're overlooking something." She skimmed through the summary Melanie had made of the trial transcript, then took out the accountant's report. "Based on the overages charged for the jail, and on the amount of monies Joe and Quince took for themselves, there had to be three other people who profited from the scheme. Let's assume Paul Scoby is one. Maybe Frank Reynolds is another. That leaves one other person." She looked up at her colleagues. "Any guesses on who the last person is?"

"I vote for the judge," Melanie said. "He clearly had bias toward Molly, and maybe it's because he's covering up his involvement."

"I have to say, the thought occurred to me as well. But he wasn't completely out of line with his rulings," Dani said. "That's what concerns me with the appeal. I'm afraid the court will find he exercised appropriate judicial discretion. Besides, judges in New York make decent money."

"So do builders," Tommy pointed out.

"Okay. So the judge is a maybe. Who else is a possibility?"

They were all silent. Dani knew it was because they, like herself, had no idea who else could be involved. And maybe that unknown person was the real killer.

Dani, Melanie, and Tommy walked together over to Joshua Cosgrove's office. Instead of yesterday's pristine covering of bright snow, brown slush marked the roadways. Just like every other day in Manhattan, the streets were crowded with people hurrying to their destinations.

"Ah, the whole contingent today," Josh said as they were ushered into his office.

"We're hoping you have good information for us."

Josh shook his head, his mop of blond hair falling over his brows as he did so. He brushed it aside, then said, "Afraid not. Without proof that the two men you asked me to check out have a committed a crime, I can't get the Belize banks to open their records."

Dani had held out hope that, with the power of the US government behind him, Josh would at least be able to confirm that Paul Scoby and Frank Reynolds were complicit. "So, nothing."

"Well, not completely nothing. We looked into domestic banking records of Scoby and Reynolds. Everything looked in order for Scoby, nothing unusual there. But thirteen years ago, Frank had monthly deposits of nine thousand nine hundred dollars into his savings account for ten months."

"Just under the ten-thousand-dollar limit for the bank's reporting to the IRS," Tommy noted.

"Right," Josh said. "It's not the millions that Singer and Michaels pocketed, but the timing is perfect for a payoff."

"So, will you bring him in for questioning?" Dani asked.

"Once again, it's not enough at this point. It could have been a gift from a relative; it could have been an inheritance, paid out over time in accordance with the will. There's nothing about it by itself that says fraud."

"It must be, though."

"Come back to me with more. Then maybe I can do something. In the meantime, our office will start an action to recover the money that Michaels stole from Hudson County."

"Can you hold off on that a bit?" Dani asked. "I don't want the others to know yet that your office is involved."

Josh leaned back in his chair and crossed his arms. "I suppose I can freeze Michaels's Belize account so nothing's taken out. I'll have to start something soon, but maybe I can hold off a month or two."

"Thanks, Josh."

They said their good-byes, then walked back to the office glummer than they'd been when they'd started out. When they arrived back at HIPP, they all settled once again in Dani's office.

"Suggestions, anyone?" Dani asked.

Tommy chewed on a nail, Melanie twiddled her thumbs, and neither spoke up with any ideas. Finally, Tommy said, "We know that Scoby blackmailed Mary Jane Olivetti. What if we confront him, pretend that we have proof he was on the receiving end of the money. He doesn't know we have squat."

"If we do that, he'll probably alert the fifth conspirator."

"Not if he's smart. Michaels got himself killed by doing that."

"Okay," Dani said. "Why don't you pay him a visit? Shake him up a bit."

Tommy nodded. He loved playing the bad cop, especially with no good cop to cramp his style.

T his time, Tommy didn't call ahead for an appointment. He drove up the New York State Thruway to Andersonville and, once off the exit, headed straight for Riverside Hardware. He pulled into the parking lot and walked into the store.

A pretty cashier, no more than eighteen, Tommy figured, was behind the register. She smiled at Tommy as he walked in. "Welcome to Riverside."

Tommy gave her a half wave of his hand, then casually ambled around the aisles, looking for Paul Scoby. When he didn't see him, he went back to the front.

"Boss in?"

"He's in the back. Can I help you?"

"Nah. Got to speak to him." Tommy headed to the back office as the cashier called after him. "Hey, you can't go back there." Tommy kept walking, knocked once on the office door, then opened it and strode inside.

Scoby looked up from his desk and Tommy saw his back stiffen.

"What are you doing here?"

Tommy settled himself into a chair across from him. "Got a few more questions."

Scoby fidgeted and cleared his throat. "Look. You've wasted your time. I told you everything I know about the Hudson County jail. Which is nothing."

Tommy just sat there, looked directly at Scoby, and smiled.

"Really, I'm busy here. Please leave."

Again, Tommy said nothing, just smiled.

Scoby rubbed the back of his neck and looked toward the door, as though waiting for an invisible savior to rescue him. When no one appeared, he looked back at Tommy and asked, "What are you grinning at?"

"You."

"You're nuts."

Finally, Tommy spoke. "I'm smiling, just thinking about the squirming you're gonna do."

"Look, I've told you. I'm busy and I don't know anything."

"Sure you do."

Scoby scowled at Tommy and started to rise from his seat. "Either you leave now or I'll call the police."

"Sit down, Scoby." Tommy's voice had changed from light to dark. "I don't think you want to call the cops, unless it's to confess to your blackmail of Mary Jane Olivetti."

Scoby sank back into his chair. "Wha—what are you talking about?" Just like that, his face had turned a bright shade of red.

Tommy grinned again. "There you go. I knew you'd be squirming." Just as quickly, his smile disappeared. "Now, let's get serious. I'll tell you what I know, and then you have a choice. You can tell me what you know, or I go to the police. Let me correct that, since for all I know the police here are just as corrupt as you: either come clean, or I go to the feds."

Beads of sweat had appeared on Scoby's forehead. "What do you think you know?"

"I know that you threatened to expose Mary Jane's mentor if she didn't approve the jail invoices. I know that when Molly was on trial,

Mary Jane told you she was going to confess to the police. And I know that on her way over there, she died in a car accident. So, fact—you're a blackmailer. Supposition—you personally pocketed millions from the jail. Question mark—you murdered Mary Jane, and maybe also Joe and Sarah Singer and Quince Michaels."

Scoby's red face had now drained of all color. "I swear; I had nothing to do with those deaths."

"But you did steal millions from the county."

Scoby sat silently.

"Look, Scoby, I told you, either you talk to me or you talk to the feds. I think I'm your better option."

Suddenly, the door to the office opened, and the cashier stepped inside. "Dad, there are a lot of customers in the store. You need to come help."

"I'll be out soon, honey. Do the best you can."

Suddenly, the pleasure Tommy had been feeling in bringing down this man dissipated. He was a crook, maybe a murderer, too, but he was also a father. When he went to jail, and Tommy was certain he would, the impact wouldn't just be on him. He'd leave a daughter, maybe other children, maybe a wife, behind. They'd be exposed to the vitriol of the community, tarred by their father's or husband's misdeeds.

"I can't talk to you," Scoby said, his voice subdued. "You know what happened to Joe and Quince. Maybe even Mary Jane, I don't know. I honestly thought Molly had murdered her parents, and Mary Jane just had an accident. Until Quince died. And then Mary Jane's death no longer seemed like an awful lucky break."

"The feds can protect you."

"How? By putting my whole family in witness protection? Cutting us off from everyone we know? I've lived here my whole life. I know half the people in town. I'm too old to start over. I care too much about my family to do that to them."

"Then talk to me. No one has to know who I got my information from."

"I can't."

"You don't have a choice. Let's just talk about you. How much did you skim from the jail monies?"

"I don't know what you're talking about."

Tommy threw up his hands. "You're not leaving me any choice. I'm going to go to the feds, and then everyone will know about it. Is that what you want?"

Scoby's head hung low and he wrung his hands. The guy was practically swimming in his seat.

"Let's try it again. How much money did you get?"

Scoby didn't move.

"I'm not bluffing you. It's me or the feds."

Scoby looked up. "Do you think I'm a fool? Talking to you is the same as talking to the feds. You'll go right to them."

"Then let's talk about the others."

"I don't have anything to say."

"Listen. If you give us the others, you know they'll go easier on you."

"I won't. It doesn't matter what you do or say, I won't give you anyone else."

"Look. I'm going to name some people. You don't have to say they're involved. But if they're not, just shake your head."

Scoby sat back in his chair and waited silently.

"Frank Reynolds."

Scoby sat unmoving.

"Eric Murdoch." Dani didn't think the prosecuting attorney was involved, but Tommy needed to throw in a name to make sure Scoby would react. He did, by shaking his head.

"Judge Bryson."

Scoby's head remained still.

"Holy cow! Bryson's really involved?" Dani said when Tommy returned to the office. "I thought I was crazy to even think it."

"Yeah, it's plenty crazy. So what do you do with that information?" Tommy asked. "Go to the Appellate Division? The feds?"

It was a good question, one Dani didn't have an answer to. Scoby had made it clear that he wouldn't go on record naming his coconspirators. According to Tommy, it didn't seem likely Scoby was the killer. "Too scared," Tommy had said. So it had to be Frank Reynolds or Judge Bryson, Dani thought. Unless there was a third person. Could there be?

From Tommy's description of Reynolds, he didn't seem the cold-blooded-killer type, although Dani knew from experience looks were often deceiving. Bryson was different. Maybe the revelation of his involvement had cast a dark retroactive shadow over her memories of him during the hearing, but now she was convinced there was something menacing in his eyes. Yes, she could imagine him ordering the death of someone.

She had nothing to bring to the Appellate Division, where Molly's appeal was now pending. She could share the information with Josh Cosgrove, but without Scoby's corroboration, she doubted he would move on it. It wasn't good for one's career to investigate a sitting judge without a rock-solid basis to do so.

Dani looked up at Tommy. "I don't think we do anything with it for now. Let's hope we win the appeal, and Molly gets a new trial. Then maybe I'll move to have it assigned to a different judge. I'll come up with some reason to claim he has a bias."

"And if we lose?"

"Then we go back to Scoby and tighten the screws."

37

Finn was helping Sophie with her math homework when she asked, "Why didn't the judge let Molly have a new trial?"

How did he answer his daughter when he knew the truth? And when that truth would devastate Sophie? How did he tell her that her own grandfather could ensure a new trial for Molly by coming forward, but in doing so would ensure his own incarceration? Or risk his own death?

Since her visit to the prison, Sophie had asked Finn many questions about Molly. She always called her Molly, never Mom or my mother. When he married Kim, he thought it would be best for Sophie to forget about Molly, for Kim to become her mother. And for a while, Kim did try to bond with Sophie, although if he was honest, it was never more than a halfhearted attempt. After Graham was born, Kim pushed Sophie to the side, never more to her than an annoying obligation. And so Sophie was left with a mother in the house who didn't care about her and a stranger in prison who was lost to her. And it was Finn's fault for letting that happen.

"I guess he didn't think the evidence was strong enough," Finn answered.

"But the newspaper said that her father and his partner stole money. They said he might have been killed to keep him quiet. Doesn't that mean Molly didn't kill her parents?"

"It isn't as simple as that."

"Why not? If I were on the jury, I wouldn't think Molly was guilty."

Finn leaned over and kissed his daughter's forehead. "I wouldn't either. But we don't really understand the ins and outs of the law. And the judge does."

"The paper said it was being appealed."

"That's right."

"Maybe the new judge will give her another trial."

"I hope, so, Sophie. I really do."

Sophie finished her homework, and Finn left to find Kim. On his way, he stopped by Graham's bedroom. He was already asleep, and Finn straightened the blanket over him, kissed his cheek, then walked downstairs to the living room. Kim was in front of the television, absorbed in some reality show that he couldn't bear watching himself.

He sat down next to her and said, "How about turning off the TV?"

She pressed "Pause" on the DVR remote and turned to him. "What's up?"

"Nothing. I just thought it would be nice to spend some time talking, instead of watching a show."

"But this is my favorite."

He didn't understand how it could be her favorite when it seemed identical to every other show she watched. "It's on DVR. You can watch it anytime."

"You don't appreciate how busy I am every day. This is the only time I get to relax and watch some shows."

Finn suppressed a smirk. She was busy all day at the gym and mall, with a few spa treatments thrown in every week. A woman from town came in three times a week to clean the house, and the meals Kim threw together at night required as little effort as possible. But he didn't want to start a fight. They'd done enough of that lately.

"Come on. Just one night, let's turn the TV off."

Kim made a show of raising the remote and, with a flourish, turning off the TV. "So, what's so important to talk about?"

"It's nothing special. Do you want a glass of wine?"

Kim gave him a grudging nod, and Finn went off to the kitchen, grabbed a corkscrew, and opened a bottle of cabernet. He brought two glasses into the living room and placed one down in front of her.

"Sophie's having a hard time over Molly."

"Well, of course. Her mother's a murderer."

Hold your temper. Hold your temper. "I don't think she is. But even if it were true, we still need to be sensitive to Sophie."

"You need to be sensitive to her. She's your daughter, not mine."

Hold your temper. Hold your temper.

"You don't mean that."

"I don't, huh? Well, she doesn't treat me with any respect at all. You spoil her, so of course she's nice to you."

"I don't spoil her. I just show her I love her."

"Well, I hope Molly does get out of jail. Then she can take care of her."

At that, Finn's attempt to remain calm failed him. "Do you ever think about anyone but yourself? God, you're the most self-centered creature that ever walked this earth. How could I possibly have thought you'd make a good mother? Or even a decent mother. I must have been out of my mind."

"Stop shouting. You're going to wake Graham."

"Just Graham? You're not concerned about how Sophie will react to my shouting? Let me tell you something, you may think you're a good mother with Graham, but you're suffocating him to death."

"Shut up," Kim said as tears started to roll down her cheeks.

It was her favorite gambit—begin crying whenever they fought. It ensured that the argument would end without their reaching the issues that prompted the fight. Finn picked up his glass of wine and walked out of the living room, stopping as he reached the foot of the stairs. "Go watch your TV show," he said, then retreated to his study.

This time, Molly walked toward the visitors' room with steps as quick as she could make with shackled ankles. Despite the metal cuffs, she felt as though a cushion of air were below her body, carrying her to her daughter. The guard didn't need to push her into the room. She gladly entered, and, when she spotted Sophie, rushed over to the chair opposite her.

With a big grin, she said, "I'm so happy you came back."

Sophie bit down on her lip and shifted in the chair. "Yeah, well, I heard about the hearing. I wanted to tell you I was sorry."

Molly's smile dimmed, but just a bit. "Yes, it was disappointing. But it's been appealed. There's a chance I'll still get a new trial."

"I really want you to. I hope you get out."

Molly's heart soared. Her daughter wanted her.

For so many years, she'd tried to block out thoughts of her, mostly unsuccessfully. She'd imagined her as a toddler, running around the playground with her friends, her blonde hair blowing around her face. She'd pictured her entering school, beginning to read, reveling in the joy of learning. She conjured up visions of her surrounded by loving parents and an adoring brother, ensconced in a cocoon of warmth. In Molly's mind, she saw her daughter on the brink of adolescence, confident and cheerful, ready to embark on the next step toward adulthood. Now she saw a child, still a child, uncertain, tentative, enshrouded with a cloak of sadness.

"Is there a room here with toys?" Sophie asked.

"There is. For mothers who gave birth here in prison. They play with their children in that room. After I had to give you up, you would visit me there."

"I remember it."

"Are you sure? You were so young then."

"I don't remember a lot. Just snapshots, like a picture that's frozen, with no movement. But I see myself sitting on your lap, with you reading me a book, in that room. And another picture of you helping me with a puzzle."

Molly smiled, amazed at her memory, all of it so true. "When I get out—and I know I will, I really believe it now—I hope you'll visit me."

"I, um, I was thinking. Maybe when you get out, I can spend weekends with you."

A feeling of weightlessness breezed through Molly. "Of course, you can stay with me as much as you want." Then gravity reclaimed her. She had no right to Sophie. She'd allowed Kim to adopt her. "Of course, your father and Kim will have to agree to it."

Sophie scowled. "That's just it. Kim doesn't want me around. It's bearable on school days, but on weekends I'm just in her way. She only wants to spend time with Graham."

"Oh, honey. I'm sorry."

"I mean, Dad loves me and I love him. And I love Graham, too. It's not his fault. Dad always tells me family is more important than anything else, and I suppose that's true, but you're my family, too, aren't you?"

"Yes. No matter where I am, I'm your family, and I love you dearly."

Sophie's chin dropped down and she brushed her hair away from her face. She took a deep breath, then lifted her head up, and slowly a smile crept across her face.

CHAPTER

38

They only had to wait three weeks for oral argument on *The People of the State of New York v. Molly Singer*. Dani, Melanie, and Tommy drove up to Albany the evening before. Their case was scheduled for 9:30 a.m., too early for them to leave the same morning, especially given the vagaries of New York traffic. Although it was the capital of New York State, the city had been in decline for many years. The elegant Empire State Plaza, which housed the court, along with most other New York State government offices, stood in stark contrast to their fading surroundings.

There was only one hotel within walking distance of the court, and the three checked into their rooms, then met in the lobby for dinner. The evening was pleasant, and so they walked the few blocks to the restaurant suggested to them by the desk clerk.

Dani knew that the next day's argument was crucial. If the appellate court didn't grant a new trial, it would be over. Molly would remain behind bars until she was old enough to collect social security. Only she wouldn't collect—she'd never worked and so never contributed to the fund. She'd never had a chance to finish school, start a career, raise her daughter.

Bruce had warned Dani when he hired her that she needed to keep her emotions out of the job. "Don't get drawn into your client's plight," he'd told her. It was especially so with clients on death row. If she'd established an emotional connection with a death-row client, and if HIPP wasn't successful in freeing the client, attending the execution could take an unbearable psychic toll. "And then you'll end up leaving HIPP, because it would just become too painful," Bruce had told her. He was right, of course. And, by and large, Dani had succeeded at maintaining a professional posture. But not always. And not with Molly Singer.

The moment Donna Garmond told her Molly had a daughter, she knew she'd fail miserably at keeping her feelings at bay. Her own maternal instincts shuddered at the thought of losing a child along with her freedom, a torment she knew would be made a thousandfold worse if her incarceration were wrongful. Tomorrow, though, she'd have to keep those emotions in check. When she stood to argue on Molly's behalf, she'd remain focused and in control. The facts and the law. Win or lose, that's all that mattered.

The restaurant was only half full, and they were seated immediately. Tommy and Melanie ordered cocktails, but Dani never drank before an argument. She needed to get a good night's sleep, and alcohol disrupted that. The food was better than expected, but they didn't linger over it. They ate quickly and walked back to the hotel. When they reached the lobby, Melanie asked, "Do you want me to pepper you with some more questions?"

"No, I'm going to turn in."

"Are you feeling all right?"

Dani nodded, although the truth was, she'd felt queasy since finishing dinner. She said good night, then went up to her room while Melanie and Tommy stayed downstairs in the bar.

As soon as she unlocked the door and stepped inside, a wave of nausea overtook her and she rushed to the bathroom, threw open the toilet seat cover, and deposited her meal inside the bowl. Finished, she stood up, rinsed her mouth and looked at herself in the mirror. Her face was drained of color, and beads of perspiration dotted her forehead. "This can't be," she muttered.

She undressed and put on her pajamas, then got into bed with her notes for tomorrow's oral argument, fervently hoping she wouldn't be too sick to deliver it.

The ringing of the telephone woke Dani the next morning. She picked up the receiver and heard a digital voice announce that it was her wake-up call. She glanced at the bedside clock, saw it was seven thirty, and groaned. She'd been up much of the night heaving into the toilet bowl, finally falling asleep after three a.m.

She dragged herself out of bed, brushed her teeth, then stepped into the shower, making the water as hot as she could tolerate. She quickly dressed, then rode the elevator to the ground floor. Melanie and Tommy were already in the hotel coffee shop when she walked in.

"You don't look so good," Melanie said when she saw her.

"I think I had food poisoning last night. I didn't get much sleep."

"Are you up for the oral argument?"

That was the question Dani had wrestled with ever since she had awoken. Melanie had been lead on cases before, but always those where DNA evidence was in play. She knew the argument, though—she'd worked closely with Dani on the brief and had prepped her with questions. And, she was smart and quick on her feet. Still, today was crucial if they had any hope of freeing Molly.

"I'm not sure. How would you feel about doing it?"

Melanie straightened her back. "I can handle it. I know the points we have to make."

"Okay, let's see how I feel when we get to the court."

Finished with breakfast—just hot tea for Dani—they walked over to the courtroom. Before going in, Dani said, "I think you're going to have to handle it, Melanie. I'm still feeling shaky."

"Sure," Melanie said, and they walked inside. Eric Murdoch was already seated, and he nodded to them. Slowly, the room filled with attorneys scheduled to argue their cases that morning. At nine thirty promptly, the door to the back rooms opened, and five justices entered the courtroom and took their seats. Dressed in the traditional robes, they looked like a sea of black, indistinguishable from each other, despite the fact that the chief judge was a woman. With her dark hair pulled back in a severe bun, she could have passed for one of her male colleagues.

The first case was called, and the attorneys for both sides took their seats in front. It was a "hot" bench, the justices showering the attorneys with questions from the outset. When their fifteen minutes apiece were up, the lawyers left the courtroom, and Dani, Melanie, and Eric Murdoch moved to the front. The bailiff called their case, and Melanie stood up and moved to the lectern.

The chief judge, sitting in the center, nodded for Melanie to proceed.

"Your Honors, may it please the court, my name is Melanie Quinn, and I represent Molly Singer. Ms. Singer was convicted twelve years ago—"

"Ms. Singer confessed to the murders of her parents, isn't that so?" the chief judge asked.

"Yes, but she quickly recanted. And there was no forensic evidence which tied her to the crime. Based upon newly discovered evidence, a 440 hearing was held. The defendants only had to show a probability that the new evidence would lead to a more favorable verdict. In this case—"

Another judge interrupted. "Assuming that your evidence is sufficient to show that Mr. Singer had been involved in a crime, why would that necessarily lead to a different verdict?"

"Because he wasn't alone in committing that crime. And we introduced evidence that he had considered coming forward about the crime. Certainly a juror could conclude that he was killed to silence him."

"Isn't that speculative?"

"Yes, Your Honor. It's always speculative. One can't know with certainty how a jury will respond. But the court must look at what a reasonable person would do, and a reasonable person would have to consider the possibility that there was a motive for killing the Singers that was far more plausible than the one conjured up by the prosecution for Molly."

As Dani listened to Melanie's responses, she felt more and more comfortable that she'd made the right decision to let her handle it. She still felt out of sorts and hoped her rumbling stomach settled down soon.

"I have a more serious concern," said another judge. "Why couldn't the defendant have discovered this evidence at the time of her trial? It seems to me nothing has changed since then. The same steps she took now to uncover the fraud could have been taken then."

Melanie hesitated. Dani knew they hadn't prepared for this question, since the trial judge accepted that it couldn't have been discovered before. Years of standing before a row of judges had prepared her to field the unexpected questions, but Melanie was relatively inexperienced at this.

"Because, uh, because they had no reason at that time to suspect there had been wrongdoing in connection with the jail. The state had done an audit and said everything was in order."

Good girl, Dani thought.

The judges peppered Melanie with a few more questions, which she handled easily. When the red light came on, she sat down next to Dani and let out a huge breath. Murdoch stood up and moved to the lectern. His argument consisted of a repeat of Judge Bryson's reasoning in his decision. He, too, was showered with questions, but to Dani they seemed more like softballs, designed to allow him to expand on his explanations. Only the chief judge came down on him hard.

"A juror from the first trial testified that if he had known of Mr. Singer's criminal activity, he wouldn't have voted to convict Ms. Singer. Isn't that definitive evidence of the probability that the verdict would have been more favorable if they'd heard about this?"

"I don't believe it would have overcome Ms. Singer's confession. Jurors have a difficult time ignoring that."

"But there was also testimony from an expert about false confessions. If he testified at a new trial, wouldn't that serve to alleviate the jurors' concerns and allow them to focus on the other evidence?"

"No, I don't believe it would."

The chief judge didn't appear convinced.

Dani managed to make it through the end of Murdoch's argument. They stood up to leave, and as soon as they exited the courtroom, she excused herself and rushed to the bathroom. She wasn't finished being sick. She hoped it was the remnants of food poisoning and not because of her sinking feelings about Molly's chances.

Chapter 39

Five weeks had passed since Molly's appeal was argued and still no decision. That wasn't unusual—it sometimes took months. Still, the anxiety ate at Dani. There was nothing she could do, though, to speed it along, and so she turned to other work piling up on her desk. She began with a review of letters from inmates seeking representation by HIPP. The first seven she reviewed were typical. They began with a protestation of innocence, blamed the system for being against them, then offered no facts to support their claim. Even without those facts, there was something about some of the letter writers' voices that piqued her interest, but most times she sent back a routine sorry-we-can't-help-you letter.

She picked up the eighth letter and began reading. "My name is Tyrone Watkins. I been in prison in Illinois since I was fifteen years old. I be thirty next month. The Chicago police said I killed a woman. When they took me in, they kept at me so many hours I lost track. Then they said if I confessed, I could go home to my mama and sleep in my bed. They told me what to say and I signed my name. I never did hurt any woman. But the judge didn't believe me. Can you help me?"

A false-confession claim. Once, Dani hadn't believed in false confessions, then she was proven wrong by the nephew of her childhood nanny, who had confessed to a rape and murder it was eventually proven he didn't commit. Still, she thought it an isolated phenomenon. Molly Singer was the first false-confession case she'd handled at HIPP. And now Tyrone Watkins. She marked his file as "Accept," and decided to do some research on false confessions.

Dani was startled to learn that a full 25 percent of exonerated inmates had confessed to their crimes. The reasons for doing so varied, but the one thing they all had in common: the confession, even retracted, had trumped all other evidence in their trials, including DNA evidence. As a lifelong New Yorker, Dani recalled the case of five teenagers convicted of the rape and brutal beating of a Central Park jogger. The woman had been so badly injured that she had no memory of the crime. Dani had been as outraged as the rest of New York at the night of "wilding," as the police dubbed the perpetrators' activities, and gratified by their convictions. For months, the newspapers printed stories about the crime, the criminals, and the trial. Almost absent from the newspapers were the reports of their exoneration many years later, following the confession of another man known as the East Side Rapist. When the teenagers' trial took place, the police had a DNA sample from the victim. It didn't match any of the teenagers. The confessions they obtained from the teens didn't match the facts of the crime scene and were inconsistent among them. None of that mattered. It only mattered that the teens—who were between fourteen and sixteen at the time of the arrest—had confessed. When, twelve years later, the East Side Rapist, who was then in prison, admitted to the crime, they tested his DNA. It matched that found on the victim. He gave details of the night that were accurate and could have been known only to the attacker. Four young men had spent years in prison because they confessed to a heinous act they hadn't committed.

And they weren't alone. Dani read about the sixteen-year-old who spent fifteen years in prison for the rape and strangulation of a classmate, even though jurors had been informed that DNA evidence didn't match his. But he had confessed, as had the man who was sentenced to death for the murders of his parents, only to be exonerated three years later when two gang members were convicted for their deaths. A father who confessed to the murder of his three-year-old daughter was eventually exonerated when DNA evidence later identified a neighbor, who by then was serving a sentence for sex crimes, as the perpetrator. The list of cases went on and on, some famous as a result of their causes being undertaken by celebrities, but most anonymous men and, yes, a few women, who languished in jail as a result of confessing to a crime they didn't commit, and later exonerated when new evidence came to light.

Why did they do it? Dani kept digging to ferret out the answers. Some confessions were given freely, to protect the actual perpetrator. Some, like the young man whose letter she'd just read, were given because of a promise made by their interrogator—perhaps to go home, or to get a lighter sentence. Or, often, because they were desperate to end the hours upon hours of relentless interrogation. And some, like Molly, fed lies by their interrogator, came to believe they were guilty. And once made, no matter how quickly recanted, that confession became the truth in the eyes of jurors.

In many of those cases, DNA ultimately exonerated the defendant. In others, the true perpetrator was arrested on different charges and evidence was found linking him to the other crime. In rare cases, the true culprit confessed.

None of those factors were present in Molly Singer's case. If only they knew who had written the anonymous letters. He was right about hanky-panky with the jail. He obviously knew more. They needed him to connect the dots between the jail funds and the Singers' murders. Then, maybe, Molly would have a real chance at freedom.

John Engles popped his head into Frank Reynolds's office. "Want to get some lunch?"

Although Engles had an office in the county jail, he had a second office in the county government building, at eight stories the highest building in downtown Andersonville. Frank's office was on the top floor.

Frank looked at his watch. He didn't particularly care for Engles, but better to stay on his good side. "Sure, but let's make it a quick one."

They rode the elevator down to the lobby, then strolled over to a coffee shop one block away. Settled into their booth, Engles asked, "What do you think will happen with the appeal?"

Frank shrugged. "Have no idea."

"I think she did it."

Frank eyed him carefully. Once, he thought she was guilty, too. But someone killed Quince Michaels, and it certainly wasn't Molly Singer.

"Even after Michaels?"

"Who knows if those investigators were right? It could have been an accident."

"Maybe." Frank didn't want to say more. He didn't trust anyone now. He tried to change the subject, but Engles wouldn't let it go.

"You know, right now they only know that Singer and Michaels profited from the jail. If she doesn't get a new trial, it stays that way."

"Even if she does get a new trial, it should stay that way. If you're right, and Michaels's death was an accident, they can say that he killed his partner to stop him from talking. Case closed and Molly goes free."

"I don't think so. If they get a new trial, her lawyers.are going to keep digging. I know the type."

Frank didn't want to think about it. He wanted this mess to be over. He looked up and saw Darlene, his favorite waitress, approaching his table. She was someone who always wore a smile and made him feel welcome.

"Hi, Frank, what'll it be today?"

"I'll have today's special."

"Good choice. And how about you, Sheriff?"

"The same."

Before Darlene left with their orders, she turned back to Reynolds. "So what do you think will happen with Molly Singer?"

Frank remembered that Darlene had gone to school with Molly. He just shrugged and held open his two palms.

"I sure hope she gets out," Darlene said. "I never thought she was the kind of girl who'd do something like that."

"I hope so, too."

When the waitress left, Engles said, "See what I mean? Everyone's talking about it. The sooner it dies down the better."

"Better for us, maybe, but not better for Molly."

Engles just shrugged, as though that issue couldn't be more beside the point.

Frank returned to his office and tried to settle down to work, only he couldn't concentrate on anything. He worked with no success at the tightness in the back of his neck. *Calm down. Everything will be okay.* Only he didn't believe it. Whatever happened, everything had changed for him. He realized now he'd fooled himself twelve years ago. He'd wanted to believe the Singers' deaths had nothing to do with the deal he'd made. The day he told Alan Bryson he'd do what was asked of him, he lost himself. The man who prided himself on his integrity, who vowed to work hard for his constituents, had disappeared, gone in a puff of smoke, and replaced with a selfish, cowardly shell. He'd convinced himself over the years that his act was justified because of the good he was accomplishing as county executive. And he had accomplished much for the county. But it wasn't enough to erase his shame.

The phone on his desk buzzed and Frank picked it up.

"Don't forget, you have a two o'clock with the controller," his secretary said. "It's five of now. It's in Conference Room A."

"Thanks for the reminder."

He needed to clear his mind before he walked into the meeting and put aside all thoughts but government business. He stood up and shook out his hands, blew out a series of short breaths, then gathered up his papers and walked to the Conference Room.

"Hi Harlan," he said to the county controller, then nodded to the others in the room. They had gathered together for another in a long line of meetings to discuss the next year's budget. He took a seat and placed a notepad and pen on the table. "So, where are we?"

"Well, as we've covered, we anticipate revenues will be down again this year. We'd hoped housing prices would have started to come back and increase our share of property taxes, but it seems unlikely."

"You know I won't impose any new taxes," Frank said.

Harlan had his calculator in front of him and punched in some numbers. "I'm well aware of that. We're going to need to streamline expenses. I've put together a list of the cuts we'll need from each department."

Harlan handed Frank a sheet of paper with names and numbers on it. The county executive looked it over, but it all seemed a blur to him. Thoughts of Molly and his role in the fraud against the county rose in him like flood waters. He tried to control his growing sense of desperation, but it seemed like a mammoth task. He was walking a tightrope. On one side lay self-preservation, on the other, integrity. He knew he would fall. He just didn't know on which side.

Dani had to read the Appellate Division's decision twice before it sank in.

Denied. No new trial.

The court had been split three to two. The majority wrote:

> *At the outset, we find that the defendant exercised due diligence in coming forward with her new evidence. However, although the revelation about the fraud perpetrated by one of the victims and his partner is certainly troubling, no compelling evidence tying that crime to the murders has been presented. Furthermore, the fact that one juror, who had doubts during the original trial, claims he would have voted differently had he been made aware of the victim's wrongdoing, is simply not probative of what a reasonable man, the standard required by law, would do with that information. The defendant has failed to provide a sufficient nexus between the two events for it to have a probability of creating a more favorable outcome for her. Accordingly, her request for a new trial is denied.*

The minority were more sympathetic.

> *Our system of justice abhors the notion of keeping a person incarcerated if there is the possibility she is innocent of the crime. With that in mind, it is within the power of this court to review the findings of fact made by the county court judge. With respect to the finding that the tactics used by the police were insufficient to trigger a false confession, we must disagree. Since the only significant evidence tying Ms. Singer to the murder of her parents was her confession to those crimes, evidence relating to circumstances resulting in false confessions, and therefore whether her confession was false, is highly germane and should have been left for a jury to consider. Since these studies of false confessions were not available at the time of her trial, it constitutes newly discovered evidence, as is the now clear evidence of criminal wrongdoing by Ms. Singer's father and others. For these reasons, we would remit this case back to the county court for a new trial.*

There was no place left for them to go. Except in death penalty cases, the New York Court of Appeals, the highest one in the state, wouldn't question a judge's exercise of discretion in a 440 hearing. She picked up her phone, buzzed Melanie, Tommy, and Bruce, and scheduled an impromptu meeting in fifteen minutes. While she waited, she called Josh Cosgrove, hoping against hope that he had some news for her.

"I'm afraid not," he said after Dani filled him in on the appellate court's decision. "We have good news for us, but it's not going to help you."

"What's that?"

"Lisa Michaels has agreed to turn over the unlawful proceeds from the jail construction, including the amount used to purchase their house. We don't have to bring an action against Quince Michaels's estate."

"It's nice to know someone has a conscience. Although I guess it's easier to be noble when you're wealthy in your own right."

"I guess we'll never be tested that way, given the careers we've chosen," Cosgrove said. Dani knew that was certainly true. Government and nonprofit lawyers were at the bottom of the attorney pay scale. College professors were only marginally higher. She ended the call and went into the conference room. Melanie and Tommy were already seated and Bruce entered moments later.

"We lost the appeal on Singer," Dani announced to them. "It was a three-two verdict. No new trial."

"So it's over?" Melanie asked.

Dani had been thinking about that question. "Maybe not. Paul Scoby blackmailed Mary Jane Olivetti. He must have been in on the scheme. We also think Frank Reynolds was in on it. But the big fish—at least for us—is the possibility that Judge Bryson was part of it. If we can prove that, Molly would have to get a new trial. He was the original judge on her case and presided over her 440 hearing. If he'd been involved in a criminal enterprise with the victim, he would have to have recused himself. He didn't."

"Scoby didn't actually confirm Bryson was part of it," Tommy said.

"I know. But if he is, we've got to find out."

"What are you proposing?" Bruce asked.

"Look, we struck out with Tommy trying to squeeze Reynolds and Scoby. Maybe Josh Cosgrove would agree to bring them in to see if he can get more out of them."

"Have you discussed that with him?"

"Not yet. But what if Cosgrove is willing to make a deal with them? 'Fess up, implicate the judge, assuming it's true, and they'll get a reduced sentence. It's the judge we want."

Tommy had been tapping his fingers on the table, but now stopped. "If it was me, I wouldn't admit anything without a demonstration of their proof. And that's the problem. They don't have any. If they could find their bank accounts, then they could offer a deal."

"But they don't know that the US Attorney's Office hasn't found the bank accounts. Maybe Josh can bluff them. It's probably in the Caribbean somewhere."

"Okay," Bruce said. "Ask Josh if he's willing to bring them in. If the answer is no, or if he can't get anything from them, then you need to move on to other cases." Bruce turned to Dani, and with his voice soft, said, "You knew this would be a tough one. You fought hard for Molly, and I know you'd like to free her, but it doesn't always work out. I'm sorry."

Dani nodded. Tears welled up, but if she spoke, they would likely overflow. Instead, she picked up her papers and went back to her office.

After a ten-minute conversation with Josh Cosgrove, Dani hung up the phone relieved. He agreed with Tommy that it would be pointless to bring in Paul Scoby and Frank Reynolds for questioning without something solid to hang over them. But he would work with the IRS. They now had authority to require all foreign banks to report to them the existence of offshore bank accounts held by American citizens. Josh felt confident he could convince the IRS that, as part of a federal fraud investigation, they should scour their records first to see if they already had information of large sums held by those individuals and, if not, send out a blanket request to Caribbean banks. It would take weeks, maybe months, but at least Dani felt like there would be movement. She needed to make a trip up to Bedford Hills to give Molly the bad news. Now she had something to temper that news with.

Dani worked through the morning and early afternoon polishing some appeals for different clients. At two, she gathered her files to work on at home and set off for Bedford. She reached the prison in record time, thanks to the rare absence of traffic or accidents, and ninety minutes later was seated in front of Molly.

"I'm sorry. It's bad news."

"We lost?"

"Yes."

Molly blinked. "Are there more appeals?"

"I'm afraid not."

Molly slumped down in the chair. "So it's—it's over." She paused, opened her mouth to say something, then stopped, as though speaking took a monumental effort. Finally, she said, "I'm going to stay here until I'm old."

Dani took Molly's hand in hers. "I'm not going to stop fighting for you. There are some more things we're trying. Maybe something will turn up from them."

Molly just hung her chin on her chest and didn't answer.

"Molly? Don't give up hope."

Molly lifted her head. Her eyes looked vacant. When she spoke, her voice was devoid of emotion. "No. I can't keep hoping. It's too disruptive. I have to accept this is my fate."

"But look how things have changed for you. Before, you hadn't seen Sophie since she was four. Now, she's come to visit you twice, and I'm sure she'll continue to see you. Isn't that something to look forward to?"

Molly shook her head. "It'll just remind me of what I've lost."

42

Frank Reynolds read the news of the appellate court's decision with a combination of relief and dismay. Maybe Engles was right. Maybe if a new trial was granted, more would come out about the jail finances. But did he care anymore? He wanted it to be over—the unrelenting guilt that washed over him every time he saw his granddaughter. The excuses he'd used to justify his actions twelve years ago meant little to him now. Then, he thought Molly was guilty. Now he knew better.

He didn't know who of the others had murdered Molly's parents, but it had to be one of them. Otherwise Quince Michaels wouldn't be dead now. Was it Paul Scoby? He'd use every underhanded tactic available to get his candidate elected, but beyond politics he seemed spineless. John Engles? Tougher than Scoby, that was certain. But he'd dedicated himself to a career of law and order. And then there was the judge. Alan Bryson. Frank had never met anyone whose eyes seemed so cold, whose will seemed so strong. He could see Bryson orchestrating the murder of Joe and Sarah Singer. He wouldn't do it himself. No, he'd never get his hands dirty that way.

He worked late into the night, reluctant to go home and have the conversation with his wife that he dreaded. He needed to have it, though. When he turned himself in, as he'd come to realize he must, everyone would know he was a thief—and a heartless one at that. Betsy had to be told first.

He pulled into his driveway after ten o'clock. The light over the door had been left burning for him, as well as the light inside the foyer. The rest of the house was dark. He knew Betsy often went to sleep before ten. He hung up his coat in the hall closet, then went into the kitchen and poured himself a drink. He brought it into the living room and turned on the television, then switched the channel to the evening news. He sat back, sipped his drink, and let his mind go numb.

He stayed up to watch Letterman's monologue, then turned off the TV and walked quietly upstairs. He left the bedroom light off, guiding himself by the light from the hallway. After he undressed, then washed up in the bathroom, he slipped into bed next to his wife.

"Frank?" came her drowsy murmur.

"Shh, go back to sleep."

Betsy stirred in bed. "What time is it?"

"Midnight."

"You okay?"

"Sure."

Betsy rolled over to the side of their king-size bed and turned on the lamp. She sat up and looked at him. "What's wrong?"

"Nothing. I told you, everything's fine."

"Frank Reynolds, we've been married almost thirty-five years. I can tell when something's bothering you."

"What are you talking about?"

"It's your tone. It always tells me when something's off."

Frank hadn't wanted to get into it tonight. He knew he'd have to soon, but not yet. He wasn't strong enough yet.

"Just some county business. Nothing for you to worry about. Go back to sleep."

And to Frank's great relief, she did.

Paul Scoby kept waiting for the FBI to show up, an arrest warrant in their hands. When the investigator from HIPP left his store, he knew it would come. At the least, they had him for blackmail. It wouldn't take much for them to learn he'd gotten seven million dollars for his part in the fraud. Like most Americans, he expected their tentacles were far reaching, including into GBT Bank in the Cayman Islands, where he'd hidden the money. It probably also didn't matter that the money was in the name of a company instead of his own. They were magicians, the FBI. He was sunk.

It was taking longer for them to come than he'd thought it would, though. And the longer it took, the more frightened he became. He considered walking away from his store and disappearing. But where would he go? He supposed he could fly down to the Cayman Islands, buy a little house with his money there, and live the rest of his life lying out on the beach, with no cares. He'd worked hard his whole life and deserved that. But his daughters and grandchildren lived in Hudson County. He'd never be able to fly back and see them. That would be unbearable. Better than prison, though, he reminded himself.

Once, he would have turned to the judge for advice. He'd called him whenever a wrinkle popped up. Like when Mary Jane said she was going to the police. Her mentor had called Paul that night and told him of Mary Jane's intentions, begging Paul not to reveal his secret. And then, after her accident, everyone felt safe again.

Only now he was afraid to call the judge. If he told him that the investigator knew about him, about his role, would he be marked for death? Like Quince Michaels? He didn't know for certain that Bryson was behind it. Or even behind the Singers' murders. Who else could it be, though? Frank Reynolds wasn't invested in it the same way as the rest, and although John Engles had the guts, Scoby didn't think he'd do anything without Bryson's okay.

He thought about the investigator's offer. Turn himself in and get a deal. Hand him the others on a silver platter. Then maybe he'd serve a little time, maybe in one of those Club Fed prisons he'd read about. When he came out, he'd be able to live near his family. The money would be gone, though. That was the only thing that kept him from running away—trying to decide which path was worse. And since he hated both choices, he did nothing.

The restaurant he'd chosen was tucked into a hillside on the other side of the Hudson River. Frank had asked Finn to meet him there for lunch and was already seated when Finn walked in the door.

"Hi, Dad," Finn said when he sat down. "Why'd you pick something so far away?"

"Let's order first."

Finn looked through the menu, and when the waitress approached their table, both men gave her their orders.

"So, what's up?"

"I've made a decision, and I want to tell you first. I haven't even told your mom yet."

Finn raised his eyebrows.

"I'm going to the FBI. I'm going to tell them about the fraud."

"You do that, you'll go to jail."

"I know. But Molly will be freed. Or at least she'll get a new trial."

Finn placed his elbows on the table and dropped his head into his hands, as though praying. After a few moments of silence, he looked up at his father, his eyes moist.

"Why are you doing this?"

"Because it's the right thing to do. It needs to be done for Sophie."

"No, Dad."

"And it needs to be done for me."

The waitress came to their table with their meals then. When she'd walked away, Finn said, "You'll be locked up."

Frank sighed deeply. He pushed the food around on his plate. One day, he hoped Finn would understand. He couldn't go on, knowing what his actions had led to. Although prison frightened him, the person he'd turned into frightened him more. "I'm prepared for prison, Son."

Finn looked at him with clear eyes. "If you're certain about this, I think you should talk to Molly's lawyer first."

Frank nodded. They finished their lunch in silence. There was little else to be said.

Instead of returning to the office, Frank went straight home. As soon as he walked in the house, Betsy called out, "What's wrong? Why aren't you at work?"

She'd always been intuitive. He'd often wondered if she'd sensed, back so many years ago, that he was about to do something despicable. Probably not. If she'd known, she'd have talked him out of it. He walked into the kitchen where Betsy was busy preparing a pie, pulled her into his body, and planted a big kiss on her lips.

"I need to tell you something," he said, then confessed the whole sordid mess.

When he finished, she had only one thing to say. "You're doing the right thing."

CHAPTER 43

Even without a window in her office, Dani could hear the wind whistling outside. It had been raw this morning. Just the few blocks she'd walked from the parking lot to HIPP's building put a chill in her that she hadn't yet shaken, despite two cups of coffee.

She was at her desk, typing a brief on her computer, when Tommy walked in.

"You'll never guess who I just got a call from."

Dani turned away from the computer and looked at him. "Who?"

"Frank Reynolds. He wants to come in and talk."

Dani fell back in her chair and barely contained the whoop fighting its way out of her throat. "Oh my *gosh*, Tommy. This could be the break we've waited for. When's he coming?"

"Today. He'll be here in two hours."

Dani buzzed Melanie and asked her to come into her office. When she arrived, Dani told her Tommy's news. "Let's think about this. Should we hear him out first, or do you think we should ask Josh Cosgrove to come over?"

"Having a US attorney here might spook him," Tommy said.

"It might. But if he wants to make a deal, then Cosgrove's the one to make it happen."

"Still, we don't know what he's going to say or where his head is. I say we wait."

"Okay. But I'll give Josh a heads-up. Maybe he can be on standby and come over if Frank is willing to talk to him."

Tommy nodded. "That makes sense."

They returned to their offices and Dani turned back to her computer and struggled with just about no success to concentrate on her brief for the next two hours. Finally, her phone buzzed and the receptionist told her Frank Reynolds had arrived.

"Bring him into the conference room and tell Melanie and Tommy to meet me there."

Dani picked up her coffee mug, now filled with a third cup of coffee, and went to the conference room. She found a tall man dressed in a suit, biting at his lips.

"Mr. Reynolds?"

He stood up and held out his hand.

"I'm Dani Trumball. Thank you for coming in." As she introduced herself, Tommy and Melanie entered the room. "I believe you know Tom Noorland, and this is my associate, Melanie Quinn.

"Pleased to meet you," he mumbled as he shook Melanie's hand.

"Can we get you something to drink? Some coffee or water?"

Reynolds shook his head, then cleared his throat. "I'm set."

"Okay, then why don't you tell us why you're here," Dani said.

Reynolds cleared his throat again, then rubbed his hands on his thighs. "I, um, I'm here, because, uh, I want to tell you everything, I mean, what I know."

"We're listening."

He leaned forward. "I'm going to go to the FBI after this, you know, to turn myself in. I just thought I should tell you first, so you could get started on helping Molly."

"We appreciate you coming here."

Dani sat back and waited for Reynolds to continue. After a few moments, he began.

"Back then, before the jail was built, I was very ambitious. I'd been in the county legislature for eight years and felt it was time to move up. The state legislature next, then congressman, then senator. Or maybe governor. Even the presidency was within my reach, I thought." He rubbed a hand, hard, over his face and smiled weakly at them. "So, yeah. Ambitious.

"Still, when Judge Bryson came to me and asked me to look the other way when invoices for the jail came in, I said no. It was out-and-out fraud, and I didn't want any part of it. But he wouldn't let it go. Kept badgering me about it. 'Badgering' isn't the right word. He demanded that I do it. And then he laid it out for me. If I did what he asked, he promised I'd be the county executive. If I didn't, I'd never run for elective office again."

He sighed and looked miserably out the window for a moment. When he turned to them and spoke again, his voice was almost hushed. "I didn't want any of the money. I just wanted my career. Being part of government would allow me to make better all the things I thought were wrong. So I told him to keep it."

"Then what about the hundred thousand dollars you were paid during the first year of the jail construction?" Dani asked. "Where did that come from?"

Reynolds's mouth fell open. "How did you know about that?"

Dani waved the question away. "Later. Tell us where the money came from."

"Bryson wouldn't let me take nothing. He said I had to be invested in it to ensure my silence. The money came from Quince Michaels, but the source was the jail payments."

Dani did some quick calculations on the paper in front of her. If Singer and Michaels each took seven million, and Judge Bryson took the same amount, there had to be two others.

"Was Paul Scoby part of the group getting payments?"

Reynolds nodded. "He took the same amount as the others."

"There must be one more."

"John Engles." Dani would've been tough to surprise at that point, but the revelation that a lawman was involved drove a disgusted grunt from Tommy. "Back then he was chief deputy sheriff. Building a new jail for the county was controversial. John mobilized the support of the guard's union, got them all behind the need for a new jail. That provided the support for the legislators to vote in favor of building it. Bryson considered him essential and gave him a full share."

So that's it, Dani thought. Five men, two of them dead. One of the others was a murderer.

"Frank," Dani said softly. "Do you know who murdered the Singers?"

"I thought Molly had. But now I realize I was kidding myself all along."

"Why do you say that?"

"Because of Quince. And because my son reminded me of a phone call twelve years ago."

Dani looked at him quizzically.

"The state was looking into the cost overruns on the jail. It made all of them nervous, me, too, but Joe the most. He wanted us to come clean about it. Kept saying it would be better than them finding out on their own. I'd known Joe since high school. We'd stayed pals over the years. His daughter was dating my son. Alan called me one night and told me I better convince Joe to keep quiet or someone else would shut him up. I brushed away the memory of that remark after Molly was arrested. I mean, she'd confessed. Why would she have done so if she was innocent?"

"Do you think Judge Bryson killed the Singers?"

Frank looked down at the table. His hands were clenched tightly together. "I don't know," he whispered.

The silent glances between Dani, Melanie, and Tommy made it clear they all believed Frank. Only one question was left. "Would you be willing to tell this to an assistant US attorney?" Dani asked.

"Shouldn't I go to the FBI?"

"They would turn it over to the US Attorney's Office."

"Whatever you think is right. This will help Molly, won't it?"

Dani smiled at Frank. "Yes. She'll definitely get a new trial now. Even if we can't prove Judge Bryson murdered, or had murdered, the

Singers, it was improper for him to preside over her case when there are allegations of his involvement in criminal activity with the victim. He clearly had a personal interest in seeing Molly convicted."

Frank exhaled deeply. "You know, her daughter is my granddaughter. Finn is raising her."

"Yes, I know."

"This will make Sophie very happy."

"Yes. She'll be happy to be with her mother. But I suspect she'll be unhappy about you going to prison."

"I will, won't I?"

"I can't say. Maybe you can work something out for your testimony. That's out of my hands."

Frank nodded.

Dani left the room to call Cosgrove.

"That son of a bitch. Bryson really was involved?" he said after Dani filled him in.

"Appears so."

"Keep Reynolds there. I'll be right over."

"Trust me, he's not leaving here until we have his sworn affidavit."

"Well, congratulations. Looks like you got what you needed."

Dani wished that were true. It was enough to get Molly a new trial. It was still an open question whether it would be enough to get her acquitted.

Two hours later, Assistant US Attorney Cosgrove emerged from the HIPP conference room and made his way to Dani's office.

"He's a solid witness," Josh said. "My office is preparing arrest warrants for Bryson, Scoby, and Engles. Before we serve them, though, we're going to see if we can track down the money they hid."

"Was Frank any help with that?"

"A little. He doesn't know what they actually did, only that he was told to set up a dummy corporation and open an account for it in one of the Caribbean islands that had banking secrecy laws. Alan Bryson gave him a list of possibilities. He didn't do that for himself, but he assumes the others did."

"Makes sense. That's what Singer and Michaels did."

Cosgrove looked around Dani's small office. "So this is what you left us for."

Dani smiled. "Can't beat the ambiance."

Suddenly, Cosgrove turned serious. "You did a good job on this. Without your digging, they would have gotten away with it."

"Thanks, but it wasn't just me. I have a great team here."

Cosgrove stood up to leave. "It's good working with you again."

As he reached the doorway, Dani called after him. "What's going to happen to Frank?"

Cosgrove turned around. "He'll do some time, but it'll be a slap on the wrist compared to the others."

"I'm glad. It was brave of him to come forward."

"No. It would have been brave twelve years ago. It's too late for it to be bravery now."

Dani sat in the waiting room at the US Attorney's Office. She hadn't seen or spoken to Cosgrove for six weeks when he'd called last night and asked her to come in. Every time someone walked past, she jumped up, hoping it was Josh. Ten minutes later, he popped in and brought her to his office.

"I wanted to let you know that we're going to execute arrest warrants today for Alan Bryson and John Engles," he said.

Dani exhaled deeply. "Finally! Did you find the money?"

Cosgrove reached behind him to a batch of folders on top of a file cabinet. "Enough to go forward. Reynolds's information was invaluable but just a starting point. Do you know much about banking laws in many Caribbean islands?"

Dani shook her head.

"Well as you know, they've been a tax haven for years. Many of them allow individuals or groups to incorporate there as an international business company, or an IBC. Not only are the assets held by them free of taxes, but the names of the owners, directors, and shareholders are not made public. In fact, in some countries, they don't even need to register the names of the true owners. They can use the names of nominee directors and shareholders. To top it off, US subpoenas aren't enforceable in those countries."

"So how did you get the money?"

"The IRS has been cracking down on these accounts. They first went after some accounts in Switzerland and India. Just recently they started with Caribbean banks."

"But how? You said the subpoenas weren't recognized there."

"Yes, but—and this is a big *but*—many foreign banks have a relationship with one or more US banks. Either they have an actual presence on US soil, or they use the American bank for certain transactions, such as wiring funds to their American clients. The subpoena gets served on that bank, and the foreign bank must comply."

"So, what did you find?"

Cosgrove opened one of the folders. "Based on Reynolds's affidavit, we got a judge to sign a John Doe subpoena for four islands—the Bahamas, Belize, the Cayman Islands, and Dominica—targeting only those banks that had a relationship with a bank in the US. Fortunately for us, Paul Scoby parked his money in one of those banks in the Bahamas and didn't use nominees. We had him cold."

Dani knew what came next. When she was an assistant US attorney trying to crack a group of conspirators, she'd work on the weakest one and offer a deal. "So you brought Scoby in?"

Cosgrove nodded, then smiled. "It was hardly any fun at all. He was like a volcano ready to erupt. As soon as we sat him down and said, 'Your bank account in the Bahamas with seven million dollars has been frozen,' he started talking. It was like he couldn't get it out fast enough."

"Did he say he killed the Singers?"

"No. And he doesn't know who did. He thought it could be any one of the other three. Since it's not Reynolds, that leaves Bryson or Engles."

"Did he lead you to the bank accounts for them?"

"No, but we're going ahead with the arrest warrants without their money. Now that Scoby corroborates Reynolds's account of the enterprise, it's enough for a conviction."

Dani twisted the ends of her hair, her mind racing as she plotted her next moves. A new trial for Molly—that was a certainty. With evidence of the criminal scheme Joe Singer was part of, Reynolds's testimony that Singer wanted to confess, and Bryson's veiled threat against him, and with the expert testimony on false confessions, Dani felt optimistic about Molly's chance for acquittal.

As she headed back to her office, her feet seemed to skim over the pavement. She would file the papers for a new trial tomorrow, and then visit Molly to tell her the good news.

Hudson Valley Dispatch
February 17
Hudson County Shocker!
Byline: Shannon Evans

FBI agents arrested County Court Judge Alan Bryson and Hudson County Sheriff John Engles and charged them with theft of government funds, fraud and RICO violations. Both were removed in handcuffs from the courthouse and jail, respectively. According to the warrant, the men were part of a five-man group that stole more than $35 million from Hudson County through inflated and fraudulent invoices submitted in connection with the building of the Hudson County jail. Joseph Singer and Quince Michaels, the principals of the company that built the jail, were part of the conspiracy, as was local Democratic leader, Paul Scoby, and County Executive Frank Reynolds. Scoby and Reynolds have been charged as well, and sources say they've agreed to a plea bargain.

Spokesmen for both Bryson and Engles vehemently deny the charges and say they will vigorously defend themselves at trial.

Twelve years ago, Joseph Singer and his wife, Sarah, were found brutally murdered. Their daughter, Molly Singer, who was

the only other person in the house with them during the time of
the murders, first confessed to the crime and then recanted. She
was convicted of both murders and is serving two consecutive life
sentences at the Bedford Hills Correctional Facility in Bedford,
New York. Quince Michaels was recently killed in a boat accident
ruled suspicious by the Coast Guard.

Back in the familiar motel room, Bryson waited for Engles to arrive. The unthinkable had happened. Now he had to manage it. Engles wasn't capable of doing so on his own. He paced back and forth in front of the two beds. Even the shot of scotch hadn't calmed his nerves.

He pounced on the door when he heard the soft knock.

"About time."

"I had to give Kathy an excuse," Engles said. "She didn't want to leave me alone. Thought I was suicidal or something."

Bryson looked at him coldly. "You're not, I assume."

Engles answered with an equally cold stare. "I'm fine. So now what? It's your meeting."

"We need to coordinate our responses. They don't know where our money is or else they'd have put that in the indictment. And frozen the accounts. Without the money, they have nothing concrete on us."

Engles snorted. "Nothing except the word of Scoby and Reynolds. Damn! I knew Reynolds felt all guilty over Molly Singer. I should have taken care of him before it came to this."

It all came back to those murders. He never should have brought Engles into the deal. The sheriff's whole adult life had been spent in close proximity to criminals. It must have rubbed off on him. Bryson hadn't wanted Joe Singer murdered, just frightened into silence. That's all. If Engles hadn't overreacted, they'd all be looking forward to retirement soon, each with seven million dollars paving the way for a luxurious end to their time left on earth. He'd be damned if he would spend it in prison instead because he'd aligned himself with a Neanderthal.

"It's still their word against ours," Bryson said. "It's easy to dismiss Scoby. We say since he knew he was going down himself, he thought he'd try to take down the leaders of the Republican party in Hudson County along with him."

"Reynolds is a Republican."

"As you said, he wants Molly out. Figured if he fingered the judge who presided at her trial, it would get her a new one."

Engles eyed Bryson warily. "How do I know you're not going to make a deal with them? Throw me under the bus for a lighter sentence?"

He really is an idiot, thought Bryson. "Because our fates are tied together."

"Really? You didn't murder them. Seems like it'd be real easy for you to hand me over to them as the one who killed all those people and cut yourself some sweet deal."

"You forget. I asked you to take care of Quince. That makes me just as culpable."

Engles spotted the bottle of scotch on the dresser, walked over, and poured himself a drink, then took a long draw on it.

"If we remain firm, we won't be convicted," Bryson said, his voice stern. "But you raise an important issue. They're going to tell each of us that the other has made a deal and squealed, implicating the other. Don't believe them. It's a trick."

"And how will I know if it's not a trick?"

"Because I'm telling you right now. I will not talk to them. I will not give them any information. About the money or the murders. Can you promise me the same thing?

Engles took a second swig, then placed his glass down. "Sure."

"Say it."

"What is this, kindergarten?"

"Just say it!" Bryson felt like he might literally explode.

"Okay. Okay. I promise."

Bryson sat back and studied Engles. "You know, we can ensure our acquittals. In fact, we can ensure that we never even get to trial."

Engles took another swallow of his scotch. "How's that?"

Bryson smiled and his coal-black eyes almost seemed lively. "Without Scoby and Reynolds they have no case."

"So?"

"So, why don't you take care of that problem like you took care of the other problems?" Bryson had thought about this all through the wait leading up to his arraignment. He wished it hadn't come to this, but he'd been backed into a corner—by two political flacks, no less—and so they'd brought it on themselves. Sure, there was a risk. The spotlight was bound to be on him and Engles. But he'd make sure they had plenty of alibi witnesses. Hadn't they pulled it off with Quince? The coast guard may have had their suspicious, but they hadn't proved anything.

Engles stood up and began pacing. He started to speak, then stopped and paced some more. "Before they didn't know anything about the money, about our involvement in that. If I off them, they'll know it's us."

"They may suspect it, but they'll have no proof. Do it carefully and they won't get any."

Engles sat down on the bed and gulped down the rest of his drink. "I'll think about it."

The sheriff walked up Thirty-Fourth Street toward Macy's. He'd told Kathy he'd meet her there in an hour, and it was almost time. He knew the only way to get her to leave him alone was with the promise of shopping. As he walked, he kept his eye out for one of the numerous electronics stores that popped up every few streets in Manhattan. At the first one, he ducked in and purchased a burner cell phone. He couldn't make the call on his own cell phone—for all he knew, it was being monitored by the feds. No, he needed secrecy for this call. Once he'd activated the phone, he tapped out a number and, when the call was answered, said, "I have another job for you."

"I still haven't collected on the last one. And from what I hear, you're not going to be in a position to deliver."

"Do these jobs for me, and I'll be back as sheriff before you know it. And ready to deliver on our deals."

The silence on the other end lasted only a minute, but Engles held his breath for what seemed an eternity.

"Okay. Same arrangement as before, right?"

"Right."

"Tell me who."

"Paul Scoby and Frank Reynolds."

"Shutting down the leaks, I see."

"That's right. And it needs to happen *now*. No later than tomorrow morning. After that, I expect they'll be buttoned up in protective custody."

"Consider it done."

Engles breathed a sigh of relief. He took a handkerchief from his pocket and wiped the phone clean, then dropped it in the first trash receptacle he passed.

Hudson Valley Dispatch
February 18
Arraigned
Byline: Shannon Evans

Judge Alan Bryson and Sheriff John Engles were arraigned yester-
day afternoon in the U.S. District Court in lower Manhattan be-
fore the Honorable Judge Edwin Gleeson for theft of government
funds, bribery and RICO violations. Both men entered pleas of
not guilty. Although Joshua Cosgrove, the assistant U.S. attorney
prosecuting them, requested that they be held without bail, argu-
ing that they each had at least $7 million secreted in an offshore
bank account, Judge Gleeson released them on bail of $250,000
and ordered them to turn over their passports.

Frank picked up his cell phone on the first ring. He'd just finished
reading the morning newspaper and had broken out in a sweat when
he learned Bryson and Engles were free. Shaking, he said, "Hello."

"Frank, this is Josh Cosgrove. I wanted to let you know the judge allowed them to post bail. They did and were released late yesterday."

"I just read that."

"I want to put you and your wife in protective custody. We'll do the same for Paul Scoby."

"What does that mean?"

"We'll put you up in an obscure hotel room and post an FBI agent outside around the clock."

Frank's stomach was doing somersaults. "How long can that go on?"

"I'm going to convene a grand jury in the next few days. Once your testimony there is on record, they'd have no incentive to harm you. If they did, we'd still be able to read your testimony at the trial. And I'll make sure they know that. Where are you now?"

"I'm still at home."

"Stay put. Don't go outside. An agent will be there in two hours."

Frank started to breathe more easily. It would be okay. He would come out of this.

Two hours later, right on cue, a black SUV pulled up in front of Frank's house. Betsy had packed a suitcase for both of them and placed it in the front foyer. Frank watched through the glass at the top of the door as a tall, muscular man exited the passenger side and walked up to his house. When the doorbell rang, he was about to open it when Betsy tugged on his arm.

"Make sure he's the FBI first," she whispered.

"Let me see your ID first, "Frank said. "Hold it up to the window."

Frank watched as the man opened his jacket. Instead of pulling out a badge, the man whipped out a gun that had been slipped inside his pants and raised it quickly toward the glass. Frank had just grabbed Betsy and pulled her to the floor when the gun and window exploded, raining glass upon them. A volley of shots rang through the wooden door as they crawled madly along the floor into the main hall.

"What's happening?" Betsy cried. Frank could feel her body shaking.

"Stay down. I'm going to try to get to the phone."

"Don't leave me."

"Shh. It'll be okay."

Just then, they watched in horror as a gloved hand pushed out the remainder of the glass and reached inside for the doorknob.

Frank yanked Betsy to her feet and shouted "Run!" as he led her toward the back door. As they neared it, they saw the face of another man, gun in hand, standing outside. Frank knew he could do nothing but pull Betsy into his arms and hold her tight, prepared for the inevitable. He could offer no words of solace. He'd aligned himself with a killer, and his silence had led to this. He couldn't bear the thought that he'd put his wife's life at risk.

They heard a loud gunshot outside, and someone shouted, "Freeze! Move away from there." Then footsteps running, the sound of car tires squealing, more shots, and finally, a knock on the front door.

"It's Agent Hawkins, with the FBI. You okay in there?"

Betsy burst out crying and stayed close to Frank as he walked back to the front door, where they found the agent holding his badge open through the empty window.

With wildly shaking hands, barely able to operate the deadbolt, Frank opened the door.

Hawkins looked them over as he pocketed his badge. "You folks sure you're okay?"

"I think so," Frank said. He turned to Betsy. "You all right?"

"Oh sure," she said, her voice wobbling, then held out her hand so they could see it shaking. Frank lifted his quaking hand beside hers, and they shared a choked laugh.

"Plenty of reason for that," Hawkins said. "That was way too close. Those guys were sent to silence you. Permanently. I wounded one of them. They took off and my partner's gone after them."

Hawkins quickly took out his cell phone and punched in some numbers. "We just had an attempted hit here," he said. "Be careful picking up your package." When he hung up the phone, he turned back to them. "They're moving quickly. Here's hoping they stopped here first instead of Scoby's."

"What now? For us?"

"If my partner catches the shooters, he'll bring them in to the police. Then he'll come back and pick us up."

"And if he doesn't catch them?"

"Then it's a good thing we have you under protection."

Two minutes later, Hawkins's cell phone rang. He looked at the number, then answered. "All okay?"

Frank saw the agent's lips clench, then heard him say, "Understood," before he ended the call. Hawkins turned to Frank and shook his head. "They hit Scoby first. He's dead."

The two men met in a diner an hour north of town. The judge was dressed in a neatly pressed suit, as he wore every day going to work. Only he had no job to go to. Of course he'd been suspended pending the trial. With pay, fortunately. Engles showed up in ragged jeans and a flannel shirt. He hadn't bothered to shave that morning. He, too, had been suspended pending the trial. Without pay. If he were acquitted, he could apply for back pay. Maybe he'd get it, maybe not.

"What went wrong?" Bryson asked, fingertips tapping on the Formica table. "I thought you could handle this. I told you it had to be done quickly."

Engles glowered at him. "Scoby's dead enough, isn't he?"

"This isn't a baseball game," Bryson said. "Batting .500 won't win you a trophy."

Muttering unintelligibly, Engles turned his scowl on his coffee.

"Any idea where Reynolds is now?"

Engles shrugged. "Protective custody somewhere."

"You have sources. Can't you find out where?"

"I've tried. I'm a pariah now. And besides, what are you going to do, order in an air strike? Short of that would be suicide."

Bryson picked up his coffee cup and took a sip. This wasn't good. It left them vulnerable and that was not acceptable. Still, at least Scoby was out of the picture. He was by far the more dangerous of the two. Unlike Frank, Scoby had been a full partner in their endeavor and privy to more details. With him gone, as long as the feds didn't find the money, it was the word of just one man—Reynolds—against theirs. He felt confident he could find an accountant who'd testify that the excess payments only amounted to twenty-one million, not the thirty-five million claimed by Ms. Singer's forensic accountant. And during the months leading up to the trial, he would come up with some reason why Reynolds fabricated a story against him and Engles. It might work—as long as the money stayed hidden.

"We've got to move our accounts," Bryson said.

"Why?"

"Because the others were found in some Caribbean islands. The feds have got to be all over the other islands looking for ours. We need to get it someplace else."

"Have any ideas where?"

"Dubai."

Engles looked at him with a blank stare. "Where the hell is that?"

"Doesn't matter. It's safer than Switzerland. But we'll need an agent to go there, present a passport and visa, and set it up."

"So who've you got in mind?"

"Someone I trust. Who can't be traced back to us. I just need to know if you're in."

"Is there any choice?"

"Not really."

Engles nodded.

"Then I'll take care of everything. Just remember, we're innocent and have nothing else to say."

"Did I hear you right?"

Dani smiled broadly. "Yes. It may only be temporary, but you're getting out."

"When? How?" Molly asked. Her heart was hammering, and she put a hand to her chest as though that could slow it down.

"The judge granted our new 440 motion. With the indictment of Judge Bryson, and the allegations of his involvement in a criminal enterprise with your father, there was really no choice. The judge ruled that even if a conviction didn't result, the claims of Reynolds and Scoby, especially since they were against their own interests, were credible and warranted a new trial. Unless the DA decides not to retry you."

"Is that possible?"

Dani nodded, then added, "But unlikely."

"In the meantime, the judge said I could go home?" *Thump, thump*—it felt like her heart was singing with joy at this impossible news.

"He said you would be released on bail of one hundred fifty thousand dollars."

That quieted her heart. "I don't have that kind of money."

"Your sister does—or at least her husband. They've already posted it."

"When? When can I leave?"

"Tomorrow morning."

"Oh my God. I can't believe it," she said. She pinched the flesh on the back of her arm, hard. Nothing. "It must be a dream, but if it is, don't wake me up."

"No dream. I'll be here tomorrow morning to pick you up."

"But where will I go?"

"To Donna."

She sank in her seat as though the room's gravity had just been reactivated. "I guess I don't have any choice, do I? I have no money, no job, no home."

"No, not really."

Despite twelve years of shutting her sister out of her life, Molly recognized that Donna's home was the only workable solution. She had no other family nearby, and with the possibility of a new trial starting soon, she couldn't leave the county.

"It'll work out," Dani assured her. "You'll see."

Molly looked at Dani skeptically. Her sister was a virtual stranger to her.

The next morning, Molly walked outside the gates of the Bedford Hills Correctional Facility for the first time in twelve years. The sun shone overhead and the temperature had warmed up to a balmy forty-eight degrees. She was dressed in a pair of jeans, a pullover sweater, and a wool jacket, all purchased for her by Donna. None of her old clothes had been saved, and if they had, wouldn't have fit her anymore. She had gone into prison a child and was now a woman. Her eyes, unused to much time outdoors, burned from the brightness.

Dani had met her in the front vestibule, and together they walked away from the concrete building to the mass of cars in the visitors' lot. Molly carried only a small paper bag. During twelve years of incarceration, she'd accumulated little of worth. She'd wanted to leave everything associated with the prison behind, to wipe it clean from her memory. At the last minute, she'd grabbed the notebooks she'd written in over the years. If her reprieve were only temporary, if she had to go back to that filthy institution, she'd want her recorded musings with her.

"I'm so nervous," Molly said as she slipped into Dani's car.

"Of course you are. But your sister will help you through it."

Molly was quiet for a time as Dani put the prison behind them. She didn't look back.

Then she found herself thinking of what Dani had said. *Your sister will help you through it.* It was such a foreign concept that she could hardly make sense of it. "Donna and I haven't spoken in so many years. We're both different people now. I don't know her husband, her children. How can I possibly fit in there?"

"Look, it's going to be an adjustment no matter where you live. Don't expect everything to fall into place all at once. Take baby steps. And let Donna help you. She really does love you."

Molly sighed, then leaned back in the car and closed her eyes. After a while, she opened them and saw they were on the New York State Thruway. Everything looked both familiar and yet fresh to her. After an hour of driving, she caught her first glimpse of the mountains she'd loved. From a young age, her parents had taken her and Donna hiking in those mountains during the warm months, skiing down them during the winter. The memory of those times pained her. They had been such a happy family. Now her parents were gone and her relationship with her sister had shriveled and died.

She didn't speak again until they pulled up in front of Donna's house. As they pulled into the driveway, Molly took in the house, the grounds, and the view of the mountains. "It's beautiful," she said.

"Len's business has done well."

"Have you met him?"

"Not yet."

"I hope he doesn't mind my being here."

Dani turned to Molly and put her hand on hers. "They both want you here. Come on. Let's go in."

Slowly, Molly exited the car, then stopped. "I can't."

Dani came over to her and said softly, "You can. You withstood twelve years in prison. You can do this." Together, they slowly made their way to the front door, then rang the bell. Within seconds, the door flew open, and Donna threw her arms around Molly. She didn't say a word as she held Molly tightly.

"I'm so sorry, so sorry," Donna said when she finally found her voice. She stepped back and took a long look at her sister. "You're still so pretty. I didn't know what to expect." Donna glanced downward. "I mean, I didn't know what prison had done to you."

"It made me stronger."

"Oh, no, honey. You were always strong."

Molly looked her sister over. "You look different. More like Mom."

Donna laughed. "As long as you don't tell me I *act* like Mom."

Molly laughed, too, and at that moment, a weight was lifted. Her years of thinking of Donna as the enemy melted away, and they were teenagers again, allies against their parents' rules.

"Come in and meet the family. You, too, Dani. Len will be home later, but the kids are here."

Molly stepped into the foyer, and Donna took her hand to lead her into the living room. It was furnished simply, with contemporary furniture in the soothing colors of an island retreat. Seated on the couch, along with Donna's children, was Sophie. Molly's hand flew to her mouth. She rushed over to her daughter, who'd bounced to her feet, threw her arms around her, and kissed her forehead. "I can't believe you're here."

"I hope you don't mind my asking her," Donna said. "I wasn't sure if you would have preferred to settle in first."

"Mind? No, I'm thrilled." Sophie sat back on the couch and Molly sat down next to her and wrapped her hand around her daughter's.

"This is Sarah and this is Jacob," Donna said, pointing to her two children.

Molly's eyes moistened. "You named her after Mom."

Donna nodded. "I miss her. Dad, too."

Molly looked at her niece and nephew. She'd never even seen pictures of them before, and now they were before her in the flesh. Sarah looked like childhood pictures of her namesake, with blonde hair, a pug nose, and a round face. Jacob was more angular, with light-brown hair that flopped over his eyes and covered his ears and neck. Molly leaned over and held out her hand to Sarah. "Nice to meet you. How old are you?"

"I'm nine. Almost ten. And it's serendipitous to meet you."

Molly looked at her sister quizzically. "Sarah likes big words," Donna said.

"That's because I have Williams syndrome," Sarah piped in. "It makes me special."

Dani, who'd taken a seat at the end of the coach, laughed quietly at that and beamed at Sarah.

"I can see you're special," Molly said. "And how old are you?" she asked Jacob, who'd been squirming on the couch ever since she walked in.

"I'm six and I'm in the first grade."

"Well, I bet you're learning a lot of good things."

"I can read," Jacob said, sticking out his chest.

"Maybe you can read me a book later?"

"Sure."

"Okay, kids, scoot," Donna said. "Let Molly get settled."

Molly held on to Sophie's hand to make sure she didn't leave with the younger children, then looked up at Donna. "Thank you," she whispered.

"What for?"

"For posting bail, for letting me stay here. I've been pretty horrible to you, never answering your letters or letting you visit me."

"Oh, Molly, I'm the one to ask for forgiveness. I never should have doubted you." She stood erect over her sister. "And I promise. I'll never doubt you again."

Dani had hoped the district attorney would choose not to retry Molly. She had already served twelve years for a crime of which the evidence was flimsy. But the prosecutor knew that, no matter what any expert said, jurors were spellbound by confessions. And so he had chosen to go ahead.

Now, six weeks after Molly's release, Dani, Tommy, and Melanie were booked into rooms in the local Holiday Inn. Even though their homes were only two hours away, it was too long a drive to go back and forth each day during the trial. Juror selection was scheduled to begin the next morning. Unlike high-powered firms with wealthy clients, there was no jury consultant who'd sit in the courtroom and advise Dani on which men and women were more likely to be sympathetic to Molly. She had only herself to rely on. Although she rarely tried jury cases at HIPP, she expected to call on her years of experience prosecuting cases at the US Attorney's Office.

"All set for tomorrow?" Tommy asked.

"Yep."

"Nervous?"

"Yep." Dani was always nervous at the start of a trial, just as she always had to calm her nerves at the start of an oral argument on her appeals cases. But she knew the nerves would die down, and instinct and skill would take over once she began.

"I told the witnesses it would probably be at least a week before we got to them," Melanie said.

"That sounds right." Dani calculated two days for juror selection, three days for the prosecution's case, and four days for the defense. Given the lack of forensic evidence, the district attorney should be able to get in everything he needed in one day, but Dani knew from experience he would drag it out.

They ate dinner together, Dani foregoing any alcohol, then retreated to their rooms. Once again, Dani looked over her notes. She was prepared, ready to give Molly her chance for freedom.

The next morning, they headed over to the courthouse together. The courtroom assigned to them was as airless as the building that housed it. Dani and Melanie took seats up front, with Molly sitting between them. Acting Chief Justice Arnold Silver presided over the proceedings. Forty prospective jurors were seated, ready to be called for voir dire. Dani had considered moving the judge for a change of venue to a different county but decided against it. The publicity surrounding Judge Bryson and Sheriff Engles's arrest would more likely work in her favor.

The first six prospective jurors were called to the jury box. After they took their seats, Assistant District Attorney Eric Murdoch began his questioning. He went through the jurors methodically, asking their names, whether they had any relationship with the defendant, her attorney or the ADA, their occupation, and about their family. He asked them if they'd read about the case or if they'd read about the arrests of Bryson and Engles. He asked if they could keep an open mind and judge the case on the evidence and not on any knowledge or experience they brought to the jury room. When he finished with each one, Dani had only one question: do you believe a person can confess to a crime when she didn't commit it? At the end of two days, they had their jury.

After the day in court ended, she drove Molly back to her sister's home. Once settled in the car, Molly asked, "Do you think we have a good jury?"

"I hope so. You can never tell, though. Sometimes jurors answer what they think you want to hear and then do an about-face during deliberations."

"I'm frightened."

Dani glanced over at her client. Her face was pale and her hands shook. Keeping one hand on the wheel, Dani covered Molly's hand with her other. "You have a right to be scared. And when you're at home, let it all out. Cry or scream or run around in circles. But tomorrow, in the courtroom, I want you to look calm, but resolute. You want the jurors to see you're taking the trial seriously, but you're not afraid because you know you're innocent. Can you do that?"

"I'll—I'll try."

"Good girl."

"It's just—I can't go back there. Now that I'm free, now that I have a chance to be with Sophie, now that I'm getting close to Donna again, getting to know my niece and nephew—I just can't do it."

Dani understood. She also understood it was up to her to make sure Molly didn't go back to prison.

"Ready, Mr. Murdoch?" the judge asked.

"Yes, Your Honor."

Murdoch walked over to the jury box, ready to begin his opening statement. He stood a foot away from the jurors and looked solemnly at each one before beginning.

"Ladies and gentlemen of the jury. You are here to decide whether Molly Singer, when she was seventeen years old, murdered her mother and father. You will hear testimony that on the night her parents were murdered, she was the only other person in the house. You will learn that no doors or windows were broken or tampered with. Her classmates at the time will tell you that she often complained about the restraints placed on her by her parents. And you will see on videotape her confession to the crime. When you hear all the evidence, you will realize that no other conclusion can be reached but that Ms. Singer murdered her parents. Thank you."

Murdoch walked slowly back to his seat and sat down. Judge Silver nodded at Dani and she stood up, then walked over to the jurors.

"Good morning. Mr. Murdoch would like you to think that this is a very simple case. And it is. It is simple because you will find, as the prosecution presents its case, that there is absolutely no evidence that ties Ms. Singer to the crime. There is no weapon with her fingerprints on it. There was no blood on Ms. Singer from the bodies of her parents. There is no evidence of psychological disturbance in her history. The complaints she made to her classmates are the same that you probably made when you were a teenager. The only basis they have for believing Ms. Singer committed this horrible crime against parents she loved is her confession, which she immediately recanted when she was no longer in police custody. You will hear a great deal of evidence about the phenomena of false confessions and realize that Ms. Singer was tricked into believing she'd done something she hadn't. Listen to the evidence carefully, and when you do you'll conclude that the state has not come close to meeting its burden of proving guilt beyond a reasonable doubt. Thank you."

Dani walked back to her table and sat down. Melanie nodded at her.

"Call your first witness," the judge said to Murdoch.

"Detective Dylan Baxter."

A broad-shouldered man with thinning hair combed over a bald spot, dressed in casual cream-colored slacks and a striped button-down shirt, ambled to the front of the room and took a seat in the witness box. After he was sworn in, Murdoch said, "Please state your name and occupation."

"Dylan Baxter, detective first grade with the New York State Police."

"And how long have you been a police officer?"

"Twenty-two years, the last fourteen as a detective."

"Were you present at the home of Mr. and Mrs. Singer the morning they were murdered?"

"Yes, sir. I was called to the scene and was lead detective on the case."

"And what did you observe when you arrived?"

"The first thing I saw was their daughter, Molly. She was sitting in the living room with the first police officers that arrived at the premises."

"Would you describe how she looked?"

"Very calm. She just sat on the couch quietly. When she saw me, she nodded."

"Thank you. Now what did you do next?"

"I went upstairs and viewed the bodies. Mr. Singer was fully in bed, and Mrs. Singer was lying partially out of the bed."

"And what did that indicate to you?"

"That Mr. Singer was murdered first and Mrs. Singer was awakened by it and tried to escape."

"Isn't it true that suggests there were two murderers?"

"Not necessarily. Mrs. Singer might not have awakened until the attacker had finished with her husband and come over to her side of the bed."

"But she was half out of the bed, trying to escape, you said. If the attacker was standing over her, wouldn't he have just pushed her back down on the bed?"

"She," the detective said, emphasizing the pronoun "may have been on her way over to that side when she awoke. Only the murderer"— he pointed to Molly—"the defendant over there, knows exactly how it went down."

Bristling, Dani considered objecting to Baxter's description of Molly as the murderer—after all, that's what this trial was to determine—and decided to let it pass, fearing that an objection would only highlight his characterization further for the jury.

"Did you examine the premises for signs of a break-in?"

"Yes. My men and I examined every window and door and found no evidence of a break-in. I questioned Molly Singer as to whether the front door had been locked the night before, and she told me it had."

"At some point did your attention turn to Ms. Singer?"

"Yes, right away. Her demeanor was strange. She didn't appear to be upset or disturbed. She just sat on the couch and seemed very cool to me."

"Did you bring her to the police station for questioning?"

"Yes."

"Please describe what took place then."

"Well, at first she kept saying that she went to sleep after one a.m. and didn't hear or see anything until she woke up the next morning and found her parents dead. But after a while, she told us she'd taken Ambien the night before. She'd read about people doing things while they were on Ambien and started to question whether she could have killed her parents without knowing about it. We talked some more and she began to realize that that's what she'd done. Little details came back to her, and she put those details in her confession."

"Was her confession videotaped?"

"Yes, sir, that's standard practice."

Murdoch turned to the judge. "Your Honor, I'd like to show the videotape now."

"Go ahead."

The videotape was played. In it, Molly looked like the frightened teenager she was. Dark circles rimmed her eyes, and her face was pale. Dani knew the impact it would have on the jury as they heard her speak, her voice meek, confessing to the murders. Murdoch finished with a few more questions for the detective, then sat down.

Dani rose and approached the witness.

"Mr. Baxter, have you ever seen someone in shock before?"

"Sure."

"Isn't it true that someone who's just witnessed a traumatic event can appear unnaturally calm?"

"I suppose. But most seventeen-year-olds would be hysterical if they saw their parents murdered."

"Did you listen to the 911 call that Molly made?"

"I did. And she was agitated on that call, but she could have been putting it on. She was nothing like that when I saw her."

"And how long after the call did you arrive?"

"About thirty minutes."

"So, isn't it possible that during those thirty minutes a state of shock could have set in?"

"Anything's possible."

"Now, turning to the doors and windows. Do you know if the Singers kept a spare key anywhere outside the house, in case they were locked out?"

"No. I don't. But if they did, how would the intruder know where to look?"

"Do you keep a spare key for your house?"

Murdoch called out, "Objection. Irrelevant."

"It goes to the commonality of keys and their hiding places, Your Honor."

"I'll let him answer."

"Yeah, I have a key. It's in a fake rock by the front door." He allowed himself a small grin at the jurors. "Though I guess now I'll have to move it."

"And where did you purchase that fake rock?"

"Home Depot."

"Isn't it true that many people purchase fake rocks to hide keys to their house?"

"I wouldn't know."

"Have you ever heard of someone hiding a key to their house under a doormat?"

"Sure."

"How about under a decorative item near the front door?"

"I guess."

"In your experience, isn't it common for people to keep spare keys outside their house in case they lock themselves out?"

"I don't know. I never polled most people."

"Let's move on and talk about your questioning of Molly at the police station. Did you tell Molly that you had evidence she'd committed the crime?"

"Sure. It's standard police interrogation to do that to get a confession."

"And didn't you say you found the murder weapon, and her finger-prints were on it?"

"I did."

"Isn't it true that you told Molly she didn't remember murdering her parents because she'd taken Ambien?"

"That's not how I remember it. I recall her suggesting it first."

"How long had you been questioning Molly before you began telling her about this so-called evidence you had?"

"A few hours."

"Exactly how many?"

"I'd say about nine hours."

Dani allowed that to sink in before she went on.

"And was Molly able to talk to anyone, a lawyer or a family member, during those nine hours?"

"She waived her right to counsel."

"So, she was a seventeen-year-old girl who'd discovered her parents murdered, had been all alone for nine hours while she was being questioned and told that you had proof she'd murdered her parents, then given a reason why she couldn't remember, is that right?"

"Yeah. Only she's the one who told us about the Ambien and not remembering things."

"And how long after you told her you had proof she'd committed the murders did she confess?"

"About another two hours later."

"Was her entire interrogation videotaped?"

"That's not standard procedure. We just video the confession."

"So you don't have on video the hours she spent denying involvement in the murders."

"They all start out saying they didn't do it."

"Thank you. I have no further questions."

The morning continued with Murdoch's questioning of the other police officers at the scene and Dani's cross-examination of them. At noon, the judge called a recess for lunch. Dani and her team, along with Molly and Donna, headed over to the same nondescript luncheonette with gourmet food they'd found during Molly's first 440 hearing.

"How do you think it's going?" Molly asked when they were seated.
"Exactly as expected so far." She turned to Tommy. "Were you keeping an eye on the jurors?"

"Yeah. Jurors five and seven concern me. They were listening real intently when Murdoch talked about her confession."

Dani sighed. No matter how many experts she brought in to explain why people confessed to a crime they didn't commit, it would still be a battle to convince the jurors. It was especially true in New York State, which held the distinction of having overturned the most wrongful convictions for murder since 2000. In many of those cases, where DNA later proved they had not committed the crime, the defendants had confessed.

She wished Judge Bryson and Sheriff Engles had been tried and convicted before Molly's trial. Then, with both Finn and Frank's testimony about the overheard conversation, the evidence would be strong that others had a motive to kill Molly's father. But an arrest didn't carry the weight of a conviction.

With the murder of Paul Scoby, Cosgrove had decided to go slowly with their prosecution, stall for more time to search for the money they pocketed from the fraud scheme. Cosgrove had told Dani that the state police had been tracking down every lead in the murder of Paul Scoby but, so far, had come up empty-handed. The car involved in the shoot-out at Reynolds's house had stolen plates that led back to an elderly woman who rarely took her car out of her garage. And despite knocking on every door near Scoby's home, no witness came forward with any useable information. Still, they hadn't given up on the investigation.

They finished up their sandwiches and headed back to the courtroom. It would be a long afternoon of the prosecution's witnesses, stretching out their testimony to make it seem like they had a case. Smoke and mirrors, Dani thought. Confuse the jurors with enough words that it would become a jumble in their minds, leaving room only for the image of Molly Singer on video, saying, "I killed my parents."

His finger hovered over the doorbell as he wondered whether she would see him, speak to him. If she refused, he'd understand. His mouth felt dry and his stomach did acrobatics.

"Come on, Dad, what are you waiting for?" Sophie asked.

Finn closed his eyes, tried to calm himself, then pressed the button. Within a few moments, Donna opened the door. She stared at Finn, then pasted on a bright smile when she spotted Sophie.

"Hi, sweetie. Molly's in the living room."

Sophie stepped around her father and entered the house. Donna continued to stare silently at Finn.

"I know you didn't expect me, too," he said. "And I get it if Molly doesn't want to see me. But"—he glanced downward, bit his lip, then looked up again—"but I'd really like to see her. Would you ask Molly if I can?"

Donna paused, then nodded. "Wait here."

It seemed like an eternity, but then she was there, standing in the doorway, smiling at him. Her hair had darkened from the light blonde of childhood, but it still shone. She'd changed from the black skirt and flowered blouse he'd seen her wearing on the evening news coverage of her trial. Now she wore jeans that hugged her hips and an emerald cashmere sweater that deepened the green of her eyes.

"Of course I'd like to see you," Molly said. She waved him inside and he followed her into the living room. "Have you met Len, and my niece and nephew?"

Finn nodded. They all lived in the same small community, and he'd run into them many times over the years. At first Donna, believing Molly had killed their parents, had been cordial to him. By the time Donna realized that Molly would never re-establish contact with her, she began to hold Finn responsible for the verdict. After that, they only spoke on the few occasions when he dropped Sophie off to spend time with Donna's family.

"It's good to see you," Molly said as she sat down on the couch and motioned for Finn to sit next to her.

"I wasn't sure how you'd feel, you know, because I testified for the other side at your trial."

"We talked about this a long time ago. You didn't lie on the stand."

"But you didn't know then that I was trying to protect my father."

Molly could see Finn squirming. She knew this conversation had to be difficult for him, especially in front of her whole family. She took his hand in hers. "You thought you were doing the right thing. I'm not angry at you. If anyone, it's my own father I should be angry at." She stopped speaking and the room was silent. She let go of Finn's hand, picked up her glass of water from the cocktail table, and took a sip. After placing the glass back, she looked up and quietly said, "I spent twelve years in prison because my father was a crook. If he hadn't cheated the county, no one would have felt threatened; no one would have killed him. I lost my daughter because of what he did."

Donna came over to Molly, pulled her up from the couch and gathered her into her arms. "He did something terrible, that's true," Donna said. "But he wanted to make it right. He shouldn't have been killed for it. Or Mom either. Be angry at the men who murdered them."

Molly pulled away from her sister, sighed, then sat back down on the couch. "You're right, I guess. It's just—I want those years back. I didn't allow myself to be angry when I was in prison. It made it too hard. Now that I'm away from it, it's all coming to the surface."

"Maybe that's good," Finn said. "Maybe you need to let it out."

Molly smiled. "Well, I just did and I feel better already."

The conversation returned to the idle chatter of families. No one spoke about the ongoing trial. Instead, there was an easy, relaxed rapport among the family members. Even laughter at times. Finn watched Sophie's face as she joined in the conversation, already a part of this family, it seemed to him. She looked happy, something he hadn't seen in a long time. As it approached nine o'clock, he motioned to Sophie that it was time to leave.

"Just a little longer," she begged.

"School tomorrow."

Sophie stood up, gave Molly a hug, and said good-bye to the rest of the family. Molly walked Finn and Sophie to the front door, and when they got there, Finn said to Sophie, "Go sit in the car. I'll be with you in a minute."

When she left, Finn turned to Molly. For a long time he'd wanted to tell her he'd been wrong. Wrong about so many things, but most of all for convincing Molly to give up Sophie. It had hurt both of them. Mothers and daughters shouldn't be separated, he'd realized too late, long after it had been clear that Kim didn't want to be Sophie's mother. "I—" He paused, looked down at the ground, then up at Molly again. "I—" The words wouldn't come. He felt like they were tied up in a knot inside his chest, and he couldn't untangle them.

Molly put her hand on Finn's. "It's okay. I know what you want to say."

Finn mumbled, "You don't."

"You want to say you're sorry."

The knot loosened, his words began to flow. "I should never have asked you to give up Sophie. She's been so unhappy. And I see her now with you, with your family. Her face lights up around you."

Molly continued to hold Finn's hand. She brushed her hair away from her face, and said, "I should never have agreed to it. Mothers shouldn't give up their children. Ever. But"—her voice softened—"we both thought we were doing what was best for Sophie. And we were both mistaken. There's no point in looking backward now. It can't be undone."

Finn nodded. Still, he'd raised Sophie since she was a year old. He'd seen Kim's treatment of her, the subtle rejection after Graham was born. He could have done something about it, and he hadn't. Molly may have forgiven him, but he wasn't ready to forgive himself.

"When the trial is over, if I'm acquitted—" Molly said.

"Oh, you will be, how could the jury not see that."

"If I am, I'd like Sophie to be in my life."

"Of course."

"I'd like to share custody of her."

Finn had never thought about that. Sophie was his child. He'd had sole custody since he stopped bringing her for visits at the prison. He knew, though, that Sophie needed Molly. He nodded slowly. "We'll work something out, when this is over."

They had sat through three days of the prosecution's case. Three days of hammering away at Molly's confession with very little else of substance. The medical examiner testified that the victims had been bludgeoned with a heavy object and then stabbed multiple times with a six- to seven-inch nonserrated knife. Dani got him to admit that, based upon the depths of the contusions from the heavy object, it was more likely wielded by a person weighing more than Molly's 112 pounds, although, he added, "adrenaline can give someone unexpected strength."

The crime-scene investigator testified as to the state of the master bedroom and their search for evidentiary clues. "No fingerprints were found other than the family's," she said. Under Dani's questioning, she admitted that she'd found no forensic evidence that tied Molly to the murders. Unlike Molly's first trial, Dani got in testimony that the shower and sink drains had been tested for blood residue and none was found.

A lesser parade of schoolmates than at the original trial testified about statements Molly had made about her parents but admitted during Dani's cross-examination that they'd made similar statements about their own parents during high school, yet none had murdered them. Given Frank Reynolds's complicity in the county jail scandal, Finn wasn't called by the prosecution this time around.

This morning began the defendant's case. Dani had her witnesses lined up and ready. Her most important witness, Molly, would take the stand last.

With the jurors seated and the judge on the bench, Dani called Josh Cosgrove. He was dressed for the occasion in a navy pinstriped suit and strode to the stand with an air of confidence. Once seated and sworn in, Dani ran through his credentials: a Yale Law School graduate, fifteen years at the US Attorney's Office, the last four as chief of the criminal division.

"Mr. Cosgrove, did there come a time when you learned that one of the victims, Joe Singer, had been involved in criminal activity?"

Eric Murdoch stood up. "The county concedes that Joe Singer had been involved in criminal activity. There's no need for testimony on that subject."

Dani turned to the judge. "Your Honor, the jury has a right to hear the details of that activity and the others involved in it. Since two of those people have pending criminal charges, I'm sure Mr. Murdoch is not conceding their guilt."

Judge Silver nodded, then looked at the witness. "You can answer the question."

The court reporter read it back to Cosgrove and he answered, "Yes."

"Would you describe that activity?"

Cosgrove leaned forward in his seat and turned toward the jury box. "Joe Singer and his partner, Quince Michaels, won the bid to construct the Hudson County jail, back around fourteen years ago. With the acquiescence of Frank Reynolds and Mary Jane Olivetti—they were the ranking Democrat and Republican on the county legislature's appropriations committee—they submitted fraudulent invoices for more than thirty-five million dollars over the actual cost of building the jail."

"And did Mr. Singer and Mr. Michaels pocket that entire sum?"

"No. Together, they received fourteen million dollars over their expected profit for building the jail."

"And how do you know this? Did Mr. Michaels tell you?"

"Michaels died in a suspicious boat accident five months ago. But he'd told his widow about the scam, and she provided bank records from the Caribbean bank where they stashed the money and an agreement which showed that both Singer and Michaels were the owners of that account."

"Did Mrs. Michaels tell you what happened to the rest of the money?"

"She knew others were involved but didn't know who."

"Has the US Attorney's Office arrested anyone else in connection with this fraud against the county?"

"Yes. Two months ago we filed criminal charges against Frank Reynolds. He's since entered into a plea agreement and is serving a one-year sentence in a federal prison."

"Did Mr. Reynolds know who else pocketed the remaining money?"

Murdoch called out, "Objection. Hearsay."

"I'll rephrase. As a result of information you received from Mr. Reynolds, did you indict anyone else for stealing funds related to the building of the county jail?"

"Yes. The grand jury issued indictments for theft and bribery concerning programs receiving federal funds against Judge Alan Bryson and Sheriff John Engles."

"And what is the essential allegation of that indictment?"

"That together with Quince Michaels, Joe Singer, and Paul Scoby, they bribed or blackmailed Hudson County legislators Frank Reynolds and Mary Jane Olivetti in order to defraud Hudson County of more than thirty-five million dollars. They did this by using fraudulent invoices to overbill for the construction of the Hudson County jail."

"Has there been a trial in that case?"

"No. It's still pending."

"Why hasn't Paul Scoby been indicted as well?"

"He was arrested and released on bail. We had arranged to put him into protective custody, but before our men got to him, he was murdered."

"So, let's make sure I've got this straight. Joe Singer was part of a group of men who either were known to have defrauded the county or who were arrested for defrauding the county and whose charges are still pending. Of those men, Joe Singer and Paul Scoby were murdered, and Quince Michaels's death was ruled suspicious. Is that correct?"

Cosgrove turned toward the jury and somberly answered, "That's exactly right."

Dani took a step back. She wanted the jury to take in the testimony they'd just heard. After a moment, she turned back to Cosgrove and said, "Thank you. No further questions." She walked back to her table and sat down. Melanie, sitting next to her, scribbled on a notepad, "Great job. No one could convict Molly now." Dani wished that were true. She had too much experience with juries to believe results were ever predictable.

Murdoch stood up and approached the witness.

"Mr. Cosgrove, did you uncover any evidence that any of the men involved in this scheme murdered, or arranged to have murdered, Mr. and Mrs. Singer?"

"No, not yet. But we're working on that."

"Please confine your answer to the question asked," Murdoch said, his jaw clenched tightly. "Have you arrested anyone in connection with the murder of Paul Scoby?"

"No."

"To your knowledge has any arrest been made in connection with the death of Quince Michaels?"

Cosgrove shook his head, then caught himself and answered, "No."

"Do you have any information which shows that these deaths were related?"

"Not at this time."

"In fact, isn't it true that Paul Scoby's house was burglarized as well?"

"The house appeared to have been ransacked. It's unclear whether anything was taken."

"So, Mr. Scoby's death could have been attributable to a home break-in gone bad, isn't that so?"

"It's possible."

"With respect to Mr. Michaels's boat accident, has the coast guard ruled out the possibility that the gas line was tampered with by Mr. Michaels himself?"

"They ruled it was suspicious."

"I must remind you to answer my questions. Have they ruled out the possibility of deliberate tampering by Michaels as a way to commit suicide?"

"Not that I'm aware of."

"So, let me recap. Mr. and Mrs. Singer were murdered twelve years ago, Mr. Michaels's boat exploded as a result of a gas leak that the coast guard hasn't ruled out as a suicide, and Mr. Scoby was murdered during what could have been a burglary, isn't that correct?"

"Yes, that's correct."

"Thank you. I have no other questions of this witness."

Dani stood up. "Just a few more on redirect," she said. She approached the witness box. "To your knowledge, were any attempts made on Mr. Reynolds's life?"

"Yes, when our agent arrived to take him and his wife into protective custody, an armed man was firing his weapon into their home and attempting to enter it. Our agent thwarted the murder attempt on the Reynoldses."

"And when did this attempt occur?"

"The same day that Paul Scoby was murdered."

"Were FBI agents dispatched on that day to bring Mr. Scoby into protective custody?"

"Yes, but when they arrived, he'd already been murdered."

"Now let me once again recap. Mr. and Mrs. Singer were murdered twelve years ago while the state was investigating improprieties in the cost of building the jail; Mr. Michaels's boat exploded after his wife was told by investigators for the Help Innocent Prisoners Project that he was suspected of stealing money from the county. Mr. Scoby was murdered after he had been arrested for his theft of county monies, and an attempt was made on Mr. Reynolds's life after he confessed to his role in the crime and on the same day Mr. Scoby was murdered. Is that correct?"

"That about sums it up."

"Thank you. You can step down."

Judge Silver looked up at the clock. "I think this is a good time to break for lunch. Let's resume in ninety minutes."

Dani knew she was a worrier. Over lunch, Melanie and Tommy were confident that she'd scored a bull's-eye with Cosgrove. Molly sat quietly, clearly unsure what to think. Dani couldn't shake the fear that it wouldn't matter to the jury that Joe Singer had been caught up in something despicable. Unless Dani could tie one of the participants in that scheme to the Singers' murder, the jurors would fall back on Molly's confession.

When the court was called into session, Dani called Finn Reynolds to the stand. Finn entered the courtroom hesitantly, but upon seeing Molly, smiled at her, then quickly took his seat.

"Mr. Reynolds, please describe your relationship with Molly at the time of the murders of her parents."

"She was my girlfriend."

"And are you the father of her child?"

Finn nodded.

"Please speak your answers for the court reporter."

"Yes, I am."

"Did you testify for the prosecution at Molly's first trial?"

Finn nodded again, then caught himself. "I did."

"What did you say at that trial?"

Finn described his earlier testimony.

"Now, most boyfriends wouldn't have offered that information to the man trying to lock up his pregnant girlfriend. Were you angry at Molly?"

"No."

"Did you believe she murdered her parents?"

"No."

"Then please tell the jury why you testified against her."

"I wanted to protect my father, Frank Reynolds."

"And why did you think your father needed protection?"

"Because I'd picked up the phone a few weeks before the Singers were murdered and overheard Judge Bryson tell him he had to convince Joe Singer to keep quiet or someone would shut him up. He said otherwise Joe would ruin things for everyone, including my father. I knew my father was involved in something bad."

"Thank you. No further questions."

Murdoch stood up at his table and asked just one question: "On this phone call, did anyone say that Joe Singer would be killed if he didn't stay quiet?"

"Not in so many words."

"That's all. You can step down now."

Dani had managed to track down several of Molly's closest high school friends, and they counteracted the testimony of other classmates that Molly hated her parents. One by one, Dani paraded them up to the witness stand. One by one they testified that they had all complained about their parents from time to time, Molly no more than the others. One by one they spoke about it having been obvious that Molly loved her parents. Murdoch merely rolled his eyes and tapped his fingertips on the table throughout this testimony, never choosing to cross-examine any of them.

When the last classmate had been called, it was past five o'clock, and the judge recessed for the day. Tomorrow Dani would call Derek Deegan to the stand, her expert on false confessions, and then finish with Molly. She would return to the courtroom prepared for battle but had a worried feeling that she was armed with confetti instead of bullets.

CHAPTER 50

The first witness that morning had been the psychiatrist who'd examined Molly after the murders. He testified that Molly exhibited no homicidal thoughts or sociopathic tendencies. Murdoch did little to counteract his findings. The rest of the morning had been spent eliciting testimony from Derek Deegan. He expanded on his testimony from Molly's first 440 hearing, describing numerous instances of homicide convictions based on confessions that were subsequently overturned when DNA evidence proved the defendant was innocent. He then explained to the jury the techniques used with Molly that could have led to her false confession. Murdoch scored a few points on his cross-examination when he got Deegan to admit that the techniques used with Molly more often led to an accurate confession. Now Dani would close her case with Molly.

"I call Molly Singer to the stand." Molly stood up from the defense table and slowly made her way to the witness box. She wore a cream-colored skirt with a sapphire-blue blouse. "No black," Dani had warned her. "I don't want you to look like you're in mourning."

After Molly was sworn in, Dani started with the question upper-most in the jurors' thoughts. "Did you murder your parents twelve years ago?"

Molly turned to the jury box and, with her voice steady and firm, answered, "I did not."

"But you told the police you did, isn't that right?"

"During hours and hours of questioning, I repeatedly said I hadn't. That I didn't know anyone who'd hurt my parents, but I certainly wouldn't have."

"If you didn't murder them, why did you sign a confession that you had?"

"You have to understand. I was seventeen years old. I'd just found my parents dead in their beds. I'd been taken in for questioning and was all alone. Over and over the detectives told me I was responsible, that I didn't remember because of the Ambien I'd taken. They called it a blackout. One of them—the nice one—kept telling me it was the fault of the drug. That I wouldn't have done it if I wasn't blacked out. He said I would feel better if I admitted it. If I didn't confess, I would carry the guilt with me forever. If I did confess, the jury would under-stand and go lightly on me."

"When you confessed, did you believe you had murdered your parents?"

"I was so confused. They said they found the murder weapons, and my fingerprints were on them. They told me they found a spot of my parents' blood on my pajamas. I began to believe they were right. That I'd killed them during a blackout."

"Is that why you signed the confession?"

"Yes."

"If you didn't kill your parents, how were you able to put the details of the murder in your confession?"

"Detective Baxter told me what to write. And before he turned the video camera on, he told me what to say."

"If you believed you'd murdered your parents, why did you recant later?"

"After they brought me to a cell and left me alone, I kept thinking about it. I couldn't come up with any reason why I would murder them. I loved them both. The more I thought about it, the more I became convinced that it wasn't me, no matter what evidence they had. So the next time a guard came around, I told her I wanted to take back the confession."

"Did she let you?"

"No. It was only after my sister got a lawyer for me that I was able to officially recant."

"Molly, you've heard testimony in court that your father was involved in a scheme to defraud the county. Did you know anything about that before the murders?"

"No. I remember my father being more irritable than usual, but I didn't know why."

"Were you aware that the state was investigating the cost overruns of the new county jail?"

"Only vaguely. I know the newspapers carried stories about it, but I only read the paper when I had to for a class. Sometimes my mother would bring it up at the dinner table, but my father would always shush her."

"Did you ever overhear any conversations about it?"

"Never directly, but I do remember my father and Quince arguing in my father's study more than once in the weeks before he died."

"And this was unusual with them?"

"I'd never heard them that angry with each other before."

"Thank you, Molly. I have no more questions."

As Dani walked to the defense table, Murdoch stood up, then strode confidently to the witness box.

"Ms. Singer, you said you were all alone during your questioning. But you had been told you had a right to an attorney, isn't that true?"

"Yes, but—"

"So, you could have had someone with you, correct?"

"I suppose, but—"

"And during your questioning—"

Dani stood up. "Objection, Your Honor. Mr. Murdoch is not allowing the witness to finish her answers."

"The witness has answered the questions I've asked her," Murdoch said. "I'm not allowing her to go on and answer questions I haven't asked."

"Objection sustained. Mr. Murdoch, repeat your questions and allow Ms. Singer to complete her answers."

Murdoch sighed, then turned to the jury and rolled his eyes. "Ms. Singer, you could have had an attorney with you, isn't that true?"

"I was seventeen years old and frightened. I didn't think I'd done anything wrong and thought I was there to help the police find who murdered my parents. After they pounded at me for hours, I was too confused to even remember that I could ask for an attorney."

"Did the officers ever tell you that you couldn't leave the room until you confessed?"

"No."

"Did they ever tell you that you had to put in your written confession the details they gave you?"

"No."

"Did they physically abuse you in any way?"

"No."

"So, let's be clear now. You confessed voluntarily, without any abuse by the officers."

"I confessed voluntarily because they'd lied to me and convinced me of something that wasn't true."

"So you say now."

"Objection."

"Sustained."

"Now, you've testified that you tried to recant after you were brought to your cell, but weren't allowed to. What's the name of the guard you spoke to?"

"I don't know."

"So we only have your word that you tried to recant your confession to a guard."

"But—"

"I haven't asked my question yet, Ms. Singer. When you met with your attorney, didn't he tell you to recant the confession?"

"He told me to recant it because I said I was innocent."

"But your attorney did tell you to recant, right?"

"Yes."

"Let's go back to the night of the murders. When you came home, your parents were asleep, correct?"

"Yes."

"So you were the last person to enter the house."

"Yes."

"Did you lock the doors behind you?"

"I think so."

"You normally lock the doors when you're last in the house, don't you?"

"Yes."

"Were any windows left open?"

"No. My mother was allergic to trees and grass. We always kept the windows closed."

"Did your parents keep a key outside the house in case someone was locked out?"

"Yes."

"Where was the key kept?"

"Under an antique milk can on the back porch."

"So, it wasn't by the front door, right?"

"Yes. But there was a door to the house on the back porch."

"Did you ever tell anyone where the spare key was kept?"

"No."

"To the best of your knowledge, did your parents ever tell someone where the key was kept?"

"No."

"So, the doors were locked, you were the only other person in the house, and no windows were open, is that right?"

Molly looked down at her hands and answered softly, "Yes."

"Thank you. I have no further questions."

"You can step down," Judge Silver said. "Any other witnesses?"

"No, Your Honor," Dani answered.

"Then let's end here. We'll have closing statements tomorrow."

Dani stood before the jury box. "Ladies and gentlemen. A week ago, at the beginning of this trial, I told you this was a very simple case. And that it was simple because the prosecution had no evidence which proved Molly Singer murdered her parents. They had no murder weapons with Ms. Singer's fingerprints. They had no blood from the crime scene on any of her clothing or shoes. They had no one who witnessed the crime.

"They had no answers, and so they latched onto a frightened seventeen-year-old girl who had just witnessed a horrific sight—her parents, brutally murdered. And then what did they do? They convinced this girl—barely out of childhood—that she was the one who'd killed them. Why did they do this? Because a detective thought she was too calm when he saw her at the house.

"We know so much about post-traumatic stress disorder now. We know that people can react to extreme stress by going into a state of unnatural calm. Instead of realizing that Molly was a traumatized teenager, they isolated her from everyone and systematically created a new reality—their own. Hour after hour they wore her down to the point where she began to believe the lies they told her. Until finally, she substituted their lies for her own truth and confessed to a crime she hadn't committed.

"By rushing to judgment, the police failed to investigate others who might have had a motive to murder the Singers. We now know that Joe Singer was part of a group of men who swindled Hudson County out of more than thirty-five million dollars. Finn Reynolds testified that he overheard Judge Bryson say someone would shut him up if Finn's father couldn't keep him from talking. Molly told you that Joe's partner, Quince Michaels, argued angrily with him within days of his death. Were they arguing about the jail fraud? We don't know for sure because the police never investigated them. Could one of those men have killed Joe and Sarah Singer? Maybe. We do know that three of those men are now dead. Thirty-five million dollars is a powerful motive to kill.

"Remember, it is the prosecution's job to prove Molly Singer's guilt beyond a reasonable doubt. I've told you what evidence they didn't have. Let's look at what they do have.

"There was no evidence of a break-in, and Molly was the only other person in the house. That's true. But Molly told you the family kept an emergency key outside the house, just like I'm sure many of you do. How long would it take for someone to check nearby each of the doors to the house and find that key? Not very long.

"The only other evidence the prosecution has is Molly's confession. Molly told you why she confessed. Not because she remembered killing her parents but because the police convinced her she did it during a blackout caused by Ambien. As soon as she was away from their influence, she realized she never would have murdered the parents she loved. Derek Deegan told you that what happened with Molly was not uncommon. Under almost the exact same circumstances, there are many cases of people falsely confessing to crimes they didn't commit.

"Ladies and gentlemen of the jury, when you examine all the evidence, the only conclusion that can be reached is that the prosecution has utterly failed to meet its burden. Not only is there reasonable doubt, there is considerable doubt that Molly Singer murdered her parents. Thank you."

As Dani sat down, Eric Murdoch stood and strode over to the jurors. "Ladies and gentlemen of the jury. My esteemed colleague believes that if she throws enough red herrings at you, she can confuse you enough to return a not-guilty verdict. I have more faith in your intelligence.

"There are two basic facts that are irrefutable. The defendant was alone in the house with her parents, and there was no apparent break-in. Ms. Trumball wants you to believe that an intruder skulked around the property in search of a key, politely entered through the front door, murdered the Singers, took nothing from the home, then just as politely returned the key to its hiding place. She doesn't explain, though, why no trace of fingerprints, other than family members, was found on the key.

"The second irrefutable fact is that the defendant confessed to the crime. You saw her videotaped confession. There were no marks on her, no one pointing at gun at her head. You even heard her say that she freely and voluntarily gave that confession. Ms. Trumball wants you to believe that she was tricked into believing she was guilty. Tell me, would any of you ever confess to a crime this heinous, not only murder, but murder of your parents, if you hadn't done it? Of course not. The defense offers as proof that she didn't mean it by pointing to her retraction a day later, after she'd met with her attorney and no doubt been told what trouble she was in as a result of her confession. Folks, I've lost count of the number of criminals who've tried to take back a confession when they realize how much jail time they're facing. It occurs a thousand times more often than the rare false confession.

"No one else was in the house. Molly Singer confessed. You don't need more than that to bring back a verdict of guilty. Thank you."

Three full days had passed since the jury began their deliberations. Three nail-biting days spent in the Andersonville Holiday Inn. Dani and her team couldn't return to the office—it was too far away to get back to court when the call came in that a verdict was reached.

"What's taking them so long?" Melanie asked as they waited to order lunch in their now-favorite luncheon shop in Andersonville. "It should have been a slam dunk for them."

Dani knew that nothing short of absolute proof that someone else committed the murders was a slam dunk. And it shouldn't take this long for the verdict to be returned. The delay could only mean bad news for Molly. She'd been on the phone with her an hour the night before, trying to calm her nerves despite Dani's own concern about the verdict. This was the part of her job she hated most—waiting for a decision, waiting for a verdict when she'd done all she could and it was out of her hands. It felt like tumbling endlessly down an abyss, those waits. An empty hole waiting to be filled with cheers or sobs. She always shared the joy or sorrow with her clients, celebrated or commiserated. But when the news was bad, and the tears had dried up, she went home to her family. Her clients went back to prison or, worse, to their execution.

Just as the waitress came over to take their order, Dani's phone buzzed. She quickly answered it.

"Ms. Trumball, Judge Silver would like the attorneys and the defendant to come over to the court as soon as you can."

"We'll be right over," she answered, then hung up. "That was the court. They want us back there."

"The verdict's in?" Melanie asked.

"Didn't say. Just told me to come in with our client." Dani turned to Tommy. "Would you go pick Molly up at her sister's?"

"Sure. I'll meet you over there."

Dani apologized to the waitress, then grabbed a muffin on the way out. She and Melanie walked the two blocks to the courthouse, went through security, then walked up the two flights to the courtroom. Eric Murdoch was already inside.

"Is there a verdict?" Dani asked him.

"Don't know. I was just told to come in. The court officer said to let him know when everyone's here."

Dani and Melanie sat down in front, at the defense table, and waited for Tommy to arrive with Molly. Twenty minutes later they walked in the door. Murdoch nodded at them, then stood up and walked to the door leading to the judge's chambers. He knocked twice and a moment later the judge's law clerk opened the door.

"Everyone here?" he asked.

"All accounted for," Murdoch answered. "Is there a verdict?"

"The judge will be out in a moment." The law clerk took his seat, and a minute later, Judge Silver entered the courtroom. The parties started to rise but he waved them back down.

"Counsel, it appears we have a hung jury."

Dani gasped. This was one outcome she hadn't imagined.

"I've urged them to keep deliberating, but I'm told they're intransigent. I'm going to declare a mistrial."

Murdoch stood up. "May I poll the jury?"

The judge nodded. "My court officer is bringing them in now."

The door to the back hallway opened, and twelve bleary-eyed jurors marched into the seats in the jury box.

"Ladies and gentlemen of the jury," the judge said, "I'll ask you one more time, do you think if you continue to deliberate you can reach a consensus?"

The forewoman of the jury answered, "No, Your Honor. I don't believe our opinions will change."

"Then, before I dismiss you, I'm going to ask each of you what your vote is. Juror number one?"

"Guilty."

"Juror number two?"

"Guilty."

"Juror number three?"

"Guilty."

With each guilty vote, both Dani and Molly sank deeper into their seats, barely able to breathe.

"Juror number four?"

"Guilty."

"Juror number five?"

"Innocent."

So it wasn't a complete wipeout. When the polling was finished, seven jurors had voted to convict, only five to acquit. The judge thanked the jurors for their service, and they were escorted back to the deliberation room to gather their belongings. Once they had left the courtroom, Murdoch stood up.

"Your Honor, the county requests bail be continued for Ms. Singer."

"Are you going to reprosecute?"

"We'd like time to evaluate our case and make a decision, but it's likely we'll go ahead with another trial."

"All right, I give you two more weeks to file charges again. Bail continued." With that, the judge banged his gavel and exited the courtroom, leaving Dani, Melanie, and Molly stunned by the news.

Two weeks to the day after the hung jury, Hudson County refiled charges against Molly Singer for the murder of her parents. Dani had warned Molly they weren't likely to let it go. Now, a week later, Dani was back in her office scrutinizing the trial transcript, trying to figure out what she'd done wrong, what she could do better.

"You didn't do anything wrong," Tommy had told her earlier that morning. "You've said it a zillion times. Juries are unpredictable."

It didn't matter what she'd said—it had been her failure, so she would spend every minute going over and over the transcript, knowing cold what Murdoch would do and say the next time around, trying to come up with something to throw him off. Her head was buried deep in the transcript when her phone buzzed.

"Yes?"

"There's someone out here to see you. Her name is Janine Manning."

"I'm not expecting anyone. Can you palm her off on someone else? I'm tied up here."

"She says it has to be you."

The last thing she needed was a distraction. Molly's new trial would begin in only three weeks. Still, she hated to turn someone away when thirty minutes of her time, maybe less, could help provide hope to a person who had none. She sighed deeply, then said, "Send her down."

A minute later a slim woman with brown, close-cropped hair and large round dangling earrings stepped into her office. "Ms. Trumball?"

Dani smiled and motioned her to come in. "Take a seat, Ms. Manning. How can I help you?"

"My brother sent me. He's at Napanoch."

Dani knew she meant the Eastern New York Correctional Facility, a maximum-security prison located in Napanoch, New York. "Does he claim that he's innocent?"

"No. He did it. Got caught red-handed."

Dani looked at her quizzically. "Then why are you here?"

"I wish I wasn't. Zeke, that's my brother—my twin, actually—Zeke Williams is his full name—he made me promise I'd come. I tried talking him out of it; I'm afraid for him, you see. But I made a promise, so I'm here."

Dani looked at this woman, so clearly conflicted about being in this office. She wanted to take the time to comfort her, ease her into her story, but looming in the back of her mind was Molly's next trial. "What does your brother want to tell me?"

"It's about Molly Singer."

Dani shot up straight in her chair. Now this woman could have all the time she needed.

"He's the one who sent Donna those anonymous letters. Well, it was me, actually. But he told me what to write, and I put it down on paper and mailed it. You see, we both went to school with Donna. She was always nice to us, to Zeke especially."

"What does Zeke know about the murders?"

"First, you got to tell me you can protect him."

Dani sat back and looked closely at the woman. Her hands were folded tightly in her lap, her mouth set in a taut grimace, her body stiff. *She's scared.*

"Yes," Dani reassured her. "If he knows something about the murders, if he's willing to testify about it, then we can get him protection."

Janine nodded slowly, took a deep breath, then said, "He knows the people who killed them."

Dani could barely breathe. Somehow, she managed to ask, "How does he know this?"

"Because he was one of them. And Sheriff Engles was the other."

Two days later, Dani drove to Napanoch with Cosgrove. He had arranged with the warden for Zeke Williams to be brought to his office for an interview. If his story held up, he'd be moved to a federal prison. Neither Josh nor Dani wanted to take any chance that Engles's tentacles reached the guards at Napanoch. "Unfortunate accidents" happened all too often in prisons.

When they arrived, they showed their IDs and informed the guard at the desk that they were there to see Warden Jackson. Five minutes later they were escorted to his office. Zeke Williams was waiting for them.

"Feel free to use my desk," Warden Jackson said. "I've got a guard posted outside, one I trust completely. I've work to do elsewhere."

They thanked him and he left the room. Zeke sat in a chair with his arms and legs shackled. He was dressed in regulation prison garb that hung loosely on his thin body. His muddy-brown hair hung below his ears, and heavily smudged wire-framed glasses obscured his eyes. Although Dani knew he was Donna Garmond's age, he looked ten years older.

"Okay, let's get started," Cosgrove said when he and Dani were seated. "Tell us what you know about the Singers' deaths."

"I know everything about it. I was there."

"By yourself?"

"John Engles was with me. Or, actually, I was with him. It was his job. He needed an extra man."

"Do you know why he murdered the Singers?"

"To keep Mr. Singer from talking. About the jail money."

"How do you know this?"

"'Cause John told me."

"What exactly did he tell you?"

Williams squirmed in his seat. His forehead was suddenly shiny with sweat. "Will I be protected? John has friends all over the prison system. Both guards and prisoners. Hell, half the prisoners have done jobs for him."

"If your story bears out, we'll move you to a federal prison. He won't be able to touch you there. So, what did he tell you?"

Williams looked around the room, then turned back to Dani and Cosgrove. Quietly he said, "John had been approached by some people about getting union support behind a new jail. If he came through, he stood to make millions of dollars. When the state began looking into how much it'd cost, Joe Singer got nervous. He was thinking of admitting that he'd padded the bills. John said he had to be shut up—permanently."

"Why you?" Dani asked. "Why did he take you with him?"

"I've known John most of my life. I got messed up with drugs in high school, couldn't shake the habit. Before I turned around, four years had gone by, and it was costing me a grand a week. Only choice was to sell—small amounts, you know, to friends. The first time I got nabbed, I gave up my supplier and they dropped it down. Second time, that wasn't going to fly. Under the Rockefeller drug laws, they would've put me away for life. Man, I was messed up.

"So, John comes to me. He says he can make the evidence disappear. I only have to do a small favor for him."

"Help him kill Joe Singer?"

Williams nodded. "I'd never hurt anyone in my life. But I had no choice, right? It was that or the can for good." He sighed deeply. "I should have taken the can. It busts me up what I did to those folks."

"Describe that night," Cosgrove said. "Everything you did and everything Engles did."

Williams took a deep breath and stared at the corner of the room for moment, then began talking. "We got there around two a.m. Everything was dark and closed up tight. I was ready to break a window but John said no, look for a key first. I found one by the back door. We both had gloves on, you know, for fingerprints. John brought a knife and we both had baseball bats. Everything was dark inside. We made our way up the stairs. John had a flashlight. One door was closed upstairs, two were wide open, and no one was inside, and one was a bit open. John motioned for me to check the room with the closed door. I opened it quietly and saw Molly, asleep in her bed, then closed the door again behind me. John nudged open the door to the Singers' room and swung the flashlight over the bed. There they were, sound asleep. John went over to Mr. Singer's side and bashed his head with the bat, then knifed him four times."

Cosgrove interrupted. "Where did he knife him?"

"The first was in the neck then three more in the chest."

"Go on."

"Poor bastard never even woke up. But the noise woke the missus. I stood over her, just in case. I didn't want to be the one to kill her. So, she opens her eyes and sees me standing there and tries to get out of the bed. Before she even had a chance to scream, I knocked her out with the bat, then John came around and finished her off with the knife. Man, I was so scared, I thought I was gonna pee my pants."

"How many times did he stab her?"

"Same as before. First in the neck, then three times in the chest."

"What happened next?"

"Well, John wanted me to check on Molly again. I opened her door, and she was in the exact same position as before, still asleep. You gotta understand, John never expected Molly to get fingered for the murders. But he was happy when she did. Took the heat off of us. Poor kid. It's always eaten away at me, especially her being pregnant and all."

"What happened to the knife and bats?"

"John brought a pillowcase with him. He stuffed them in the bag, our gloves, too. They had blood all over them. John brought a clean pair with him. We left by the back door, locked it up, and returned the key. We drove over to McAdams Park and gathered some rocks to put in the bag. The Hudson was just below the park, but it was a steep incline down to it, so John gave me the bag, told me to dump it in the river while he stayed on top of the bluff and watched."

"Why now?" Dani asked.

Zeke looked at her blankly.

"Why are you telling us this now? Molly's first trial was twelve years ago."

"See, I wasn't locked up then. And my habit was real bad. But a year ago, I started breaking into houses, take some stuff to fence. I needed money for the dope. It was going good, then one job, this lady walks in on me. She starts screaming, and I swear, I just wanted to quiet her down. I grabbed her head and put my hand over her mouth. That crazy lady bit my hand. I just reacted—I didn't think. I twisted her head, and she dropped to the floor and didn't move. I'd broken her neck. Never meant to. I never meant to hurt anyone. But they caught up with me, and here I am.

"It's hard in here. And I got to thinking again about Donna's sister doing time for something me and John did. I wanted to help, but, man, you know, John scares the shit out of me. Still, it didn't sit right with me that Molly was in prison, especially since I'm in for murder anyway now."

"So you sent the anonymous letters to Donna."

"Yeah. I thought it would get things going. And I guess it did. I followed the case in the papers. I thought for sure Molly would get off with a new trial. What a bunch of a-holes, those jurors. Pardon the expression, but they sure are."

"I believe you were there that night," Cosgrove said. "You know some details that were in the file but not released to the media. But why should I believe that Engles was with you?"

Williams broke out in a grin. "'Cause I never trusted that he wouldn't try to pin the whole rap on me. So, when I got down to the river with that pillowcase, I slipped one of his gloves out of the bag and into my jacket pocket. It was too dark, and I was too far away for John to catch me doing it. I bet you can get his fingerprints off it. And blood from the bodies." Suddenly, his face paled. "It'll still be good after all this time, won't it?"

"We'll see."

"You know, Engles still has others doing his dirty work. I read about Paul Scoby in the paper. I'd bet I know who he used to take him out."

"Who's that?"

Zeke grinned slyly. "Well, see, I figure I owed it to Donna to own up about Molly's parents. But this here's separate information. What can I get for it?"

Cosgrove sat back in his seat and eyed Zeke. He picked up his pencil and twirled it in his fingers, watching as Zeke fidgeted in his chair.

"Come on, man. It's got to be worth something."

"Here's the problem, Zeke. You're serving time on state charges. The murder of Molly's parents is also a state crime. I'm not sure how I can help you out."

"But the feds are interested in who killed Scoby. Aren't they? Can't you talk to the DA?"

"I suppose I can, but I can't promise you anything. If the information you give me pans out, the best I can do is ask the DA to take that into consideration in offering you a deal on the murders of the Singers. Press him for the sentence to run concurrent with what you're already doing."

"Do you think he'll go for that?"

"Probably. And we'll see that you do your time in a federal prison."

Zeke let out a breath. "Okay, then. Talk inside is that Danny Childs is doing work for Engles now."

"Who is he?"

"Danny? He runs the drugs in Andersonville. Engles keeps his crew out of jail, and Danny does jobs for him."

As Cosgrove pumped Zeke for more information about Childs, Dani tried hard to contain her excitement. Whether Cosgrove could prove Engles had been involved in the deaths or not, she now had proof of Molly's innocence—the confession of one of the murderers.

53

It took Cosgrove only a week to put together a sting against Danny Childs. "Child's play," he'd told Dani, then laughed at the inadvertent play on the target's name. "Nothing like the drug traffickers in New York City." After his arrest, Cosgrove sat down across the table from him and laid out Childs's options.

"We have you stone cold, Childs. And your friend Engles can't get you out of this one. In fact, with what I have, I should put you away for a good long time. That is, if I don't decide to go for the death penalty."

Childs, a thirty-two-year-old man bulked up by hours in the gym, glared at him. "What're we talking for, then? You're fishing."

"See, that's where you're wrong. The way your friend Engles served you up, you'd think he was law enforcement or something." Cosgrove grinned. "Said you came to him and offered to take care of Paul Scoby. Said he told you not to, was putting together surveillance to keep an eye on you, but you went ahead anyway. Said he's been building a case against you." Engles hadn't said anything of the kind to Cosgrove— they hadn't even talked since his arraignment months earlier—but he could tell by the murderous gleam in Childs's eye that he believed it.

"He's lying."

"Maybe. Maybe not. But see, who do you think the jury will believe? A loser drug dealer or the sheriff of Hudson County?"

"I ain't copping to no murder."

"See, I don't believe Engles. I think he called the shots and you did his bidding."

Childs sat still in his seat, silent.

"Of course, if you don't want to give me your side of the story, I'll go with Engles. Then it'll be you facing the needle instead of him."

After a few more moments of Childs's silence, Cosgrove stood up. "Okay, have it your way." He turned to the FBI agent in the room and said, "Book him for the murder of Paul Scoby," then started to walk toward the door.

"Wait."

Cosgrove turned back to him.

"What'll you do for me if I tell you how it went down?"

"Now you're thinking, Childs. Tell me what happened, and I'll take death off the table."

"No, man, I need more than that."

"Sorry, that's the best I'm offering."

Child's wrung his hands together, then wiped his greasy hair back from his forehead. "It was his idea. He called in some chits. I just followed his directions."

"You've got to give me proof."

And so Danny Childs laid out for the assistant US attorney every phone call, every meeting, every favor between him and Engles. It was more than enough for Cosgrove.

Dani watched through the one-way glass as Cosgrove questioned Sheriff John Engles. Engles's lawyer, Malcolm Jenner, sat by his side.

"As I told your lawyer," Cosgrove said, "we now have proof that you were responsible for the deaths of Joe and Sarah Singer as well as Paul Scoby."

"Yeah, he told me. A guy doing time for murder and a low-life drug dealer. Why would you believe them? Why would any juror believe them?"

Cosgrove looked up toward the mirrored wall, straight at where Dani stood on the other side, and smiled. Dani knew he hadn't told Jenner everything he had. He'd told her that he wanted to experience the pleasure of watching Engles's face when he realized he had no way out. He turned back to Engles and said, "You shouldn't have trusted Zeke Williams to throw away all the evidence of the Singer murders."

He let that sit there. Engles didn't respond, but his counsel did, shooting an agitated glance his client's way and then back down at the table.

"He kept the glove you wore that night," Cosgrove went on at last. "And it still has your fingerprints on it, along with blood matched to both of the Singers."

There it was: Engles's face drained of all color.

"You're bluffing," he said, his voice husky.

"Nope. It's all in here." Cosgrove pulled out a paper from his folder and handed it to Jenner. On it were the results from the forensic lab that had examined and tested the glove.

"What's it say?" Engles asked his lawyer, his voice barely above a whisper now.

Jenner stared at it, then said, "I'd like some time alone with my client."

"Sure. Take as much as you need. Just knock when you're ready." Cosgrove left the room, turning off the sound as he exited, and joined Dani, beaming.

"So, what do you think?"

"Engles looks like he's going to have a heart attack," Dani said. "He'll talk. And I bet he'll give us the judge."

After only five minutes, they watched Jenner stand and stick his head into the hall.

Cosgrove grinned at Dani. "Sometimes I love my job," he said, then left her alone in the observation room and rejoined the men on the other side of the one-way glass.

"What are you offering?" Jenner asked after Cosgrove had taken his seat.

"Since you killed Scoby to keep him from testifying against you in a federal trial, we can and will seek the death penalty, and we'll get it. I want a full recitation of facts, including everyone implicated, and I'll take death off the table."

"The glove doesn't tie him to Scoby's murder."

"True. But I don't think I'll have any trouble convincing a jury that there's a pattern here. First with Zeke, then with Childs."

Jenner turned to Engles and whispered something in his ear. Engles nodded, then Jenner turned back to Cosgrove. "Just taking death off the table isn't good enough. My client can hand you Judge Bryson. Without his testimony, Bryson will walk."

"What are you looking for?"

"Fifteen to twenty."

"Not a chance. I'll go ahead with just your client. I have enough to bury him."

Now Engles whispered in his lawyer's ear. Jenner whispered something back, and Cosgrove offered to leave the room once again so they could talk freely.

"No, it's okay. Apparently my client is unhappy about the judge getting off. Give us twenty to life in a minimum security federal prison, and he'll tell you what you need to know."

"Twenty-five to life, medium security, final offer."

Engles nodded.

"Go ahead," Cosgrove said.

Engles took a handkerchief from his pocket and mopped his brow with it. He cleared his throat, then began to talk. "Bryson planned it all, from the very beginning. He and Quince knew each other, played cards together or something. Quince told him his business was going to put in a bid for the county jail project, and Bryson said, 'What if I can promise you'll get it?' It all developed from there. Bryson brought on board Scoby and me. We each had something he needed."

"And Singer was part of it?"

"Yeah. A reluctant part. But he and Quince were like brothers, and Quince convinced him to go ahead with it."

"Why were the Singers killed?"

"'Cause Joe got nervous when the state started poking around. He thought it'd go easier on everyone if we confessed, instead of waiting for the state to figure it out."

"Did Bryson order him killed?"

Engles stared down at the table. After a few moments, his lawyer told him he needed to answer the question. "Not in so many words. But he told all of us he had to be kept quiet. I figured that was the only way to do it. Besides, the others—they all had money, from their businesses, from being a judge. I'd given my whole life to public service and had squat. I deserved that money, and no way was I giving it back."

"Why Sarah Singer?"

"She woke up. I couldn't let her ID me."

"What about Quince Michaels?"

"Childs arranged for a contact in Miami to jimmy with the boat's gas tank."

"And that was you, again, protecting your interests?"

"No. Bryson found out from Quince that the HIPP investigator knew about him stealing money from the county. He was afraid Quince would strike a deal for himself and implicate us. He told me to kill him."

"And Scoby?"

"That was Bryson also. I had Childs handle it, but it was Bryson who ordered it."

As Dani listened to Engles's confession, she wished Cosgrove would ask him about her and Mary Jane Olivetti's "accidents," although she really knew the answer. The black SUV she'd seen through her rear window was undoubtedly the same that had carried Frank Reynolds's would-be assassins to Reynolds's house. Hearing Engles admit that he'd arranged for the "accidents" wouldn't change anything for him or Bryson. Even without it, both would go away for a very long time.

Dani's stomach churned. Five people dead, solely because of greed. Not poverty, not drug addiction, not inflamed passions. Just greed. And because of that greed, a young woman had lost her parents, her daughter, and twelve years of her life.

As soon as Engles was placed under arrest and led away to a federal holding cell, Cosgrove dictated an affidavit to his secretary. When it was typed, he headed over to Foley Square, the site of the US District Court for the Southern District of New York, found Justice Marvin Wolfe in his chambers, and had an arrest warrant signed. From there, he walked it over to Federal Plaza, the New York field office of the FBI.

Warrant in hand, the FBI dispatched a field agent to head immediately to Judge Bryson's courtroom up in Andersonville. He was on the bench when they walked in, but that didn't stop the agents. The two men politely informed the attorneys arguing their cases that court was now closed.

"Who do you think you are?" Bryson began to bluster from the bench before the agents whipped out their badges. He immediately announced that everyone should clear the courtroom.

When it was empty, he smiled genially toward the men and asked, "How can I help you?"

"Sir, we have a warrant for your arrest in the murder of Paul Scoby. You have the right—"

"Enough. Don't you think I know my rights?"

"Sorry, sir, but we have to state it in full," one said and then went through the standard litany.

"This is insane. Someone's head is going to roll for this."

"Step down from the bench, please, and place your hands behind your back."

Bryson was marched from the courthouse, hands in cuffs, past the attorneys, defendants, and spectators who had just been evicted from his courtroom. He was placed in the back of the FBI vehicle and driven down to Cosgrove's office. On the way, and with Cosgrove's approval, he was allowed to call a defense attorney to meet him there. Peter Spencer arrived ten minutes before his client and was ushered into an interrogation room.

When Cosgrove entered, Spencer immediately jumped up. "This is a complete outrage. Judge Bryson is one of the most respected jurists in the state. It's preposterous to think that he'd be involved in a murder."

"Sit down, counselor. Why don't you take a look at what we have before you start grandstanding?"

Both men sat down, and Cosgrove pushed a folder across the table. Spencer opened it up and began reading. When he was finished, he said, "We'll fight this. You have no hard evidence to tie him to the crime, just the word of one man fighting to save his own skin. You have plenty on Engles, but the only thing tying my client to any of this is his word. And I promise you, I'll demolish him on the stand."

"We have one other thing. Engles told us where his and Bryson's bank accounts are. We're already working on getting access to them. Seven million dollars is going to be hard for him to explain away. With the bank account, we have him solid on the fraud scheme, and it won't be a giant leap for the jury to believe that he engineered the hit. Especially with Frank Reynolds testifying that the judge ran Hudson County. When he said jump, everyone jumped."

Just then, there was a knock on the door. "Come on in," Cosgrove said. The door opened and the two agents escorted Alan Bryson into the room.

"You can take the cuffs off now," Cosgrove said. "I suspect Mr. Spencer wants some time alone with his client."

Spencer nodded and Cosgrove stood up. On his way out the door, he said, "I'm in a generous mood today. It's your best chance for making a deal. After today, I go for the death penalty."

As he left the room, he saw a shriveled-up man, his skin a ghostly white, sunk into his chair. One hour later, a deal was in place. Twenty-five years to life in a federal prison.

CHAPTER

55

Molly's family were all gathered in Judge Silver's courtroom—her daughter, her sister, her niece and nephew, and her brother-in-law. Dani was there with Tommy and Melanie. An air of excitement filled the room and spilled over to the guards and court officers. All were smiling and relaxed.

It had been two weeks since Engles and Bryson had confessed. That had been a wonderful day. Dani had left Engles's interrogation and sped up to Donna's home in Andersonville. She hadn't yet told Molly about Zeke Williams or Danny Childs. Although she'd wanted to rush up there right after Williams confessed, Cosgrove convinced her to wait. "A small town grapevine can go viral. I don't want any information getting back to Engles before we have it all tied up."

"What's happened?" Molly asked after she'd opened the front door and seen Dani standing there, a wide grin on her face.

"Sheriff Engles confessed to murdering your parents."

Molly had stared at Dani, speechless, as though she couldn't comprehend the words. When the import hit her, she threw her arms around her.

"It's over," Dani told her. "You're free."

In the intervening two weeks, Dani met repeatedly with Eric Murdoch. He was prepared to jointly move the court to declare Molly innocent of the crimes she'd spent twelve years in prison for. But Dani wanted more.

Instead of entering Columbia University, where she'd been accepted following her high school graduation, Molly had entered the prison system. Instead of studying hard and embarking on a career path after her college education, she'd washed dishes in the prison kitchen. Instead of raising her beautiful daughter, she'd given her up, to a woman who mistreated her. Dani wanted Molly to be compensated for what she'd lost.

It would cost money for Molly to go to college, all these years later. It would cost money to rent an apartment, to buy food and clothes, to help raise her daughter. Dani wanted her to enter her life out of prison as an independent woman, not a child forced to live with her older sister.

New York State allowed payment to those who were unjustly convicted in an amount that the court of claims determined was fair and reasonable. Dani argued that those years should be valued in terms beyond mere lost income. Molly had lost her innocence. Her entry into the business or professional world, where youth is valued, had been delayed. But most of all, she deserved compensation for the devastation she'd suffered in giving away her child.

At first, the state attorney argued that Molly wasn't entitled to compensation. The law said no money would be awarded if the defendant's own conduct caused her conviction. "She confessed, and that's why she was convicted," the state attorney argued. But everyone wanted the scandal to go away. The Hudson County district attorney, embarrassed by the heinous crimes committed by public servants, bent over backward to end the ordeal as quickly as possible and urged the state attorney to settle Molly's claim. And finally he had.

Now they were all in court for the formal pronouncement of Molly's innocence. When the bailiff announced that all should rise, a hush descended over the courtroom. Judge Silver entered and took his seat.

"Mr. Murdoch, Ms. Trumball," he said as he nodded toward each of them. "I have your joint petition before me. The conviction of Molly Singer has previously been vacated based on new evidence, and she is awaiting retrial. The Hudson County district attorney has moved to dismiss the indictment against her based on the confessions of John Engles and Zeke Williams to the murder of Joseph and Sarah Singer. I hereby pronounce that Molly Singer is innocent of the deaths of her parents, and the posted bail is to be returned."

He paused, then looked directly at Molly. "My deepest sympathy goes to you, young woman, for all that you've suffered. I am profoundly saddened and disgusted that it was one of my brethren that caused that suffering." He straightened up in his seat. "I understand that a settlement agreement has been reached in which Ms. Singer will be compensated one hundred fifty thousand dollars for each year of incarceration. Frankly, it if were up to me, I'd have awarded her ten million dollars as punitive damages against the state. Alan Bryson and John Engles were public officials." He muttered, "Disgraceful," then said, "Case dismissed, and good luck to you, Ms. Singer."

Dani watched Molly's family rush to her and envelop her in hugs. Molly stood inside this circle, a look of pure joy on her face. After they'd at last disbanded, Molly turned to Dani, Tommy, and Melanie and thanked them for giving her back her freedom, throwing her arms tightly around each of them in turn.

As they started to leave the courthouse, Dani walked behind Molly and her daughter. She smiled when she saw Sophie take Molly's hand.

"I was wondering," she heard Sophie say. "I mean . . . um, I was just thinking . . . is it okay if I call you Mom?"

ACKNOWLEDGEMENTS

My thanks begin with my husband, Lenny, who is always my first reader and biggest fan. His love and support, along with that of my sons, Jason and Andy, and my daughters-in-law, Jackie and Amanda, mean so much to me. I'm especially grateful that they've given me five beautiful grandchildren—Rachel, Joshua, Jacob, Sienna, and Noah—whom I cherish.

Jason and Amanda have reliably become my second readers—the ones I turn to when I've finished the first edit of a manuscript. I can always count on them to let me know when I write something that is no longer in the current vernacular (I had no idea that pocketbooks are now referred to as handbags or purses!) or seems inconsistent.

In writing the story, two men were instrumental in my research. Ulster County Sheriff Paul Van Blarcum, who, unlike the sheriff in *Presumption of Guilt*, is a man of the highest integrity, talked to me about the building of the Ulster County jail. Although there were cost overruns in that construction, they bear no relation to the purely fictional problems in mythical Hudson County. Jeff Leonard, with the Office of the New York State Comptroller, explained to me how fraudulent schemes can go undetected, even with the most scrupulous examination.

I'm so fortunate to work with the wonderful people at Thomas & Mercer. I'm especially grateful to Senior Editor Alan Turkus for his continued belief in my writing, and to the rest of the team, including my copy editor, Laura Silver, who makes sure I haven't embarrassed myself with run-on sentences or other grammar crimes, and my proofreader,

Stephen Wesley, who catches all those misspelled words and missing commas. Thanks also to Tiffany Pokorny and Jacque Ben-Zekry for doing their best to ensure prospective readers learn about my books, Scott Barrie for designing a brilliant cover, and Patrick Fusco for writing a perfect book-jacket description that makes readers want to read the book. And special thanks to my editor, Kjersti Egerdahl, who has made the publishing process smooth and stress free. I'm especially grateful that Kjersti sent *Presumption of Guilt* to David Downing, who was invaluable in finding the holes in the story and pushing me to fill them.

Finally, my thanks to innocence projects throughout the country, and to the lawyers who work tirelessly to correct the occasional mistakes of our judicial system and free those innocent men and women who have been wrongfully imprisoned.

ABOUT THE AUTHOR

After receiving her Master of Science degree and New York State professional certificate in school psychology, Marti Green realized her true passion was the law. She went on to receive her law degree from Hofstra University and worked as an in-house counsel for a major cable-television operator for twenty-three years, specializing in contracts, intellectual property law, and regulatory issues.

A passionate traveler who has visited six continents, Marti Green now lives in central Florida with her husband, Lenny, and their cat, Howie. She has two adult sons and five grandchildren.